HERE WE GOAT AGAIN

HERE WE GOAT AGAIN

A

ZEN GOAT

MYSTERY

JANNA ROLLINS

To our very own Brady Bunch – Thank you for all your hilarious inspiration

Praise for Here We Goat Again

"I'm ready to book my stay at Haybeck Farm right now! From the delightful goat yoga sessions to Aunt Ellen's mouthwatering muffins, I don't know if I'd want to leave. This fun mystery kept me on my toes, and Callie's antics had me laughing out loud. *Here We Goat Again* made me feel like I was right in the middle of the action, and I never wanted it to end. I can't wait for the next goat adventure!"—**Annie McEwen**, author of the Northwoods Mysteries

"*Here We Goat Again* takes us back to Bobwhite Hollow with a new cast of quirky suspects, incriminating camera rolls, and a goat with a criminal sweet tooth. It's baaad news for the killer when amateur sleuth, Callie Haybeck, dives headfirst into this perfectly crafted mystery filled with more twists than her goat yoga class."—**Christina Romeril**, bestselling author of the Killer Chocolate Mysteries

Chapter One

"Argue all you want, Sunny. It won't change anything. I'm not staying here at Haybeck Farm with you. End of story. Honestly, sometimes you wear me out." Lucy Thorne, renowned landscape photographer, tucked a strand of chin-length ash blond curls behind her ear and sighed. "Nothing against you or Danae," she glanced between her assistant and the journalist traveling with them, "but it's going to be a busy week, and I need my own space to decompress. I booked my room at The Bobwhite Inn weeks ago."

"We spent six hours in the car together, and you couldn't bother to mention we were staying at separate places at some point during the long drive? How am I supposed to get around if you're in town and I'm all the way out here? Did you forget we came in the same car?" Sunny Hammond complained to her boss while pulling her long dark hair into a ponytail. "I thought we were finally going to get to spend some quality time together."

Lucy blinked at her assistant rapidly, as if surprised by her statement. "The six-hour ride wasn't enough quality time for you? We'll be repeating the same drive on the way home, you know. I don't know what kind of quality time you're talking about, but if you want to chat photography, we can do it then. There's no reason for the two of us to be tied at the hip. You're a smart, independent woman who'll do perfectly fine without me. It's time you learned to stand on your own two feet." She lowered her voice and hissed, "And we certainly don't need to be having this conversation in front of Miss Haybeck or Miss Mutasa. We're not making a very good first impression." Lucy sent me a tight smile.

I held up my hands, palms out. "Don't worry about me. It's all good. I haven't heard a thing."

If they only knew. The tension between the two women was nothing compared to a couple of other groups who had booked our guest cottage and sessions at The Zen Goat this past summer. I stared out at the goats dotting the pasture as I waited for the new arrivals to finish their conversation in an attempt to distance myself from the argument at hand. Bright orange and gold leaves decorating the towering sugar maples overhead danced in the light breeze.

Daisy, my great-uncle's Great Pyrenees farm dog, circled the women. She whined and sent me worried looks. I patted the side of my leg, calling Daisy closer and signaling for her to sit after she reached my side.

Sunny, ignoring her boss's reprimand, blew out a sharp breath and hung her head. "Never mind. You don't get it. You're never going to get it."

"Apparently not." Lucy pointed at the pearly silver Honda Civic parked in the driveway next to the Subaru Forester she and Sunny had arrived in. Early October sunlight glinted off the cars. "There's no need for all the theatrics. Danae has a vehicle here, and I'm quite sure she'll haul you to town for your kombucha and carrots, if you ask her nicely." She spread her arms wide. "If you two don't get along, I'll drive out here and get you myself. Problem solved."

The droop of Sunny's delicate features indicated there were issues running deep through the pair's boss/employee relationship, at least on the assistant's part. If I had to guess, I'd say Sunny was in her early twenties, just a few years younger than myself. I wondered if her sadness concerning her boss came down to pure idolization. Lucy didn't seem to be living up to Sunny's expectations of her. When Sunny had called to book the guest cottage for the weekend and told me her boss was the award-winning photographer, I have to admit I'd been a little fangirly myself about the prospect of meeting Lucy.

I glanced at the journalist, Danae Mutasa, but she seemed to be taking the other women's little spat in stride. Even slightly amused by it, if her wide smile and twinkling dark eyes were any indication.

"Since I'm here to follow Lucy around, I don't mind in the least," Danae said. "You can even ride with me to the lookout in the morning, Sunny. No sense in Lucy having to come out here and pick you up since we're all going to wind up at the same location anyway."

"I appreciate it." Sunny nodded, then pulled open the rear hatch of the alpine green Subaru to wrestle out a backpack and a worn duffel bag. She slammed the door with more force than was necessary. "At least there's someone here I can count on," she grumbled.

In conjunction with their photography workshop, I'd be at the lookout on Weaver Mountain doing a quick, albeit goatless, sun salutations yoga session with a friend at the crack of dawn. I swallowed back my offer to let Sunny ride with me. *Do not get involved in their drama*, I reprimanded myself. My mouth was notorious for getting myself tangled up in things I didn't need to be involved in before my brain kicked into gear, so I was proud of my restraint.

"With that settled, let me show you around your accommodations." I held the front door to our guest cottage open, gesturing for the trio to file inside. While they entered the stone cottage, I took a second to center my breath and say a quick positive mantra, hoping the women would settle down and leave their dramatics at the door. *Only good energy surrounds...*

A bellow of laughter cut my mantra short.

"Callie," Lucy called from inside. "Are you sure you didn't double-book us?"

What? No, of course I didn't. It wasn't possible. I mean, I definitely make my share of mistakes, but a honeymooning couple had checked out yesterday, and we weren't expecting anyone except for this photography group for another week. Confused, I stepped through the doorway. "Double booked? What do you mean?"

Sunny pointed to the couch, her jade green eyes sparkling with mirth. "We weren't expecting a roommate."

"Does the goat come with the cottage, or does he cost extra?" Danae asked between spurts of laughter.

Confused, I craned my neck to peer around the three women. A bleat reminiscent of a toddler's belly laugh shot through the air. My naughtiest goat, Bugsy, stood on the couch facing us and grinning like only a goat can do. His white coat gleamed as he playfully aimed his horns my way. Glee shone out of his yellow, diabolical, oval eyes.

Heat flashed into my cheeks as if my belly was on fire. "Oh, my heck, I've never been so embarrassed in my life. I have no idea how he got in here." Or out of the pasture, for that matter.

The goat and I eyed each other for a full ten seconds before I lunged for Bugsy's collar. He anticipated my move, bouncing over the back of the couch and kicking up his heels as he hollered and danced into the kitchen. On his way by the table, he swiveled his neck and grabbed a fresh sweet potato muffin out of the basket Aunt Ellen had left for our guests.

The door leading from the kitchen to the backyard swung on its hinges, letting the early autumn breeze in. Welp. One of my burning questions answered anyway. Aunt Ellen must not have gotten the door fully latched after she'd popped in to put the baskets brimming with muffins and fruit on the table to welcome the ladies to Haybeck Farm.

"Bugsy, no!" I reprimanded the goat, but he only chewed faster and swallowed his ill-gotten treat as he raced down the hallway toward the bedrooms.

I finally cornered the naughty goat in the bathroom, managed to get a tight grip on his green collar, and gave him a good lecture about behaving himself in front of the guests. Instead of paying attention, he stretched his neck, grabbed the zipper on my jacket, and tugged it down. I sighed. "Why do I even try with you? You're hopeless."

Apparently, Bugsy was finished with his little adventure, because now he followed along beside me like it was exactly what he wanted to do. Just as easily, he could've stubbornly stiffened his legs and refused to budge.

"Thank you for your cooperation," I whispered into his white floppy ear. "And for not leaving goat raisins all over the cottage." The cottage now smelled slightly of musty goat, but I'd take my wins where I could find them.

Lucy bent over in laughter while both Sunny and Danae wiped tears of merriment from their eyes as I marched Bugsy through the living room as if we were in a parade.

"Hysterical. I haven't laughed so hard in ages. Never expected our own little personal rodeo to welcome us to the farm," Lucy commented.

"Yep, it was all planned out and exactly how we've rehearsed it. Here at the Zen Goat, we aim to please." I shot them a wry smile, glad they all found Bugsy's antics funny, since I wasn't even slightly amused. "If you'll excuse me, I'll be back in a couple of minutes to give you an official tour. As soon as I get this escape artist secured back where he belongs."

"Take your time. We're fine," Sunny answered, looking around with wide eyes. "This cottage is gorgeous, by the way."

Maybe Bugsy had gotten himself a psychiatry degree behind my back. After what looked to be a rocky start, the tension between Lucy and Sunny seemed to have evaporated in clouds of goat dander.

Chapter Two

When Soul Dust, an art gallery in my adopted village of Bobwhite Hollow, New Hampshire, had started advertising a month ago about acquiring Lucy Thorne to judge their annual photography contest, the town had gone a little crazy. Every amateur photographer came out of the woodwork. Visions of being discovered and having their photographs splashed across the cover of *Wilderness Wonders* danced in their heads. Enthusiasm for the event spilled over the top when it was announced Lucy would also be teaching an outdoor workshop with limited availability. Only the first ten people to sign up would secure a coveted spot.

Brittany Shields, the owner of Soul Dust, told me that the second registration had opened a month before the event, she thought she'd been caught in a stampede. I'd been two days too late with my request to join the workshop. Brittany laughed and told me in the melee she'd even forgotten to block off a spot for herself.

She'd leaned across the counter. "But you know, I've always thought the lookout on Weaver Mountain would be a great spot for sun salutations. And if we happen to be in close enough proximity to inadvertently pick up a few photography tips…" Her voice trailed off as she shrugged and waggled her eyebrows.

"It wouldn't be our fault." I grinned.

"How's your schedule looking in October, by the way?" Brittany had asked. "I'd love to book a couple of goat yoga sessions for the photography weekend, and maybe Will and Ellen would let the photographers roam around the farm a bit to take pictures. What do you think?"

"It's a fabulous idea." I was never going to say no to more business for The Zen Goat. "I'll talk to Uncle Will and Aunt Ellen, but I'll bet they won't have a problem with it either, as long as we make sure the photographers don't leave any gates open."

We'd solidified our plans, and now the day had arrived. This morning, I was on my way to meet Brittany at the trailhead before the sun came up, heat cranked up in the truck against the predawn chill. Excitement bloomed in my chest even though I'd never fancied myself a photographer. The thrill came from being in the presence of such a well-known photographer. My mom was a huge Lucy Thorne fan. One of her framed prints—sunrise over the snowcapped peaks of the Teton Mountains of Wyoming—had hung in our living room as long as I could remember. Every year, Mom treated herself to the newest Lucy Thorne calendar so she could enjoy a gorgeous new landscape every month, and she had various other prints scattered throughout the house.

I patted the bench seat of Old Rusty, making sure I'd remembered to bring my phone. Not that I had any illusions a picture taken with my almost obsolete Android phone would win any contests, but better to have it with me. What if I just happened to snap the lucky shot? A girl can only dream.

This was my first autumn in New Hampshire, and it couldn't be more postcard-perfect. Every single day I was in awe at the jaw-droppingly glorious shades of yellow, red, and orange covering the foothills surrounding town. The photographs and calendars depicting New England in the fall didn't even begin to do the real thing justice. A person needed to experience it for themselves. I'd been calling my parents daily to let my Seattle family and friends know what they were missing out on. Mom had started answering the phone with, "Don't tell me. The colors are even better today." But every day, that's exactly what I told her—the colors were absolutely spectacular. Better than the day before. The locals warned me to soak it all in. The colors were hitting peak any day now and would start to fade before what they called "stick season" settled in, so I'd been taking their advice and latching on to any opportunity to immerse myself in the great outdoors.

When I'd bragged to Mom how Brittany and I were planning to tag along on Lucy's workshop, she squealed like a fourteen-year-old girl at a K-pop concert and made me promise to take scads of pictures. Not pictures of the landscape—I'd already sent her plenty of those—but photographs of Lucy instead. I'd promised to send a few.

The morning was still pitch black out with a starless sky as I wheeled Old Rusty into the small parking lot at the trailhead on Weaver Mountain. Lucy's Subaru and Danae's Honda already sat in the lot beside two bulky pickups with the green and white "Live Free or Die" New Hampshire license plates. A line of vehicles followed me into the lot, but I managed to find nearly the last empty spot and pulled in. My gaze flew to my rearview mirror as a maroon van double-parked behind me and cut its engine. What the heck? The driver's side door opened, and a woman dressed in a knee-length, navy blue winter coat, Pepto-Bismol pink beanie, and black gloves stepped out. She had a bulky camera strapped around her neck.

I jumped out of the truck and jogged to her side. "Excuse me, you can't park there. You're blocking me in." I hooked a thumb over my shoulder to point out her mistake.

The woman, mid-forties with shoulder-length coppery brown hair, scrunched up her face and squinted at me. "I could've sworn you just got here. Are you leaving already? Go ahead and back up and I'll take your spot if you are. There's no other place to park."

"Well, no. I did just get here, but that's not the poi—"

"Then there doesn't seem to be a problem, does there?" She arched one thin eyebrow and shot me a tight-lipped smile that reminded me of my stern grade school librarian. Before I could formulate a response, the woman swiveled on her hiking-boot-clad feet and marched off.

I stared after her with my mouth gaping open. "But that's not how this works," I sputtered.

She kept walking, but at least she raised a hand to acknowledge I'd spoken. *Or not*, I realized when another woman noticed her and mimicked the raised hand to greet her friend.

"MJ! Glad you made it." The rude woman and her friend joined a group of other people, all dressed in heavy coats and hats, with cameras dangling against their chests.

Even in early October, the nighttime temperatures this far north could dip into the thirties. By afternoon, we'd probably reach the mid-fifties and be shedding coats and hats left and right, but as for now, the entire crowd appeared to be ready for winter. I rubbed my hands against the nip in the air.

Huffing in irritation, I zipped up my puffer coat and pulled a beanie and mittens on. If her highness's van was still blocking me in when I was ready to leave, I'd figure out what to do then. With any luck, she'd get her perfect shot and be long gone by the time I was ready. I jogged in place and executed a couple of warm-up stretches while I waited for Brittany. With the parking lot filled up, a handful of locals who weren't part of the photography workshop were having to park along the side of the road in order to reach the trailhead for their morning hikes. They grumbled about the lot being full as they strode by me.

"Hey, Callie. Good morning," Brittany greeted quietly as she stepped up beside me.

"Alright, photographers, gather round." I recognized Lucy's voice from yesterday as she called out. She clapped her hands together to get everyone's attention. "The lookout is a mile and a half up the mountain, and we want to be at the top as the light starts to rise. Once we make it to the viewpoint, I'll give you some pointers to get the ideal shot, but we need to get up there first. We better get this show on the road."

Even though I wasn't officially, or unofficially for that matter, a part of the workshop group, I moved closer to listen to what she had to say.

Lucy glanced at the dark sky as she continued. "Looks like it's going to be a grey, overcast morning with a nice layer of clouds. Absolutely perfect conditions. You should all be able to get some great shots." She turned and headed up the trail. "Come on. Times a-wasting."

I wrinkled my nose and looked at Brittany. "Is she being sarcastic?"

"About what?" my friend asked.

"The cloud layer and grey day. Isn't that exactly the opposite of what you'd want?"

Brittany pulled her straight, long, dark hair into a ponytail, securing it with an elastic band she wore around her wrist. "Nope. Weirdly, overcast days make autumn colors pop way brighter than on sunny days. She was being completely serious. It's the perfect conditions."

"I'll be darned. I guess that's why you all make the big bucks."

"Don't I wish." Brittany chuckled. "Ready?"

At the start of the trail, a bright yellow sign cautioned hikers we were in bear country and warned people not to leave food in their vehicles. Check. The only thing resembling food in Old Rusty were a few muffin crumbs I'd dropped on the floor while driving and then smashed under my feet. Even a hungry bear should be pickier than that.

The crisp morning air smelled of sweet, fallen leaves, wood smoke, and the magic of fall. It made me wish I'd thought to bring a thermos of spiced cider along. As we trailed behind the photographers, a man keeping pace with Lucy turned to walk backwards while lifting his arm and a metal walking stick in the air for attention. His breath puffed out clouds in the chill mountain air.

"For any of you who don't know, those of you who aren't local or aren't hikers," he said in a voice loud enough to carry to those of us in the back of the pack, "this is a carry-in, carry-out area. There are no trash cans along the way or at the top, and the only outhouses are the ones in the parking lot we just left." The headlamp flashlight attached to the man's beanie illuminated his gestures as he pointed back toward the lot with his walking stick. "Do not let me catch you leaving any trash around. Mess with the bull, you'll get the horns." He twisted around and trotted to catch up with Lucy.

"I didn't realize Lucy had hired a guide. Not a bad idea, though this guy doesn't seem to be very personable," I said to Brittany as I stumbled over a protruding tree root in the dirt path.

Brittany reached out to steady me. "Alex Bell? He's neither personable nor a guide. Just someone who thinks he's all that and a bag of chips. Alex likes to imagine he's large and in charge."

"Ah, gotcha. A legend in his own mind. There's one in every crowd, isn't there? What does the illustrious Alex do for a living? No, let me guess. He's an attorney."

"Wrong. Alex owns Golden Bell Photography. It's on Webster Street just off Main. You've probably seen his studio. Most of his business comes from contracts with the local schools to take the kids' school pictures, and he takes a lot of senior photos." Brittany glanced around to make sure nobody was in earshot and lowered her voice. "Alex is one hundred percent convinced he's going to win the photography contest this year, but…" Her voice trailed off as she sent me a skeptical side-eye.

"You don't think so. His work isn't good?"

She made a face like she had a mouth full of vinegar and shook her head. "But you didn't hear it from me."

"Understood." I pointed out the woman wearing the pink beanie who'd blocked Old Rusty in, then filled Brittany in on my confrontation, albeit short, with her this morning. "Who is she?"

Brittany cocked her head. "How weird. That's Jen Earley. She's a friend of my mom's and usually fairly nice though she is a talker. If you don't want to be stuck for a while, don't ask her how her day's going. Jen is the secretary at the Baptist church and has a couple of teenagers. Two daughters, I think."

"Don't get me wrong. She was nice enough when she basically told me to stuff it where the sun doesn't shine." I laughed. "She was not about to park down the road like other people had to who were too late to get a parking spot. The whole interaction reminded me of trying to have a conversation with an entitled soccer mom."

Brittany nodded. "That's a pretty accurate assessment of Jen. And her daughter plays soccer."

I shrugged. "So there we have it."

* * *

"Alright, photographers, listen up." Lucy stood at the end of a weathered picnic table, her left foot on the bench seat. She rested her forearm on her bent leg and leaned in as she addressed the group. Fallen leaves skittered around her feet.

Brittany and I stood on an outcropping of rock at the lookout where we would have a phenomenal view of town as the sun rose but were still plenty close enough to hear what Lucy was teaching her workshop participants. Birds chirped high in the trees, welcoming in the new day. Remembering my promise to get a few snapshots of Lucy for my mom, I took out my phone and snapped a couple in the grey dawn light.

Lucy talked about shutter speed, exposure, composition, depth of field, the rule of three, which lens to use, and a plethora of other photography talk that flew right over my head. She flipped a camera around in her hands, pointing out various settings as she talked.

I glanced at the point-n-shoot camera function on my phone with a sigh. "I think I'm a little out of my depth here," I said to Brittany.

She chuckled but didn't take her focus off the adjustments she was making to her own camera. "You'll be fine."

I tucked mine back into the pocket of my coat and pulled out a dark chocolate and almond granola bar. While I chewed, I glanced at the people gathered around Lucy. Sunny, her assistant, wore a dark teal coat with a creamy wool beanie pulled over her long dark hair. She stood off to the side with a hunter green backpack on her back and a dark grey one at her feet. Sunny twisted a strand of hair around her finger as she listened to Lucy's spiel. Her gaze shifted around the group. When she caught my eye, she sent a quick wave in greeting.

Danae sat at the picnic table, scribbling notes on a yellow legal pad of paper. A small voice recorder and camera sat on the table next to her. The double-parking diva, Jen, stood with her friend next to Danae. Instead of listening to the instructions, Jen kept leaning toward MJ, whispering and nodding toward various members of the group. After each whispered comment, the two would share raised eyebrow glances as if they were gossiping. It seemed like no one was immune from their critiques.

Away from the rest of the group, a tall, muscular man around my dad's age stood in the shadow beneath a pine tree. A chocolate lab lounged at his feet. The man's eyes were laser-focused on Lucy. The only thing he held in his hands was the dog's leash. No camera in sight, so I guessed he must not be an official member of the workshop.

*One, two, three, four...*I counted the number of photographers gathered around Lucy. Twelve, but my tally included both Sunny and Danae, so ten people at the workshop, which was the number of spots Brittany mentioned Lucy had originally offered. Which meant I was correct about the solemn man in the shadow of the tree not being here to participate in the workshop. He didn't give off creepy vibes, so I shrugged. Probably doing the same thing Brittany and I were; trying to glean tips without officially being part of the workshop. Or simply trying to catch a glimpse of the famous Lucy Thorne. He could be a super fan like my mom. Probably displayed her work all over his house.

Most of Lucy's actual workshop participants were paying close attention to her tips. But when my eyes fell on Alex, the bossy-butt from the trail, the tilt of his head and downturned slant of his mouth reminded me of a prickly porcupine.

"It sounds like I should've let someone else take my spot in the workshop," a man said when Lucy paused. He held up a small camera like the one I'd had as a teenager. "I thought I could pick up some tips, but I don't have all the settings like you folks do. You can't even attach external lenses to my cheap camera."

"Here, let me see it a minute." Lucy wiggled her fingers for the camera. He handed it over, and she flipped through the few settings he had, showing him which ones she chose. "There you go. Try that. You'd be surprised at the great shots I've seen people get with these little babies."

Alex snorted. "This is a waste of time and money. Everybody in the industry knows you can't get a decent shot without professional equipment." He turned to the man in question. "She's blowing smoke up your wazoo, buddy. The only thing your pictures will be good for is your grandma's photo album."

Lucy bit her lip, but only shook her head, not acknowledging Alex's outburst. The woman had more self-control than I would have in the same situation.

Lucy turned her back on Alex while checking her watch. "Alright.

Everybody should be set. The sun will be coming up in about five minutes, so we need to get going. Remember, it's cloudy and grey. Perfect for fall foliage shots, but you're not going to see a splendid sunrise.

The sky will be moving from dawn to daylight with very little fanfare. Oh, and one last thing. All ten of you will have the chance to submit one of your photos from this morning to a private contest just for you. My team and I will pick one of the entrants to be included in next year's Lucy Thorne calendar for October. It'll be great for name recognition. We sell nearly one-hundred thousand of my calendars every year. On top of that, the winning entrant will receive a two-hundred-dollar cash prize."

The participants erupted with clapping, hooting and hollering that echoed back at us from over the edge of the mountain lookout.

Alex pumped his fists in the air. "Yes! This is going to be a cinch."

Lucy interrupted the premature celebrating with a loud whistle. "Time to go. Spread out. Find your own sweet spot and concentrate on getting the best shot of your life. Don't worry about what anyone else is doing. Play your own game. We'll meet right back here in an hour and a half."

As Lucy had talked, the deep grey morning light had brightened. When she turned my way, a shadow made it appear as if she sported a black eye. Probably just a trick of the light.

Except Sunny noticed the same thing I had. "Oh my gosh, Lucy! What happened to your eye? Did somebody slug you?"

Nope. Not a trick of the light. My first instinct was right. Lucy had a black eye she'd acquired sometime between dropping Sunny off at the farm and this morning.

Lucy visibly cringed before she turned to address Sunny. "No, I didn't get slugged. If you must know, I got up to use the bathroom in the middle of the night and…and…I forgot the layout of the room. Slammed into a corner of the wall. It was clumsy and stupid."

Sunny thrust her face close to Lucy's to study the injury. "Dude, it's purple and yellow. Do you need an ice pack?"

"I'm fine. Stop fussing. You're worse than an old lady." She shoved her assistant aside, ducking her head as if to hide the shiner. "It's nothing to worry about. The whole incident was ridiculous. Now drop it."

Lucy gestured to the photographers gaping at her. "Go. You're wasting time."

The photographers scattered in all directions. Alex sauntered by where Brittany and I stood, muttering to himself about being able to teach a better workshop than Lucy did and how she had nothing to teach him and probably deserved the black eye.

He noticed us watching him and decided to double down. "Seriously. I bet she doesn't even have a photography degree. There was nothing worthwhile in her speech. Ridiculous advice. A monkey could have done a better job. All professionals know the correct way to…" Alex's voice trailed away as he kept walking.

"Sunny!" Lucy's loud boss voice startled me. "Hand me my green bag and take the grey one back to the Subaru. There's plenty of time to get down there and back up here before I'm done shooting. Grab me a fresh bottle of water while you're at it. And hurry. I need to find my perfect spot. Is my tripod here?"

"Of course. It's strapped to the holder, just like always," Sunny answered as she relinquished the green backpack to Lucy. "I've got you covered."

"You're the best." Lucy hefted the bag onto her back. As she did, she caught sight of the man watching her every move from under the tree. Her jaw dropped and her face blanched pale as if she'd seen a ghost.

I glanced over at the guy. He raised a finger to Lucy as if to say hello. She frowned, shook her head slightly, and mouthed "Not here." Lucy sent him a palm-out hand before turning on her heel and striding off around the corner.

Alrighty, then. So, they do know each other. And apparently are fluent in speaking in their own version of sign language. From Lucy's reaction, it was clear she hadn't expected to see the man, but the "not here" indicated the two had something to discuss. Was her story about running into the wall just a cover? Had this stranger used his fist to give Lucy her shiner?

The man waited until Lucy was out of sight before he pulled on his dog's leash and followed. A handful of the other photographers had taken the same trail, so I shook off the slight hint of suspicion I felt. Sunny took off for the parking lot as instructed, and Brittany and I turned our attention to our sun salutations as the light began to brighten over the eastern horizon.

"Sorry to interrupt, but would you ladies mind if I joined you?" Danae approached us as we began the mountain pose and lifted our arms into an upward salute. "The whole reason I'm here is to get some candid shots of Lucy in action, but apparently she only works alone." Danae's tone was sarcastic and irritated.

"She agreed to let you do the article, but wouldn't let you tag along on her shoot?" I asked, dropping my hands to my side.

"Go figure." Danae threw her hands in the air. "Working with big personalities can be a challenge, to say the least. Since I'm stuck up here on the mountain, I'd love to do some sun salutations with you instead."

"The more the merrier," I said while Brittany nodded her agreement.

The three of us lined up on the ledge, started over, and welcomed the light in with a series of life-affirming stretches.

"You know, the only thing that would've made this better is a sweet little goat or two." Brittany shot me a teasing side-eye when we were about halfway through our routine.

"Agreed," Danae piped up. "When is the next session of goat yoga? I don't want to miss it."

"Tomorrow morning," I informed her. "It's at the farm, so you can't miss it, as long as you're out of bed in time."

I led our tiny class through nine sets of salutations. Once we finished, I was invigorated and ready for whatever the day had in store.

Chapter Three

My original plan had been to do a quick yoga session with Brittany and then head back home, but knowing Jen's van was still parked behind my truck, there wasn't any rush to get back to the parking lot. I had a fleeting vision of channeling Evelyn from *Fried Green Tomatoes* by slamming the back of Old Rusty into Jen's van over and over until there was enough room for me to angle out, then drive away shouting, "Towanda!" I tamped down the wicked impulse. The better choice was to stay put and roll with the change of plans. After all, Jen was older than me and probably had better insurance. Besides, I was enjoying spending extra time with Brittany and getting to know Danae a bit.

Soul Dust didn't open until ten, so I didn't have to do much arm-twisting to get Brittany to agree to hang back with me. "It'll give me a chance to take some more photos, anyway, and I wouldn't mind hearing firsthand what the photographers thought of their workshop. If it was a success, I'll need to think seriously about adding more classes to the gallery's schedule."

"And since Lucy thwarted my attempt at actually doing the job I was sent here for, I've got plenty of time on my hands," Danae said. Anger surged briefly through her eyes while a hint of red flushed her dark skin.

"Tell us a little more about yourself. Obviously, you're here working on a story about Lucy, but that's all I know. Do you work for a newspaper?" I asked.

Danae stuck out her bottom lip in a pout. "Seriously? Way to crush a woman's delusions that people watch my show and know who I am."

I raised my shoulders in an exaggerated shrug. "Sorry, but in my defense,

I'm from the Pacific Northwest. I've only been in New England for six months."

She let out a heavy sigh. "Don't worry about it. Have you ever watched a show called New York Vibrations? It airs Saturday mornings on CBS out of New York City. It's a magazine-style news show. You know, kind of like 60 Minutes."

I shook my head no, but Brittany's eyes lit up. "Yes! I thought you looked familiar. You're one of the correspondents who report those fun, feel-good stories on the show. I watch it with my grandma when I go up to visit her in Woodstock. She loves your show. Wait until I tell her I met you. Hey, can I get your autograph for her?"

"Of course. I always carry a few copies of my headshots with me. They're back in my car. I would be delighted to sign one for your grandmother. Remind me later. And to be perfectly clear, I'm a contributor, not a correspondent. We're the bottom rung of the ladder." Danae made air quotes around the word contributor. "Last week, I got passed over for a promotion to correspondent. The studio powers that be decided to hire someone from outside instead of promoting from within." She set her jaw, reached up and snapped a small branch off the nearest tree, clearly upset about not getting the job. She snapped off pieces of the branch in about inch-long sections and dropped them in the dirt at her feet.

"That's rough. I'm really sorry." I commiserated with her, eyeing the branch she was making short work of and thankful it wasn't me who had sparked her fury. "Hopefully you'll get the promotion next time."

Danae dropped the last of the stick on the ground and ran a hand through her thick, curly, dark hair. She took a deep breath and shook her head. "I'm trying not to be bitter about the whole thing, but I'm not going to lie, I kind of am anyway. Screw them. I'm going to keep doing my job to the best of my ability—my low-paying job that barely pays my rent—and keep my eyes open for the big breaking story that will finally launch my career. Then it's bye-bye New York Vibrations. I want to be respected as a serious journalist, not somebody who can only be trusted with cotton candy pieces. My big story is right around the corner, I can feel it. Like, it might even happen today." She straightened her spine and looked around the woods as if searching for the career-making story that was going to pop out from behind a tree and fall right into her lap. "Even if I have to make something happen myself." Danae laughed. "Just kidding. That would be unethical." She flashed a bright grin.

"For sure. Your career is going to explode, and you're going to rock their world. Boss babe power," Brittany encouraged. "Your bosses are going to rue the day they didn't give you that promotion."

"And Brittany and I will be able to say we knew you before you hit the big time."

"And my grandma will have the autograph to prove it," Brittany added.

We all went up for a high five.

"Thanks for listening to me whine. I promise I'm done acting like a big baby now. Way to bring down the vibe, loser." Danae's brown cheeks flushed pink as she gathered up her notebook and camera from the picnic table and stashed them in her bag.

"Hey, don't talk about my new friend that way." I gave her a quick shoulder bump.

"Thanks. You guys have been great. I guess I needed to vent. And now I need to ask a favor."

"Sure. What is it?"

"Would you mind watching my stuff for a few minutes? I'm going to head down to the parking lot and find the outhouse. I thought Sunny would be back by now and could keep an eye on my bag for me, but I can't wait any longer, and I don't want to lug it down the mountain until I have to." She crossed her legs and glanced at her watch. "I should be back by the time Lucy gets done with her shoot."

"Yep, no worries. If we don't see you before everyone heads back down, I'll bring your bag with me and meet you on the trail." I waved her off and took a seat at the picnic table.

Danae had only been gone two minutes when a sharp, short scream rent the air. Brittany and I swiveled our heads like a pair of tandem owls and stared at each other.

"What in the holy heck was that? I hope Danae didn't twist her ankle or something." The hair on the back of my neck stood at attention.

"I don't think so. Listen for a minute," Brittany said.

We both cocked our heads and kept still. Seconds later, another sharp scream filled the air.

Brittany pointed straight up. "There's our culprit."

A Red-Tailed Hawk circled in the sky above our heads, wings spread as the bird majestically rode a wave of air. My skin tingled again, but this time in awe as I watched the hawk soaring overhead until I got a crick in my neck.

As the photographers started to trickle back to the lookout, the excitement level among them was high. Voices and movements were more animated than they had been earlier as they greeted each other and talked about their early morning photo shoots. Brittany jumped right in, asking questions and begging to see their shots.

The man with the chocolate lab crested the hill below the lookout, hustling to the clearing where the photographers were beginning to gather. This time, I noticed he had a ham radio clipped to his belt. With it being daylight out now, I could see he wore dark green denim cargo pants and a khaki shirt under a forest-green jacket with a yellow-and-green emblem on the sleeve. He held up his hands to encompass the entire group. "Does anyone here own a maroon minivan parked in the lot at the trailhead?" he inquired.

I glanced around but didn't see Jen, so I stepped forward. "A woman named Jen Earley does. I only know because she blocked me in when we all got here this morning. It doesn't look like she's back from her shoot yet."

The man nodded. "Do you expect her back anytime soon?"

"What's going on, Garrett?" The man with the cheap camera asked before I had a chance to answer. "Did somebody break into Jen's van?"

"Somebody sure did," the first man, apparently Garrett, answered. "A big old black bear ripped the door right off, looking for a snack. I'm headed back down now. Send Jen my way when you see her." His radio chirped. He plucked it off his belt, pressed the transmitter button, and spoke into the receiver, "On my way. Come on, Buddy." He patted his leg and whistled to the dog before jogging back down the trail in the direction he'd come from.

"A bear ripped the door off her van? Fudge nuggets. I had no idea they could do that," I said to Brittany, picturing a gargantuan bear flexing his muscles before grabbing a door with both hands and tearing it off a vehicle. The bear in my mind shared a strange resemblance to Arnold Schwarzenegger.

"Oh, for sure. Jen must've left some food in her van. Black bears have a keen sense of smell and can sniff out a snack through an armored tank. They'll open a car door like it's a tin can of sardines, especially if a window is left down even the tiniest crack. They're masters at getting their claws wedged in there, then use sheer brute force to break the window and get the door off."

"Note to self. Never leave a sandwich in the truck. Do you think the bear's still down there? And where there's one, there's more, right?" I turned a full circle, a little creeped out now by the dense shadows in the surrounding forest. "We have to walk back down the trail. And there are still people out in the woods by themselves. What if a bear mauls someone?"

Brittany shook her head, her ponytail swinging. "Black bears are fairly timid and rarely attack humans. Not that it couldn't happen, but…" Her voice trailed off as she shrugged. "You can't live in such beautiful surroundings and not have any dangers to deal with. I'm sure Garrett will have chased the bear out of the parking lot before we ever get back down there. There's nothing to worry about."

"Garrett? You know him, then?"

"Of course. Garrett Rogers. He's a super nice guy. Works for the forest service. Everybody around here knows him."

Aha. Forest Service. Everybody knows him, except for me, which is why nobody else was giving him the side-eye when he seemed to be lurking in the shadows earlier.

The image of a hungry bear ripping a car door off its hinges was still front and center in my mind when Alex came back from his photo shoot with a swagger, crowing about how he'd taken the winning shot. He pulled off his beanie, causing his short, light brown hair to form a peak on top of his head reminiscent of a woodpecker. "To tell you the truth, the rest of you guys don't even need to bother entering," he bragged to the group. "I shot at least a dozen spectacular frames with incredible composition. You won't even believe how well done these are when you see them. This contest is in the bag."

"You're right about one thing. I'm sure we won't believe it when we see them," one man grumbled.

"Got lucky, did you?" A woman asked sarcastically.

Alex straightened to his full height and thrust out his skinny chest. If he was looking to intimidate his competition, he was going to have to try a different tactic. "Luck has nothing to do with it. My win will be due to pure skill and talent. You people are aware I have a photography degree, aren't you?"

I snorted. Here he goes, trotting out his degree again. I tuned the blowhard out and counted heads. Nine. Still one more photographer out in the woods, and Lucy, Sunny, and Danae had yet to arrive, though we knew where Danae had gone off to.

Moments later, Jen's face popped up from over the edge of the cliffside as she attempted to claw her way up to the clearing where we stood. "A little help here, please," she called out.

Jen's friend, MJ, jumped into action, grabbing her by the hand to help pull her up the slick rockface. "Oh, my lord, Jen. What in tarnation were you doing down there?"

Jen took a deep breath and brushed forest debris off her coat. She grinned. "You're not going to believe this. I found the best spot on a ledge about fifty yards down with an incredible view of Bobwhite Hollow. Lucy was right. These grey skies make the foliage pop. There are so many gorgeous shades of red and yellow, I didn't even know which way to point my lens first. I saw a chipmunk and a hawk, and I'm pretty sure a skunk wandered by. Pee-you! I bet I took three hundred pictures." She gushed on and on about her experience.

Once Jen took a breath, MJ asked to see some of the photos she'd taken. Jen waved a dismissive hand. "Oh, gosh, no, I need to futz with them a bit first before I show anybody. Now, tell me everything. How was your photo shoot? What did you see? How many pictures did you get?"

The friends wandered off, both of them chattering at once. I wondered if MJ would remember to tell Jen about the bear encounter and how Garrett requested her presence down at the parking lot as soon as possible. Maybe it was mean-spirited, but after the way she'd treated me earlier in the morning, I decided it wasn't my problem. At this point, I wasn't in any hurry to leave.

Another quick headcount brought the total to ten. Now we were only waiting on the workshop leader and her small crew.

Danae strolled up the path, breathing hard. Her arms hung at her sides, and she comically stuck out her tongue and panted as she approached Brittany and me. "Sheesh. I'm used to marching around city streets, not hiking up mountains." She reached for her bag and pulled out her water bottle, taking a long swallow. "Thanks for watching my stuff."

"No problem," I answered. "You went to the outhouse at the trailhead, right? Did you see the bear?"

Her shoulders tightened. "A bear? No. You're kidding, right?" Danae swiveled around as if the bear was seconds away from tapping her on the shoulder.

"Believe me, a bear isn't going to approach us here with all the noise this group is making. You're safe." Brittany filled her in on what Garrett told us about Jen's van getting broken into.

"Now that you mention it, I do remember hearing some commotion and seeing a Forest Service truck idling in the lot, but didn't pay much attention to what was going on. Now I wish I had. I miss all the good excitement!" Danae snapped her fingers to show her disappointment. "That would've made a fun addition to my Lucy story."

"Weren't we supposed to meet back here at eight?" Alex's raised voice interrupted our conversation as he yelled to be heard above the chatter. "It's a quarter after now. Where the heck is Lucy? She's wasting everybody's time. This is no way to run a workshop. Super unprofessional."

"And where in the world is Sunny? I hope she didn't get herself lost," Danae inserted, her eyes flaring as she studied the woods surrounding us.

"No need to worry. I'm right here." Sunny emerged from the woods on the far side of the picnic table where there wasn't a marked trail. Pine needles were caught in her hair, and a smear of dirt marred her cheek. The grey backpack Lucy had ordered her to take back to the Subaru was still flung across one shoulder. She slipped the bag down her arm and took a seat on top of the picnic table.

"Were you with Lucy? Is she on her way?" Danae asked the assistant. "The natives are getting restless."

"No, I haven't seen her since she left here earlier. My guess is she's having a great shoot and lost track of time. That's a normal occurrence with Lucy. I've gotten used to it. Hang on. I'll try to call her." Sunny pulled out her cell phone and thumbed it on, then frowned. "Scratch that. My phone doesn't have any service up here." She stood and tucked her phone back into her pocket. "Alright, then. I'll go look for her instead."

"Uh, somebody should go with you, so we don't have two lost people," I piped up.

"Sounds like you volunteered. Come on, then." Sunny waved me over.

"Me? Okay. Sure." My knees quivered at the thought of the bear wandering through the woods, but I'd gone and opened my big mouth once again. I shot a what-have-I-done look at Brittany.

"Wait for me. I'm coming, too." Brittany untangled her legs from under the picnic table. "Gotta keep my buddy safe." She hip-checked me.

I sized her up, wondering which one of us could run faster. Was it wrong to sacrifice a friend to a hungry black bear in order to save myself? Thankfully, according to Brittany, black bears weren't usually aggressive when it came to humans, unless a mama bear was protecting her cubs. She was probably safe. Time would tell.

"The rest of you stay here and wait for us," Sunny ordered, interrupting my devious plans to trip Brittany if a bear started chasing us.

Fictional planning, of course. I would never really sacrifice a friend. Well, probably not. I sighed. *Let's hope I don't have to find out.*

The three of us headed up the trail in the direction we'd seen Lucy take earlier. I grabbed two sticks and banged them together as we walked to make enough noise to let the bear know we were coming. Wasn't that the advice the twins gave to their almost stepmother in *The Parent Trap*? Not for bears, but mountain lions. *Wait? Are there mountain lions in these woods?* I shivered and decided to concentrate on finding Lucy instead of picturing a predator hiding behind every tree.

"Lucy? Where are you?" We called her name as we walked, listening between shouts to make sure we didn't miss her answering.

"Callie, stop with the banging sticks. We won't even be able to hear her if she does bother to answer us," Brittany said. "We're yelling loud enough, bears aren't going to come within ten miles of us. Trust me."

"Fine." I tossed my only bear protection down by the side of the trail. "But let the record show I'm not happy about it."

The left side of the trail offered an open panorama of the valley below with breathtaking views of the Presidential range of mountains in the distance. The sight of the spectacular crimson, orange, and gold foliage nearly brought tears to my eyes. I could barely believe I truly lived here. To our right, trees fanned out as far as the eye could see. Which, granted, wasn't super far in the dense woods. The heavy forest thinned out as we climbed toward the summit. Glancing over the cliff edge every so often, I was amazed at the variety of woodland fauna from slick granite rock walls to brush-filled ledges and outcroppings hovering over deciduous and conifer forests. It wouldn't take much for someone to lose their bearings and get lost in these woods.

We'd only hiked about a half mile when the trail turned into a series of rugged steps carved out of the dirt. Around one final bend, the trail came to an abrupt halt. A four-foot-long wooden fence curved around the peak with a yellow and black sign warning hikers about the danger of falling.

"Lucy," Sunny gripped the fence and screamed into the wind. "Where are you? Answer me!"

A rustle of dry leaves was the only response.

"Do we head back and check the sides of the trail more carefully?" I asked.

Sunny pinched at her lower lip and squinted as she studied our surroundings. "Yeah, I guess so. We should focus on the edge since that's where the best shots would be taken from. Let's spread out, but stay within shouting distance of each other."

Sunny trotted about ten feet down the trail before she veered off, disappearing over the edge. Brittany started searching from the danger sign, and I scrambled over the edge halfway between the two of them. We all called for Lucy and made sure we stayed within earshot of each other like Sunny had suggested. We meticulously worked our way back toward the lookout.

I held onto a tree for balance and scanned the area below me. *What is that?* A glint of silver and green caught my attention. I carefully crouched down, reaching for the object and skittering loose stones down the side of the embankment as I did so. When I stretched a hair more trying to will my fingers to reach the object, the loose shale under my feet shifted. The next thing I knew, I was sliding down the side of the mountain. A chunk of dirt flew into my eye as I frantically grabbed for anything to stop my trajectory. Miraculously, I managed to wrap my fist around a sturdy tree root seconds before I plummeted over the edge. A rock I'd kicked loose crashed and banged down the slick rock ledge. I caught my breath, thankful I hadn't followed the same flight path as the rock. Yet. My heart thrummed in my throat as I executed tiny, careful movements, slowly turning myself around so I was facing the rock wall. Once there, I closed my eyes and rested for a second before searching for anything I could use to leverage myself up the wall. *You've got this, Callie. Today is not the day you die. Keep going.* My arms and legs shook as I clawed my way back to solid ground using tiny crevices for hand and foot holds. Rock climbing had been on my bucket list for several years, but the opportunity hadn't come up until today. The first thing I was going to do when I got home was cross that nonsense off my list.

"I almost died just now," I yelled to my companions, once my footing was secure.

Brittany's concerned face popped over the edge of the trail above my head. "What are you talking about? Do you need a hand?"

"I'm good." I struggled the rest of the way to the trail and dropped my butt into the dirt to take a minute or three to center myself. "There's something shiny by that rock." I pointed to the object I hadn't managed to get a hold of.

"It might be a piece of Lucy's equipment, but I nearly landed in town trying to get to it."

Brittany, using a little more caution and a lot more coordination than I had, managed to grab the item and pull it out of the crevice it had been wedged into. "Just a flat rusty Rolling Rock beer can. Circa 1980, if I had to guess." She tucked the piece of garbage into her backpack to dispose of later.

"I almost died over a beer can?"

"Yep. You sure did."

We were both getting to our feet when Sunny yelled out. "Over here. I think I found her."

Brittany and I sprang to our feet and sprinted down the trail until we caught sight of Sunny's dark hair disappearing over the lip of the trail edge.

"Lucy!" Sunny yelled her boss's name, followed immediately with a heart wrenching wail. "No!"

Brittany and I gaped at each other, a growing sense of dread knotting in the pit of my stomach. Together, we crept closer. Sunny knelt beside Lucy, who was propped against a large pine tree, the sharp, spiked leg of a camera tripod embedded in her heart. Lucy's vacant gaze stared out over the kaleidoscope of autumn splendor displayed in the mountains and foothills surrounding Bobwhite Hollow. The crimson stain spreading across her chest was reflected back in the leaves shining above her head.

Chapter Four

"Don't touch anything," I warned Sunny. "One of us needs to call the police, but there isn't any cell service here." With shaking hands, I pulled out my phone to double-check. Not a single bar.

Brittany pointed back up the trail toward the summit. "There might be a signal at the top. It's a little more open up there."

"Definitely a good possibility. I'll give it a try." As Sunny continued to wail, I sprinted up the trail, my phone held as high in the air as I could stretch in an attempt to find a connection. Even though my lungs felt like they might explode with all the racing around at high altitudes, I thanked the yoga goddesses for providing me with strong legs.

Brittany was one smart lady. It took me a minute to find the sweet spot at the top of the trail, but if I stood on the left-hand side of the barrier, faced town, and crossed my eyes just right, two bars of cell service begrudgingly flickered onto the screen. After reporting the accident—accident? No way was what happened to Lucy an accident—I hotfooted it back to where Sunny and Brittany waited with Lucy's motionless body.

By the time I got back, Brittany had coaxed Sunny away from Lucy's side, but her eyes were frantic, and she hiccupped between sobs. Her rapid and shallow breathing, coupled with the fact she was shaking like a leaf in the wind, indicated she was on the edge of a full-blown panic attack. I was two seconds from freaking out myself, but giving in to panic wouldn't help the situation one tiny bit. Instead, I drew on my training as a yogi and touched Sunny lightly on the shoulder while looking into her eyes.

"Let's sit over there for a minute." I nodded my head to an outcropping of large rocks on the far side of the trail, then led Sunny to them and forced her to sit, despite her jittering limbs. From our new vantage point, we didn't have a view of Lucy's body.

"Let's take a minute to help you focus on your breathing so you don't pass out. We're going to take a deep breath together and begin to calm our bodies. Is that okay?" When she nodded, I continued, "Okay, inhale, hold it...and exhale. Good. We're going to repeat the same thing a few more times." After about ten repetitions, Sunny's breathing settled into a much more natural rhythm, and I was no longer worried about her toppling over.

Brittany had raced to the lookout to alert the others, then joined Sunny and me when she returned. "I told everybody there was a delay and said Lucy asked them all to be patient until she gets back." She sucked in a sharp breath and jammed her shoulders up around her ears. "I hate lying to everyone, but didn't want to tell them the truth and have the whole group panic."

"You did the right thing," I assured her.

"I don't understand how this could have happened." Sunny's voice was barely above a whisper. "Who would want to kill Lucy? All she does is release beauty out into the world."

"The police are on the way. Chief Barnhart will figure this all out and find the person who's responsible," I assured her. "Did you happen to notice if any of her equipment is missing?" When Sunny sucked in a sharp breath, I added, "We don't have to talk about it right now if you don't want to."

"No, I want to. We need to figure out who did this." Sunny glanced between Brittany and me. "Her camera is gone. She was using her Nikon D850 today, and it's not there. I already looked. It should have been attached to the tripod."

"Maybe the camera tumbled down the cliff when the tripod fell over?" I was tempted to go in search of the missing equipment, but after my own near tumble, decided to hang tight and let the authorities sort it out.

"No. Lucy used a clamp that had to be unlocked to remove the camera from the tripod. It doesn't make any sense for somebody to kill her for her camera. It's a professional unit, but a run-of-the-mill variety. It's not like the thing was worth a fortune." Before I could answer, Sunny kept talking.

"The only thing that made the camera special was the person using it. Lucy was amazing and super talented. I was finally getting closer to her, getting her to trust me. She was starting to open up, and now I'll never have the chance to really get to know who she was deep down."

I frowned. Sunny was talking about Lucy as if the woman was a feral cat whom she'd been attempting to tame a little at a time. Lucy hadn't given off skittish vibes to me, and with her popularity as a photographer, she was often in the spotlight. The small amount of interaction I'd had with Lucy led me to believe the woman could be somewhat standoffish and more than a little stubborn, but not timid by any stretch of the imagination. With her staying at the inn instead of at the farm with Sunny and Danae, it stood to reason Lucy might have been protective with her time and personal space, which seemed perfectly understandable to me. Maybe Sunny wanted more out of her relationship with her boss than she was ever going to get.

"How will I ever know what Lucy had been thinking? Why did she do it?" Sunny continued. "How could she have walked away without a second thought? You can't treat people as if they're disposable and not realize there's going to be consequences for your actions later on, even if it takes years."

Confused, I glanced over at the trail where Lucy's body lay concealed over the edge. Sunny seemed a little confused. Lucy most definitely had not walked away. "What do you mean? Walked away from what? Did Lucy do something you think could've made someone mad enough to murder her?" I asked.

Sunny pressed a palm to her heart and squeezed her eyes shut. "Don't listen to me. I seriously don't even know what I'm saying right now. Probably talking complete gibberish. I'm just so shocked, you know? I've never seen a dead body before."

"Me either," Brittany said, wide-eyed. She shivered. "And I never want to again."

"You never really get used to it," I added.

Two pairs of eyes swiveled my way, staring at me as if I'd suddenly sprouted an extra head.

"What? I've seen a couple now, and I'm telling you, it doesn't get easier."

Sunny dropped her head into her hands. "I can't believe someone used her own tripod to kill her. I always told her it was dangerous to keep those spikes on the tripod, but Lucy didn't want to have to fiddle with them once she found the perfect location for her shot, so she always had me attach them ahead of time."

"Do you guys think her death could've been a terrible accident, then?" Brittany asked. "Maybe Lucy slipped and somehow jammed the spikes into her own chest?" Before she even finished speaking, Brittany was shaking her head along with Sunny and me. "Yeah, you're right. There's no way that could be possible, not with the angle."

"Not to mention it would take a huge amount of strength to shove a tripod spike into someone's chest. If she'd fallen forward onto them, maybe, but Lucy was lying on her back." I pressed a fist to my racing heart and took a gulp of mountain air.

The calm our breathing exercise had given the three of us had worn off with our conjecture about Lucy's death. Sunny's grief boiled over into a mournful sob and ran in streaks down her face.

I reached over and rubbed her back. "How long had you worked for Lucy?"

She swiped at her eyes. "About a year. Not nearly long enough. There was so much more she needed to tell…I mean, teach me."

"I'm so sorry," Brittany said. "Even though your time with her was short, it sounds like the two of you were close. Her death must feel like losing a member of your family."

"You have no idea." Sunny jumped to her feet and paced up and down the trail until law enforcement arrived.

Chapter Five

For a man the size of a retired linebacker, Chief Dale Barnhart arrived at the crime scene looking as if he casually strolled a couple of miles up a mountain every morning before breakfast. A male officer a good twenty years the chief's junior trudged fifty yards behind. Once he caught up, the man held a hand to his side and doubled over, panting like a dog.

"Geez, Chief. You didn't tell me we were going to be moving at mock five with our hair on fire," the officer panted out.

Chief Barnhart threw him an irritated scowl before glancing around. "Where the heck is Bishop?"

"Almost there, Chief," a wheezy voice called.

We all swiveled to watch a portly officer who was nearly as wide as he was tall, struggling up the hill. He had a high and tight military-style haircut above a face as red as a ripe McIntosh apple.

The chief sighed. "Take your time, Dave. The last thing we need is to be packing two bodies out of here." He turned to me. "Morning, Callie. We have to stop meeting like this."

"I agree a thousand percent."

"Show me where you found the body. The paramedics are ten minutes behind us."

I walked over to the edge of the trail and pointed. "She's over here."

Chief Barnhart scooted down to where the body lay and studied her. "Do you know who she is, by any chance?"

"Yes, Lucy Thorne. That's her assistant sitting over there with Brittany." I pointed to the two women who were perched on a log behind us.

Chief Barnhart asked Sunny to verify Lucy's identity, then directed the three of us to go back to the lookout and wait with the photographers until someone came to talk with us.

As I swiveled to obey his orders, the chief tugged on the sleeve of my jacket and leaned down, keeping his voice low. The scent of peppermint from the gum he chewed wafted over me. "Do me a favor, will you?"

I nodded enthusiastically. "Sure. Anything."

"I'm assuming the group of people gathered at the lookout were Ms. Thorne's workshop participants?"

"Yes, they were supposed to wait there for Lucy," I affirmed.

"When we went by, a few tried to ask questions, but I managed to hold them off and told them to stay put. Until either myself or another one of my officers gets back to the lookout, keep your eyes and ears open for me. Pay attention to anyone acting overly nervous. You can tell them there's been an accident, but let us report the death. Just listen to the chatter for anything that seems out of place. Once we get the victim off the mountain, I'll touch base with you."

"Got it." I tried not to let my emotions show, but inwardly, I glowed with pride. After getting myself embroiled in a couple of his cases since my arrival in Bobwhite Hollow, it seemed Chief Barnhart was beginning to trust my instincts. I wouldn't let him down.

As Sunny, Brittany, and I marched down the trail, we ran into a crew of paramedics carrying a stretcher and supplies. We moved off the trail to allow them to pass by. As soon as we came into sight of the gathered photographers, we were hit with a barrage of questions.

"What's going on? I don't have time for this garbage. I have a full schedule and am three seconds away from calling an Uber and sending Lucy the bill. She's costing me time and money." Alex knit his eyebrows together and scowled. "This whole fiasco has been wildly unprofessional. You can bet I'll leave a scathing review on her website." He ran a hand through his light brown hair, causing it to stand up even more than it already was.

An Uber? Good luck, buckwheat. Even if Alex miraculously managed to find a ride share in Bobwhite Hollow, no way would one agree to pick him up clear out here on Weaver Mountain.

Danae's dark brown eyes narrowed as she marched over to us. "Is Lucy okay? Why have law enforcement and paramedics arrived? I tried to follow them, but the Chief of Police told me to stand down. Those flipping jokesters. I should've realized there was something bigger going on and followed them anyway. I need to learn to be more assertive. Why is everyone trying to thwart me simply doing my job?" Her amber cheeks flushed a feverish red while a vein down the middle of her forehead pulsed, making it clear she was in full reporter mode and furious about being cut out of the action. She whipped out a voice recorder and pushed play. "What can you tell me about what happened on the mountain today? Don't hold anything back."

Before any of the three of us had a chance to answer, Jen raced up and shoved Danae aside. "Chief Barnhart wouldn't tell us anything when he went by. The guy's a schmuck. We need to know what's going on. You know, Alex is absolutely right, and that's saying a lot since I usually don't agree with anything that comes out of that guy's mouth. We all have busy lives. I have so much on my plate right now that I really can't stay here much longer. I mean, I hope Lucy's okay and whatever happened is just a minor setback, but, not that it's anybody else's problem, I stayed up way too late last night watching a documentary about the disco scene back in the 80s and didn't get my laundry done. It was super good, you know. Those Gibb brothers, I tell you. Gives an old lady like me hot flashes." She grinned and fanned her face with her hand, "I mean, I'm only forty-five, so was just a baby during the disco era, but man alive. I had to go wake up the hubby, if you get my drift." She winked and grinned.

I did, but I didn't want to. Why complete strangers felt the need to share tidbits of their intimate lives with others was beyond me. My eyes glazed over, and I checked out of the conversation as Jen's voice droned on and on. I mean, I tend to ramble myself, but this woman was next level. When she started in on what seemed to be a recitation of her grocery shopping list, I stepped away from her, raised my hands and shouted. "Hey, can I get everybody's attention for a minute? As you guessed from seeing the police and medics, there has been an accident up on the trail. Chief Barnhart asked for us to all hang out here. One of them will be down to give us an update as soon as they can."

"I've had enough of this nonsense. As a member of the media, I have every right to be on the scene of an accident." Danae lifted her chin and glared at me as if I was the one holding her back.

"Don't worry, girl. I'm not going to stop you. Do your thing." I wasn't about to stand in her way. Sure, I'd promised Chief Barnhart I'd keep the group away, but what a reporter chose to do was out of my control.

In one fluid motion, Danae swung her bag onto her back and raced up the trail, eager to uncover the truth of what had happened and share the breaking news with the world.

I'd barely closed my mouth when Jen opened hers and started in again. "You know, I don't know why I have to stay. I wasn't even up here most of the time. I had to use the restroom, so I'd gone back to take advantage of the outhouse at the trailhead. I mean, I know you said it was an accident, but there's nothing I can tell the police to shed any light on…well, whatever the problem is that needs light shed on it. To be perfectly honest, I don't even know Lucy."

I interrupted, "You were down at the trailhead? You must know about the bear breaking into your van, then, right? Aren't you supposed to be down there taking care of things?"

Her blue eyes flared as wide as saucers. "What? A bear in my van?"

"Yeah, your friend must have forgotten to tell you in the kerfuffle. The Forest Ranger, Garrett, wanted you to head down to the parking lot as soon as you could. It must've happened after you'd used the outhouse and came back up the mountain to take photos, since you don't know a thing about it."

Jen eyed me with a horrified expression before she scurried off down the trail. Chief Barnhart might be irritated with me for sending her away, but oh, the blessed silence. Even with a dozen of us still milling around, the conversations were all muted and low. I could actually hear the wind through the trees again. It wasn't until she was gone that I wondered if Jen always talked so much or if her incessant chatter could be chalked up to nerves. I'd be sure and mention her diarrhea of the mouth to the chief.

I perched on the edge of the picnic table, my eyes and ears on high alert as we waited for law enforcement to give us the all clear. Brittany and Sunny sat on a fallen log away from the rest of the group, their heads together as they talked. I was glad Brittany was there to give Sunny someone to mourn with, since we were the only three who knew about Lucy's demise.

The photographers milled around, some talking amongst themselves and others taking the opportunity to snap more photos. I heaved myself off the table and wandered around, trying to pick up on any suspicious conversations, but it turned out to mostly be chatter about photography techniques and equipment. *Shoot.* Looked like I was already failing at the covert mission Chief Barnhart had tasked me with.

After what had to be a couple of hours, the chief and Officer Bishop finally strode into the clearing, with Danae right on their heels.

"Listen up, people." Chief Barnhart projected his voice like a bullhorn. "I understand you all took Lucy Thorne's workshop this morning—"

"Where is Lucy?" Alex interrupted. "I'll be demanding a refund, and I want to see the money today."

The chief held up a beefy palm to stop the tirade. "I'm sorry to inform you that Ms. Thorne has met with an accident and is deceased."

Accident? I swung my gaze to Sunny. By her ramrod straight posture, it was clear she'd picked up on the terminology as well.

A collective gasp came from the group of photographers.

"Oh my gosh. Did she fall over the cliff?" a woman asked.

"She did not," the chief answered. "I misspoke. We will be investigating Ms. Thorne's death as a homicide and expect your full cooperation." Chief Barnhart jerked a thumb at his cohort. "Officer Bishop here will be taking down names, phone numbers, and addresses for each one of you. When he is finished, you will be free to go, but we will be conducting individual interviews with all of you. Do not, under any circumstances, leave the county until we've had a chance to speak with you. You will be hearing from either myself or one of my officers within the next twenty-four hours. Most likely much sooner. Make sure you're available."

Danae thrust her recorder into the chief's face. "Chief Barnhart, what can you tell me about the homicide? Can you describe what happened and who you think was involved? Do you have any viable suspects at this time?"

The chief swiveled and stared directly into Danae's eyes. "Once again, Miss Mutasa. No. Comment."

Danae huffed and lowered her recorder.

"My hands are clean, I can tell you that much," Alex said. He shivered and zipped his thick coat up to his chin. "For all of you who were expecting to have your work from today critiqued, I will step in and take up the slack Lucy left behind. And in lieu of this terrible tragedy, I'm offering my professional assessment of two of your photos for only a hundred bucks. That's an incredible deal at half my normal rate."

"Would you just shut your stupid mouth?" Sunny screamed. "Lucy's dead, and you're standing here trying to cash in on her death. I bet you've never even critiqued someone else's photographs before, have you?"

A mumbling from the rest of the group seemed to agree with her.

Alex sputtered and stomped his feet like a toddler. "Fine. Whatever. I was just trying to help. You all are on your own." He started to walk away, but then turned to Brittany. "It might not be the best time to bring this up, but what's going to happen with the contest at Soul Dust, now that the great Lucy Thorne isn't in any shape to judge the entries?"

Brittany held up both hands, palms out. "You're right. It is absolutely horrible taste to bring that up right now, but the contest will continue. I'll make sure of it."

Was it only a couple of hours ago we'd followed Lucy up the trail, hanging on her every word? My gaze traveled over the outlook to the vibrant display of autumn leaves in the valley and mountains beyond. The contrast of the beauty of the morning slammed up against the evil act of someone snuffing out Lucy's life was hard to wrap my mind around. Who would do such a thing, and why? Was her killer someone taking the photography workshop? I eyed the group of people with suspicion. What could possibly have driven someone into such a rage they would stab Lucy in the heart with her own tripod spikes? The act was brutal and full of hate.

After Officer Bishop gathered personal information from each of us, it was a solemn group who arrived back at the trailhead an hour later. I'd been hoping to get a glimpse of the damage the bear had managed to inflict on Jen's van, but neither she nor the Forest Service Rangers were anywhere in sight. Instead of dispersing and warming up, the cloud layer had grown heavier. Just as I slid into the driver's seat, fat raindrops drummed on the roof of the truck, beating out a solemn rhythm. With a heavy heart, I cranked up the heater, flipped on the headlights and windshield wipers, and headed for the comfort of the farm.

Chapter Six

My stomach rolled and my whole body thrummed like I was a human fidget spinner. My neck and shoulders were taut with tension. Maybe food would help get the anxiety under control. It was past lunchtime by the time I flew down the gravel road leading to the farm. The waves in my stomach had morphed into loud rumbles.

Aunt Ellen's car was pulling out of the driveway when I pulled in. She slammed on her brakes, rolled down the window, and stuck her head out into the rain while shouting something at me.

I rolled down my own window and threw Old Rusty into park. "What? Sorry, I couldn't hear you."

"We expected you back hours ago." Aunt Ellen's voice was gruff and cranky, completely out of the norm for her. She shook raindrops out of her short, champagne-pink hair.

"I'm sorry. There was a problem on the mountain, and not much for cell service. Did I forget about something I was supposed to be doing?" I'd tell her about Lucy's death later, when she returned from wherever she was going in such a hurry. And hopefully in a better mood.

"I left a note on the table for you. I'm running your uncle into the emergency room."

"The emergency room?" I leaned over and noticed Uncle Will in the passenger seat for the first time. My heart jammed against my rib cage as I took in the ghostly pallor of his skin. His head hung to his chest, and his eyes were squeezed shut. "What happened? Was there an accident? Is he going to be okay? I'll meet you at the hospital." All thoughts of Lucy's murder immediately flew out of my head in my concern for Uncle Will.

"I didn't mean to alarm you, ladybug." My great-aunt's tone changed to one more recognizable. "He's having another one of his headaches, but worse than ever. He can barely function, and it's past time he had them checked out. This time I'm not taking no for an answer. I had one heck of a time getting him into the car by myself, but we're on our way now."

My jaw dropped open as I pictured my tiny great-aunt trying to maneuver the nearly unresponsive six-foot-tall Uncle Will into the car.

"Why didn't you call for an ambulance?"

From the passenger seat, a weak but gruff voice mumbled. "I don't need no dang ambulance."

I reached for the handle of the back door. "I better go with you to help you get him into the hospital."

Aunt Ellen shook her head. "They'll bring a wheelchair out when we get there. We'll just see you at the hospital in a bit."

"I don't need no dang wheelchair," Uncle Will grumbled again.

"You two get going. I'm going to change, check on the animals, and I'll meet you there."

"Fix yourself a sandwich, too. We don't need you fainting from hunger."

Highly unlikely. Like my goats, I was food-motivated and rarely went too long between snacks. "Drive safely, and I'll see you soon."

Aunt Ellen nodded grimly and floored her car. Gravel from under her tires sprayed the old rock wall lining the driveway as she squealed onto Old Canal Road without stopping to check for traffic.

Inside, I hurried up the stairs to my bedroom in the two-story white farmhouse and swapped out my yoga outfit for a pair of jeans and a cozy sweatshirt before heading for the kitchen to find something to eat. A good old-fashioned PB&J seemed like the quickest option. I slapped peanut butter and grape jelly on a slice of white bread, layered crunchy potato chips on top, and squashed a second piece of bread over the concoction. I poured myself a glass of cold milk and ate my lunch standing over the kitchen sink, staring blindly out the window at the backyard.

My head spun with worry, concerned about Uncle Will's health. At eighty-four, he was no spring chicken. His words, not mine. He claimed he'd never had a headache in his life until this past August when his first one hit. Ever since, the headaches had been his nearly constant companion, with one or two a week leaving him prone on the couch. Ice packs, rest, Aunt Ellen's lavender essential oil, and a lot of fussing on her part usually had him feeling better in a few hours. Today, apparently, even her remedies and hovering weren't doing the trick. My brows knit together as my brain scrolled through a list of medical conditions that could cause debilitating headaches, each item on the list worse than the last. My mouth was dry thinking about the terrible possibilities, and I nearly choked on the last bite of my sandwich. I gulped down the glass of milk, wiped off my hands, and headed out to the barnyard to do a quick check on the animals.

Chapter Seven

"Should I call Tristan?"

Uncle Will had been whisked away to have an MRI, so Aunt Ellen and I sat in uncomfortable chairs in the emergency waiting room of the squat brick hospital. The chairs were cushioned but so deep that if we sat against the back of them, neither of us could reach the floor with our feet. Aunt Ellen perched on the edge of her chair like a chickadee on a branch while I chose to scoot back, leaving my feet swinging six inches off the floor.

"Not yet, ladybug. There's no sense worrying my grandson until the doctor comes back with a diagnosis." Even in times of trouble, Aunt Ellen was always the voice of reason.

After what seemed like a lifetime, a tall, male nurse wearing luminous lime green scrubs called to Aunt Ellen from the door to the ward. "The doctor's ready for you now, Mrs. Haybeck. Follow me, please."

"Am I allowed to go with her?" I asked.

The nurse glanced at Aunt Ellen for confirmation, then flashed me a quick smile. "Yes, of course. Come on."

I jumped up and tagged along. He led us to a tiny room not much bigger than a coat closet. "The doctor will be right in," he said in a cheerful tone as he left us to deal with his next patient.

Uncle Will was propped up in a hospital bed, looking a thousand times better than my last glimpse of him through the car window. His skin tone was almost back to that of the man I knew and loved. Two bags of fluid hung on a rack above his head and dripped into his arm through a port placed in the crook of his elbow. "There's my favorite ladies," Uncle Will said with a crooked grin. His voice shook slightly and wasn't as robust as normal, but the twinkle in his eyes was back.

Aunt Ellen bustled to his side. "Well, look at you. Sitting up and talking like you have good sense." Her teasing smile reflected her relief.

The ringing in my ears that had been there since Aunt Ellen announced she was driving him to the hospital settled into a quiet hum.

"I told you I just needed to rest a minute and would be right as rain in no time. Didn't need to make all this crazy fuss over this old geyser." His eyebrows rose in expectation when the doctor walked into the room. "What do you say, Doc? Are you going to take this thing out of my arm so I can get out of here?"

"Not quite yet, Will." The doctor greeted Ellen by name, then held out a hand to me. His short hair, styled into a traditional business cut, was so black it glinted blue under the fluorescent lights. "Dr. Perry Luo. You must be Callie, the niece."

I nodded, knowing the comment didn't require a reply.

The doctor waved a hand at the lone chair squeezed into the small space between Will's bed and the window. "Please take a seat, Ellen." He sat on a stool placed in front of a computer screen on the opposite side of the bed and swiveled to face us.

Aunt Ellen settled into the chair while I stood against the wall beside her.

Once we stopped rustling around and turned our attention his way, the doctor glanced at Uncle Will and then back to Aunt Ellen. "Will here is a lucky fellow. You got him to us in the nick of time."

"I did?" Aunt Ellen asked, a breathless tone to her voice.

"She did?" Uncle Will repeated, sounding confused.

For once, I kept my trap clamped shut.

Doctor Luo nodded and pulled up an image on the screen that appeared to have been taken from the top of the skull. "She did. This is the image of the MRI we took of Will's brain moments ago. See this black spot here? It looks like a bubble, or a balloon, if you will." He pointed the area out and turned to make sure Aunt Ellen and I were looking at the spot he referred to.

Aunt Ellen gasped and covered her mouth with a shaking hand. "Are you telling us my Will has had a stroke?"

The doctor lifted his index finger in the air. "Not yet, which is exactly why Will is a lucky hombre. Currently, he has no brain bleed to speak of, but we don't want to waste any time getting in there to fix this problem area and ensure a stroke doesn't occur."

"Whoa. What are you saying, Doc? I need brain surgery?" Uncle Will's face, already as pale as the sheets he rested against, drained of every last drop of color until it was difficult to tell where he stopped and the pillowcase began.

"Because we caught it early enough, and your overall health is excellent for your age, I propose we do an endovascular repair, which is far less invasive than brain surgery. We go in through a vein in your leg and insert a coil to open the blood vessel and allow the blood to flow normally, thus preventing a stroke."

"You can get to my brain through my leg?" Uncle Will asked in a wobbly yet incredulous voice.

Doctor Luo chuckled. "I know it sounds like science fiction, but yes, we access the problem area of the brain through your leg."

"And how soon should this procedure be done?" Aunt Ellen asked.

The doctor pressed his lips together in a tight smile. "To be perfectly honest, there's no time to waste. I'd like to get Will into surgery as soon as possible. Within the hour would be best."

"Once I have this surgery, my prognosis is good?" Uncle Will asked.

"Absolutely," Doctor Luo replied straightforwardly. "The headaches should cease, and you'll be back to yourself in a few weeks. Without the procedure, I'm afraid it's just a matter of time before you experience a major stroke."

"And how long will I be laid up? There's a lot of farm work I've got to get done before winter sets in."

"You'll be staying here with us for two or three days, depending on how well you do during surgery. At home, you'll be taking it easy for a good two weeks, at the very least. I prefer six weeks, but we all know how stubborn you can be. We'll also be discussing a few lifestyle changes you're going to need to be making, as well."

"Six weeks is simply not acceptable. There are things I need to get done," Uncle Will started to bluster, but was shut down by his wife of sixty-two years.

"William Martin Haybeck." Aunt Ellen stood to her entire five feet nothing, fists on hips, chin up, and a defiant glint in her eye. "There is no question about it. You are having this procedure done. You won't be doing any chores if you're dead. I'll hear no argument from you, old man. End of conversation."

In the face of his wife's ultimatum, his bluster blew itself all the way out. "Fine. I guess I've been told. Let's get 'er done, Doc."

"Good man. I'll get everything set up, and someone will be here to get you in a short time. Don't worry. We're going to take excellent care of you." Doctor Luo stood, patted Uncle Will's foot, and spun out the door, a man on a mission.

As soon as the doctor was gone, I spoke up. "Okay, so I know we were going to be moving the sheep to winter pasture in a few days. What needs to get done before I can move them?"

Uncle Will blew out his cheeks and studied me for a minute. "The sheep shed needs to be cleaned out and a thick layer of straw laid down. The fence around the field needs to be thoroughly checked for any weak spots and fixed. If any posts need replacing, it's imperative to get them set before the ground freezes solid. Once the freeze comes, we're out of luck."

"Easy enough. I'm good at cleaning and can hold my own when it comes to fixing fence. What else?"

"Check the water lines going into the troughs. Make sure they're working right, and the insulation is tight around the lines. Dealing with frozen pipes in the middle of a blizzard isn't a fun chore. There should be plenty to keep you busy until I'm recovered. Maybe you can rope our strong young veterinarian you've taken a shine to into giving you a hand."

Despite the worry over my great-uncle, a grin cracked my face at the thought of Levi McClure. I wouldn't say we were in a relationship necessarily, but we were exploring the possibility. We'd been on a few dates in the last month or so, swapping stories and getting to know each other. For our first outing, we'd driven north to a great little Irish pub Levi knew where we'd both indulged in rich bowls of lamb stew with a side of foot-stomping traditional Irish music. The evening had been pure magic, and I couldn't wait to go back one of these evenings in the near future. While we'd strolled hand in hand along the river later, I'd learned Levi rarely stopped moving and was hyper-focused on doing everything he could to make his practice—Stonefield Veterinary Clinic—successful. I'd rolled with laughter when I found out the charismatic vet's only pet was a box turtle named Zippy. Just imagining the contrast of Zippy meandering through life to Levi's hectic energy left me wiping tears off my cheeks. We'd discovered Levi relaxed by reading enormous tomes of nonfiction with a preference for history, while I preferred fast-paced thrillers and quirky cozy mysteries. He loved folk and bluegrass music as opposed to my dedication to Seattle grunge. The two of us were polar opposites in a million different ways, but none of our differences made the spark of electricity jolting through my system any less powerful whenever Levi took my hand.

"Not a bad idea," I conceded. "Though I'm not sure when Levi would find the time. His practice has really taken off lately."

Within half an hour, the tall, dark-haired nurse whooshed back into the room. He rubbed his hands together and introduced himself this time. "I'm Skip Morales. Will, I'll be taking care of you once you come out of surgery." He circled his face with a long, slim, tawny finger. "This face will most likely be the first thing you see when you come out of the anesthesia. Do you have any questions for me before we roll you into surgery?" He flashed a grin with teeth so white I expected to hear a ping like in the dentist commercials on television.

"When are they taking me away?" Uncle Will asked.

"Any minute now." Skip checked Uncle Will's vitals, then documented them on the computer.

He'd just finished when a second nurse entered the room and began to wheel Uncle Will away. Aunt Ellen and I both kissed him on the cheek and promised to be close by when he woke up.

"Let me show you to the room Will's going to occupy after surgery," Skip said. "Then I suggest you go get something to eat. They're going to have him three to four hours, and then he'll be in recovery for a bit, so you have plenty of time to fill your bellies. I've got your number right here in my phone, Ellen, in case I need to call about anything before you return. But don't you worry. Your husband is in the best hands."

Aunt Ellen refused to leave the hospital to eat. "You go ahead, ladybug. I'm going to make some phone calls. Tristan and Jim both need to know what is going on."

"Would you like me to talk to Tristan while you tell Jim?" I asked.

"Thank you, but no. I want to tell them myself."

In order to give her some privacy for her phone calls, I decided to run out and get us both sandwiches and coffee.

When I exited the hospital, an ambulance was parked at an entrance to the building I hadn't noticed when I'd arrived. Chief Barnhart stood on the sidewalk as the medic crew unloaded a stretcher with a sheet-clad body lying on top. He disappeared through the doors behind the stretcher and medic.

Curiosity got the better of me, so I hopped in Old Rusty and turned right instead of using the left-hand exit to the parking lot. I slowed at the door where the ambulance was parked, nearly folding myself in half to read the discreet sign above the door. "City Morgue."

With Uncle Will's health scare, Lucy's brutal murder had taken a backseat in my thoughts. Now, the whole sordid affair came crashing back in stark detail.

Chapter Eight

Normally, I loved cruising through the quaint streets of Bobwhite Hollow. The five blocks of the village's Main Street were lined with historic brick buildings housing various businesses alongside a handful of clapboard-sided vintage homes turned into charming coffee shops, antique stores, and boutiques. The historic Bobwhite Inn, circa 1850, with its majestic white pillars in the Greek Revival style, took up one full block smack dab in the village center. Two weathered, white church spires rose into the sky, one on each end of Main Street, holding court over the quintessential New England village. With colorful fall mums and pumpkins set out in front of shop doors, and the background of trees alight in full autumn splendor, our village made me feel like we were moving through a movie set.

Today, though, I was hyper-focused on fetching an easy take-out dinner and getting back to the hospital as soon as possible. I ordered Aunt Ellen and I both delicious sandwiches filled with savory turkey, sweet cream cheese, and the acidic pop of cranberry chutney layered on herbed focaccia bread from Bunny Hill Bistro.

While our sandwiches were being prepared, I plopped onto a wooden bench near the front door and checked my phone for any messages. There was a text from my mom I'd missed.

Hey! Where are the pictures of Lucy Thorne you promised me?

My stomach executed a complete somersault.

Sorry. Uncle Will in hospital. All good. Will call later.

My short response would buy me some time to get my thoughts together before having to admit to my parents I'd stumbled onto yet another murder in my newly adopted village. The news would only make Dad double down on his efforts to get me to move back to Seattle once he found out, and I was not anywhere near ready for the extra stress that conversation would pile onto my head.

"Callie, here you go." A waiter handed me a white paper bag filled with our mouth-watering sandwiches.

Sliding the bag of sandwiches onto the seat of the truck, I slammed the door and headed back down the sidewalk. My destination was Cranky Bear Coffee and their decadent maple hazelnut lattes. The coffee shop used real maple syrup sourced locally. I had never tasted a latte so delicious. Even though it was later in the day than either Aunt Ellen or I usually drank coffee, I was going on the theory that it was going to be a long night and we could use not only the comforting flavors, but also the jolt of caffeine.

Back at the hospital, I filled Aunt Ellen in on Lucy's death as we ate our sandwiches and waited for news on Uncle Will. When the waiting felt too oppressive, I turned on the television mounted on the wall for some background noise. The last person to watch this particular set had been tuned to the CBS channel from Burlington, Vermont. Instead of scrolling through channels, I left it where it was and stared blankly at the screen until a familiar voice penetrated my worried haze.

My slouchy spine shot ramrod straight as an image of Danae standing in front of the Bobwhite Hollow police station filled the screen. A red "Breaking News" banner scrolled endlessly across the bottom of the scene.

"Jeez, Louise. It sure didn't take her long."

"What's that, ladybug?"

Aunt Ellen was in a similar foggy funk as I'd been feeling, so I pointed to the television screen. "Danae. She's one of our guests at the farm. She's the reporter who was traveling with Lucy and her assistant. Apparently, now, she's swiveled to reporting on Lucy's death instead of on her career."

Aunt Ellen blinked at the screen as we watched in silence for a few minutes.

"She's doing a fine job of it," Aunt Ellen remarked. "Good for her. I'm glad the network let her take the lead on the story. She seems like a nice young woman who was fortunate to be in the right place at the right time. The same can't be said for poor Lucy Thorne."

I frowned, remembering Danae's comment shortly before Lucy's body was found about looking for her big break and creating headline news herself if a story didn't fall into her lap soon. She'd been joking, but I hadn't cared for the feverish look in her eye, joke or not. Now, only a few hours later, here she was reporting live on the homicide of the well-known photographer. With Lucy's popularity, it wasn't a stretch to think Danae's broadcast could be shared on channels around the world. Certainly in North America at the very least. Did Danae take matters into her own hands to create the destiny she wanted for herself like she'd hinted at? Would she have murdered Lucy to elevate her own career?

On the screen, Danae somberly instructed her viewers to stay tuned. She would be reporting back with any developing news the moment more information became available. Was it too much to hope the news hadn't reached Seattle yet? Or if it had made the national news, that my parents wouldn't be watching tonight?

My phone pinged with an incoming text from my dad:

Call me ASAP

Yep, it had obviously been too much to ask. I could see the entire text in my notification bar without needing to click on the message, so I turned the sound off on my phone and slipped it back into my pocket. I'd call him back…soonish.

A few minutes later, Chief Barnhart tracked me down to conduct my interview and find out if I had observed anything worthwhile at the lookout with the workshop participants.

"Ellen," he took my great-aunt's hand and patted it. "I heard Will's been rushed into surgery. Dr. Luo is the best, so we know he's in good hands. Jackie sends her best and wants you to call her if you need anything. Anything at all."

Aunt Ellen nodded. "Tell her I appreciate the thought. Will's going to be just fine. I feel it in my bones."

"I'm sure you're right." Chief Barnhart turned to me. "Are you ready?"

I led him down the hall to a quiet nook I'd noticed earlier in the waiting room. We sat in side-by-side chairs with a small table squeezed between them.

The chief took a small notebook and a pen out of his jacket pocket. "Start from the beginning and tell me everything you observed."

I took a calming breath and stared at the ceiling for a moment. "Okay, well, my truck was blocked in, so I had to wait for all the workshop participants to get back so Jen would move her van, and I could leave. Since I didn't have any other options except to sit in my truck and fume, I figured I might as well wait at the lookout with everybody else. The photographers were all back from their individual shoots when we realized Lucy was missing."

Chief Barnhart held up a hand. "I'm going to stop you there and have you reach back even further. Take me back to directly after you arrived at the trailhead this morning. What was going on? Who did you see?"

I shrugged. "Sure. It was still dark when I got there, but the lot was filling up fast. Before I even got out of Old Rusty, Jen Earley pulled up behind me in her van and blocked me in, like I mentioned." I told him about arguing with her about moving her van, to no avail. Then about Brittany meeting me at the trailhead, the hike up to the lookout with the photographers, Alex's in-charge-of-everyone attitude, and every single other little thing I could think of that had transpired before we found Lucy's body. By the time I finished, my mouth was dry. "I need water. Do you want some?"

The chief nodded, so I rose and trotted to the vending machine, returning with a bottle of water for each of us.

When Chief Barnhart finished scribbling notes, he took a long swig of water before asking more questions. "To make sure I'm clear, Brittany, yourself, and Lucy's assistant, Sunny Hammond, went in search of Lucy." He screwed up his face. "Anything unusual stand out there?"

"Nope. Everybody, well, especially Alex, was getting irritated about Lucy being so late coming back to the meet-up spot. Sunny said it wasn't unusual for Lucy to get caught up taking photos and lose track of time, but decided to go look for her since the group was getting restless. Brittany and I went along to help so Sunny didn't end up getting lost in the woods, too."

"From what you're saying, Sunny didn't seem to think anything bad had happened to Lucy?"

I shook my head. "No, not at all. Once we reached the end of the trail and Lucy hadn't answered any of our shouts for her, Sunny seemed to get a little more uneasy."

"And what was her reaction when you found the body?"

I raised one finger. "Correction. Sunny found the body, not me."

He frowned and jotted something on his paper. "Noted. Please continue."

"Once she found Lucy, Sunny became frantic, panicked almost. She nearly hyperventilated before I was able to help her get her breathing under control. But I genuinely don't think it was an abnormal reaction. I was feeling panicky myself."

"And how did Brittany react?"

"Brittany?" I asked, confused. "She was upset but remained fairly calm. But Brittany can't be a suspect. She was with me the whole time. There's no way she could've killed Lucy." It took me a second to realize what he was hinting at. "Wait. Do you think Sunny is a suspect?"

He raised his eyebrows. "Don't you?"

"Honestly, with Uncle Will's health scare today, I haven't given it much thought." I tapped my lips with a finger, then launched into my report about Sunny's seemingly obsessive interest in her boss, Danae's remark about possibly creating a story to launch her career, Alex trying to horn in on the failed workshop and scoop up business for himself, and Jen's nervous chatter.

When I finished, Chief Barnhart let out a big sigh. "Gives me a good bit to get started with. Now, what can you tell me about the black eye Lucy was sporting?"

"Sunny point-blank asked her. Lucy didn't want to talk about it, but when Sunny pressed her, she said she had gotten up in the middle of the night, forgot where she was, and ran into a corner of the wall." I hesitated.

"That lines up with what the others told me, but you don't seem wholly convinced. Why not?"

I ran a hand down one of my blond braids and fiddled with the dyed orange end. "Lucy seemed flustered and embarrassed when Sunny questioned her about the injury."

"Flustered how?" the chief asked.

"She tucked her chin down like she was trying to hide the bruise and stammered around when she answered the question. I don't know, I just got the feeling like she wasn't being totally honest. Running into a wall? Isn't that the typical answer when someone gets punched in the eye and doesn't want to admit it?"

"You have a valid point."

"Did the police happen to find Lucy's camera? Sunny was adamant it was missing from the crime scene."

"Nope. We sure didn't." Chief Barnhart shook his head and flipped his notebook shut. "Alright, I guess that's all for tonight. I've kept you away from your aunt long enough."

I stood, but had one last thought. "There were several other people on the trail today who weren't part of the workshop. One man in particular stands out. Garrett someone. I don't remember his last name, but from what I understand, he works for the Forest Service. Anyway, he was uber focused on Lucy while she was talking to the photographers. Then they shared a weird little sign language communication when she finally noticed him watching her."

"Sign language communication? Neither one of them are hearing impaired, that I know of."

"Not real sign language," I clarified. "Just some random hand gestures. It definitely seemed like they knew each other, but I also got the impression that Lucy wasn't expecting to see him. Plus, this Garrett guy followed her up the trail when she went out on her own shoot, even though she'd motioned for him to stay back and leave her alone."

"Garret Rogers." Chief Barnhart flipped his notebook closed and jammed it into his pocket. "Garrett's a good man. A family man. I've known him for fifteen years. Probably had a chocolate lab with him, didn't he?"

I nodded.

"Figured as much. He was just taking Buddy for his morning walk.

Nothing nefarious in that."

"Buddy?"

"The dog." Chief Barnhart stretched his neck to the right until it popped. "I'll follow up with him to see if he saw or heard anything while he was on the trail, but I'll eat my hat if Garrett had anything to do with this murder."

Then why had Garrett been looking at Lucy like he wanted to have her for lunch? And what about the strange interaction I'd witnessed between the two of them? My gut said Chief Barnhart better get the salt and pepper out for his hat dinner.

Chapter Nine

y the time Uncle Will was back in his room after a successful surgery, full dark had fallen, and Tristan had arrived from Boston. Nurse Skip brought in an extra bed for Aunt Ellen to stay by Uncle Will's side, and Tristan and I went home to take care of the farm.

Once all the animals were fed and watered, I checked the time. Ten o'clock, which translated to seven in Seattle. I sighed. Better deal with the conversation with my parents now instead of putting off the phone call for eternity like I really wanted to do.

"Hey Dad." I attempted to put some cheer into my voice when he answered my call, but it rang false, even to my ears.

"Callie, what's going on out there? Mom said your Uncle Will is in the hospital. What happened? Is it serious? Is he going to be okay?"

The concern in my dad's voice dumbfounded me. Even though he'd never met them, and we shared a surname, Dad wasn't a big fan of the Haybeck family. He'd often lamented that he wished his stepfather had adopted him and changed his last name. When I'd expressed interest in finding this side of our family, Dad told me to go ahead but to leave him out of it.

"It is serious, but the surgeon says Uncle Will is going to be okay. He's been having bad headaches and dizzy spells since late summer. The MRI showed he was on the verge of having a major stroke. He had surgery this evening to correct the problem, and his prognosis is good. He came through the surgery with flying colors."

"Whew." Dad gushed out a breath. "That's great to hear. I know how close you've grown to him and Ellen, and I wanted to make sure you were all okay."

"So far, so good. Tristan arrived a couple of hours ago, so between the two of us, we've got things handled at the farm."

"Good, good. I'm really glad you're there for them. It's such a relief. Anything else we should be aware of?"

Apparently, the news of Lucy's death hadn't made it across the country yet. I blew out my own breath and dove in. "If you haven't heard already, you're going to find out soon. You know the landscape photographer Mom likes so much was in Bobwhite Hollow this weekend, right?"

Dad grunted.

"Well, she was killed this morning. They think someone at the workshop she taught this morning murdered her."

"Yeah, your mom and I heard about her death on the news this evening."

"And you're not going to beg me to come home?"

"Gosh, no. Terrible things happen everywhere. We can't all run away every time things get hard or don't go the way we want them to. That woman's murder didn't have anything to do with you, and right now you need to be there to support your great-uncle. Family is everything. You're right where you need to be."

I pulled the phone away from my ear to stare at it for a second. Who in the holy haystacks was this guy, and what had he done with my dad? Should I be concerned about his sudden change of heart? Had aliens abducted him and left this imposter in his place?

"I couldn't agree more. How's Mom doing? Can I talk to her a minute?" Maybe my mom would be able to shed some light on my dad's complete one-eighty.

"You know your mother. The news of the photographer's death tore her up. She's soaking in a hot bath with her calming bath salts, a paperback, and a glass of wine. I'll tell her you called and give her an update on the family. Love you lots. I know you're busy and probably exhausted, so we'll just talk soon." My dad disconnected the call.

An update on the family? This was the first time Dad had ever talked about the New England Haybecks as if he was actually connected to them. I'd been attempting to forge a bridge between them since I'd arrived with zero luck. Or so I'd thought. It looked like my efforts were starting to make small inroads. I'd gladly take any little bits of progress I could get.

By the time I finished my call, Tristan was already snoring on the couch. I pulled a blanket over him and trudged upstairs. Changing into snuggly flannel pajamas, I climbed into bed and must have fallen asleep the minute my head hit the pillow.

My alarm jangled me out of sleep at six. I slapped it off twice before giving in and rolling out of bed fifteen minutes later. There was still plenty of time to tend to the animals before my yoga students would start to arrive. By seven, the goats, sheep, mules, and chickens were all fed, and I had a cereal bowl-sized mug of coffee in my hand. Before going to bed last night, I'd taken a half-dozen of Aunt Ellen's sweet potato muffins out of the freezer to thaw and had delivered them to Sunny and Danae in the guest cottage when I went out to feed the chickens.

Sunrise didn't come as early in October as it did in the summer, so the goat yoga session scheduled for the photography contestants didn't start until eight. Given yesterday's tragedy, it wouldn't surprise me in the least if no one showed up. Since the session was open to the public as well, I'd make sure I was ready anyway. Had I been thinking clearly, I would've canceled the whole thing if it had occurred to me. I hadn't given it a single thought before ten-thirty last night, and by then it was far too late.

I pulled on a pair of burgundy leggings with subtle mandala designs in the fabric, a black, long-sleeved yoga T with my new Zen Goat logo on the front, and a matching zippered hoodie, then headed to the barn. With the fall weather unpredictable, Uncle Will and I had removed several sections of old stalls to create a large enough space to hold sessions in the barn. It should work well until it got too cold for even the covered space. As soon as the temperatures dipped below freezing, goat yoga would come to a screeching halt until the spring.

"Which reminds me, I really need to start looking for a job to hold me over until then," I muttered as I patted Bugsy's soft nose. "Got any recommendations?"

The goat remained silent, and I had to agree with him. I wasn't sure I was going to have much luck with job hunting going into winter in small town Bobwhite Hollow, but I'd better get a little more proactive since my income stream was about to dry up for a few months.

"Hey, cuz. What do you need help with?" Tristan stretched his arms above his head and yawned as he strolled into the barn.

"I didn't expect to see you so early this morning."

He cracked his neck from side to side. "Couldn't sleep, so got up and called Grandma to check on Gramps."

"And? How's he doing?"

"Great. Grandma said he's already bored senseless and harassing the doctor and nurses to let him come home."

I laughed, relieved the crisis seemed to have passed. "Sounds like Uncle Will, alright."

"You didn't answer the question. Do you need help with anything?" Tristan asked again.

"Well, I'm not sure how many are coming. It might be just you and me sitting here looking at each other, or a whole crowd could show up since Brittany advertised this weekend's sessions at Soul Dust. Maybe you could collect the payments if a bunch of people end up coming?"

"Sure. Sounds easy enough," Tristan agreed.

I handed him my phone and showed him how to pull up the QR code I'd created. The code made it easy for people to scan with their own phones and make contactless payments that I then transferred directly into my bank account.

"There's a code for today's session, or one for four sessions if they want to pay ahead. They get a ten percent discount if they pay for four upfront. Slide to the next screen for a code for a Zen Goat T-shirt, if someone wants to purchase one." I tapped the top of a plastic storage tote. "The shirts are all in here, sorted by color and size." Pastel pink, sky blue, and mint green shirts were visible through the side of the container.

"Got it. What if someone wants to use cash?"

"The money box is on the shelf in my closet. I forgot to bring it down. Do you mind going to get it?"

Tristan ran off to do my bidding while I brought a tub of yoga mats into the barn. By the time the first car pulled into the driveway, all eight of the younger goats bounced around in the Zen Pen, and Tristan was all set to collect payments from the participants. I pranced to the barn entrance to greet the newcomers, glad there would be at least two yoga students this morning since Brittany had arrived with her husband, Chris, in tow.

"She made me come, but I don't have to participate." Chris flung his hands out, one of them gripping a travel coffee mug. Thankfully, the lid on the mug remained solidly in place. "Sorry. It's probably weird to have me here. Guys don't usually do this kind of thing, do they?"

"Guys do goat yoga all the time. There's totally nothing weird about you being here, I promise," I reassured him, then pointed to Tristan. "In fact, my cousin is going to be joining in. Right, Trist?" I swiveled to my left and raised my eyebrows at him.

"Uh. Sure. Yep."

I'd pay for roping him in later.

Brittany hip checked her husband. "See? Told you so."

Chris laughed nervously. "I wasn't sure how to dress." He had short, brown hair, a slight frame, and stood only about an inch taller than his diminutive wife. He wore a white baseball-style shirt with blue sleeves over a pair of baggy grey sweatpants and scuffed, black Adidas tennis shoes.

"What you're wearing looks perfectly acceptable to me," I said. "We're not formal around here. Goat yoga takes place in a barn, after all. You can't get too fancy when you're sitting in straw."

"Then let's get this thing done." Chris rubbed his hands together and pointed to the barn. "In there?" He took off at a trot, not waiting for my reply.

Let's get this thing done. Whatever, dude.

Brittany and I both frowned at his back as I made it my personal mission to make this the most enjoyable morning of Chris Shields' life.

More cars filled up the driveway. I recognized a handful of my die-hard goat yoga regulars, as well as some of the people who had been at yesterday's photography workshop. There were even a few folks I didn't remember ever seeing around town. It appeared the flyer Brittany had hung in her gallery to advertise the weekend yoga sessions had done their job.

I caught Tristan's eye and pointed double fingers at Brittany and Chris. "Hey, these two don't pay. In fact, please give them each a Zen Goat T-shirt as a thank you for getting all these people out here."

"You got it, boss."

Fifteen minutes later, twenty-two people stood in the mountain pose on mats in the Zen Pen, including our two Haybeck Farm guests, Sunny and Danae. The talkative Jen and her friend from the day before slid in just as we were getting started. Raindrops tinkled on the metal roof of the barn, as soft and cozy as light piano music.

"Welcome to the Zen Goat," I greeted everyone, raising my voice to be heard over Jen's chatter. "Goat yoga is all about stretching, relaxing, letting your stress fall away, and enjoying the experience. Don't worry too much about your form today, just relax and have fun. A little info about our goats before we get started. These guys love being around people. They are quite friendly and super playful with delightful personalities. The more you laugh at the goats' antics, the more they will show off for you. They're little attention hogs. They have really great lives here on the farm, which includes regular checkups with the veterinarian. They're happy and healthy, so nothing to be concerned about there."

"I'll be the first to attest to everything Callie is saying to be true," Nancy, one of my regulars, spoke up. "These goats are incredibly well-treated. And I'm a staunch animal activist, so I don't make the claim lightly."

"Thank you, Nancy. I appreciate your support and kind words." I made a mental note to give her an extra punch on her goat yoga punch card.

Tristan tucked the money box away and scooted into the pen quietly, taking the last empty spot in the far corner. I sent him a grin. No other men had shown up today, so I was glad he'd joined in to help make Chris feel a little more comfortable.

"This morning, we're going to start with the pose called warrior one. Stand on your mats facing me, feet hip-width apart. Now, take a big step back with your left foot. You want two to three feet of distance. Good. That's right. Bend your right knee. Your knee should be lined up with your ankle. Press into your back foot for balance. Now inhale and raise your arms overhead, focusing on lengthening the spine. Perfect. You've got it."

After four months of working the crowds, the goats knew exactly what to do to elicit laughter from their fans. They kicked up their heels and let out short bleats as they circled in and out between the student's wide stances. I glanced at Chris, who looked stiff and uncomfortable as he held the pose.

"From here, we're going to move into the tree pose," I directed the class. "Place your hands on your hips, now bring your right foot and place it high onto the inside of your left thigh." I demonstrated the pose, aware that it took a good deal of balance and not everyone would master it right away. Especially not with goats trying to play king of the mountain on those extended legs.

About ten breaths in, half of the class had toppled over from either poor balance or the force of goats knocking against them. Both Brittany and Chris lay sideways on their mats while two goats jumped over them in a game of leapfrog. Laughter rang up through the rafters of the old barn, bringing an enormous grin to my face.

"Alright, most of us are already down on the ground, so we're going to move into the child pose, or kiddd pose, as I like to call it." I bleated out the word kid to an array of laughter.

Goats played king of the mountain, head-butting each other and hamming it up while the class stretched.

Jen kept up a constant stream of conversation, talking to her friend, who seemed to have tuned her out. "This is so much fun. Who would have ever thought it? Can you imagine someone thinking up the whole concept? I'm glad you invited me, MJ, and happy there was a session today because tomorrow morning I have church, as you well know, and I would really hate to have missed out but this way I can still catch the sermon and it's just as important we get our souls fed as well as our bodies, you know what I'm saying? After church I've got the in-laws coming over for lunch, and you know how judgmental my mother-in-law is, so everything has to be just right, then Rae has her last soccer game of the season at three tomorrow afternoon. Oh, and did I tell you about…" Her droning voice reminded me of a hive of bees frantically making honey. The woman was exhausting, and I'd only been acquainted with her for twenty-four hours.

I moved the class from the kid pose into downward dog.

Chris was struggling with the pose, so I reminded him not to worry about it and just do the best he could. "I'm just going to hang like this, if that's okay," he said with his hands hanging a foot above the ground. While he was talking, a brown and black goat jumped onto his back and knocked him sideways. He laughed and grabbed the little goat. "Never mind, I'll stay down here and play with this guy."

"Would it be alright if I took a few photos?" Danae asked. "They may wind up on a story, so I want to make sure to get everyone's permission first."

"What do you guys think? Is everyone okay with Danae taking pictures?" I asked.

A chorus of affirmations rose up, so Danae walked around the Zen Pen, snapping photos. As she moved around the pen, she stopped to request interviews from every person who was at the workshop the morning before. When she moved close to Jen, the chatty woman reached out and grabbed her arm before Danae could make her own request.

"Hey, have you heard anything more about Lucy's death?" Jen asked, her eyes wide and curious. "Do they know who killed her yet?" She made a slashing motion across her throat with her finger.

Danae jerked her arm out of Jen's grasp. "No, nothing I can share outside of my newscast."

"Oh, come on. You were on the news last night reporting the incident. Are you sure there's nothing you can tell me? You know, friend to friend? Being there at Lucy's last workshop when the tragedy happened forged a bond between all of us. Don't you feel it? With your credentials, the police must be sharing information with you."

"I promise you, they're not. And I don't have any more information than anyone else." Danae shook her head.

Jen blinked. "I don't think you're being truthful with me. I thought you'd have all the inside scoop, especially seeing how you were the one who found the body and all." She wrinkled her nose. "What was that like?"

"I have no idea. You have your facts wrong," Danae replied, irritation ringing in her voice. "Sunny, Lucy's assistant, is the person who found the body, not me."

"Oh." Jen turned her head and gazed at Sunny with an expression of mild surprise. "I could've sworn it was you."

"Well, then you'd be wrong." Danae put her camera in her bag and settled on her mat in lotus position with a goat in her lap. "Now, what about that interview? Are you willing to talk with me?"

Jen flapped a hand in front of her face as her pale skin flushed. "Me? On camera? Oh, gosh, I don't know." The dreamy look on her face told an entirely different story. When Danae failed to beg for the interview, Jen changed her tune. "I mean, really, what can it hurt? It's just a conversation. Sure. Let's schedule a time to talk."

From my standpoint, it seemed like both women came to goat yoga this morning with ulterior motives in mind. Danae to browbeat people into exclusive interviews with her, and Jen to gather gossip on Lucy's murder. An image of Jen rushing to the phone to scatter tidbits like chicken feed to her flock of chattering hens popped into my head, and the term busybody came to mind.

We moved through a series of other poses, all strategic to give the participants and goats plenty of room to interact. Everyone was having such a good time, even I was surprised when the timer on my phone buzzed to let me know to wind the class up.

"Alright, we're going to finish this up today with a Zen Goat original; the napping goat pose. Lie flat on your mat, eyes closed, and let your arms and legs go lifeless. Good. Let's just hang out here for a few minutes. Can you feel your worries melting away?"

"Yeah, not so much," someone said in a quiet voice.

I sat up and glanced around. Sunny was on her mat, but propped up on an elbow, a look of despair on her face. Dark circles rimmed her bright green eyes, sinking them deep into their sockets. She scrambled to her feet and tore out of the Zen Pen and the barn as if she couldn't get away from the rest of us fast enough. The woman was definitely grieving the loss of her boss. Unless guilt for murdering Lucy was eating her alive.

Chapter Ten

"Sooo…" Tristan slid up beside me on stockinged feet. "What did you think of Skip, Grandpa's nurse?"

"Skip? I think he's great. He seems like he's on top of things, knows what he's doing, and his bedside manner was flawless. He really made Uncle Will feel comfortable." We'd both cleaned up after yoga and were making a quick breakfast of scrambled eggs and toast before leaving for the hospital.

"Right, but what about his looks? Tall, dark, and handsome. Just how I like them!" Tristan buttered two slices of toast, sliding them next to the fluffy piles of scrambled eggs I'd plated for us.

I carried my plate to the table and fell into a kitchen chair before blinking at my cousin. "Seriously, Tristan? Yes, Skip is some super nice eye candy." I pursed my lips.

"What's the sourpuss look about?" He scooped up a forkful of eggs.

"About you falling in love as often as I sneeze," I said. "What are the chances of you flirting with the hottie nurse but just leaving it at that?"

"About as likely as the chance you won't be sticking your snub little nose into this murder investigation."

I shot him my best mean mug. "For your information, Chief Barnhart asked me to keep my eyes and ears open. And, with everything else going on, I've barely even done that."

"Yet."

He had a point. I spooned raspberry jelly onto my toast and didn't reply.

"And, by the way, I noticed you don't sneeze very often anymore since you have your magic snake oil," Tristan replied, referring to an essential oil concoction I bought from a local herbalist. "You didn't sneeze even once during yoga this morning."

"True. That stuff has been crazy good for keeping my goat allergies under control." I shoveled the last bite of scrambled eggs into my mouth while I studied my cousin's face. "Hmm. I wonder if Althea can whip something up to keep you from falling head-over-heels for every guy that catches your eye?"

Tristan rinsed his plate in the sink, then flipped around and snapped me with the dish towel. "There's nothing wrong with a little bit of romance. What is it Alice Hoffman said in *Practical Magic?*"

"Fall in love whenever you can," we quoted together. How could I argue with a good, solid piece of Alice Hoffman wisdom?

* * *

"Get me out of this contraption!" Uncle Will swatted at the IV tube hooked to his arm. He swiveled his bare legs around so they were dangling off the side of the hospital bed and tried to tuck the too-small blue hospital gown around his backside. "There's no shred of decency left. I want to go home."

"William Haybeck, behave yourself," Aunt Ellen scolded. "You'll be back home soon enough."

"Can't be too soon for the likes of me."

"Steady there, Mr. Haybeck. You just wait for me to get over there to help you." Skip shot us all an indulgent smile as he hurried to maneuver the IV pole around. Today, he wore a pair of vivid coral scrubs that reminded me of a tropical fish. The colorful nurse took Uncle Will's elbow and attempted to help him off the bed.

Uncle Will swatted Skip's hand away. "Now you just back off, son. I'm quite capable of getting myself to the bathroom by myself. The minute I'm not, you can put me in the ground."

As Uncle Will grabbed the IV pole and shuffled to the tiny restroom, Skip hovered behind him, hands out in case he fell, but not touching my obstinate great-uncle. When the door closed behind Uncle Will, he was still grumbling about not having any privacy.

Skip didn't waste time changing the sheets on Uncle Will's bed while he was in the restroom for a few minutes. Tristan jumped up and helped pull the sheets tight on the far side of the mattress.

"Well, it seems Uncle Will is back to his feisty old self, and this room is crowded with all of us milling around, so I'm going to go back to the farm and get started on my list of chores," I said.

"Do you need help with anything right away?" Tristan asked. "I thought I'd stay and visit with Grandma and Pop-Pop a little bit longer."

And Skip being on shift this morning wouldn't have anything to do with your desire to hang out longer, would it? I kept my thoughts to myself. "Sure. No worries. I'll save all the hard tasks for you." I swung my bag onto my shoulder and fished the truck keys out of the pocket of my jeans. "Is there anything specific you need taken care of today, Aunt Ellen?"

"Nothing that can't wait for another day, but I appreciate you asking." Aunt Ellen stood and stretched. "There is one thing I'd like to talk to the two of you about, though, before you rush out of here."

"Sure. What is it?"

Aunt Ellen looked at Tristan, then glanced back at me. She opened her mouth, then hesitated and snapped it shut again.

Oh, no. The doctor *had* given them bad news, and she was trying to decide how to deliver it to us. Was Uncle Will sicker than we'd been led to believe? My stomach rolled, and I suddenly felt like I might lose my breakfast all over the floor.

"Grandma, what? Just tell us, please," Tristan begged, picking up on the same vibe.

She sighed and took Tristan's hand. "You know I had to call your dad and let him know what's happening." She paused again while we both stared at her, transfixed. "I'm sorry I didn't tell you sooner, but he's on his way. He'll be in Bobwhite Hollow this evening and will be staying at the farm."

Tristan's face went from worried to angry in two point three seconds. "Why? How dare that pompous pig even think about showing his face here after what he's trying to do to you and Gramps? I won't allow him to even be in the same room with you. No, he cannot come here."

I glanced at Skip, who was staring at the computer screen and doing his best to fade into the corner of the room.

Aunt Ellen sighed heavily. "Well, it's not up to you, now, is it? Jim is my son, and he had a right to know about his father's surgery and health scare. Listen to me, the last thing your grandfather needs right now is more stress and family drama, so if you can't control your temper, I need you to step out of this room until you can pull yourself together."

Tristan's ire deflated. "I'm sorry, Grandma. I know, and I didn't mean to upset you, but I'm just so angry at him. All I want to do is protect you."

She laid a soft hand on his cheek. "I know you do, love, but everything's handled. There's nothing for you to worry about."

"Do you mean he has dropped the petition?" I butted in.

Tristan's dad, Jim, had come up with a hairbrained notion claiming I'd tracked down his parents in order to steal the farm from them in some elaborate scheme. From his high-rise office in Chicago, where he practiced law, he'd filed a petition to have my great-aunt and great-uncle proclaimed incompetent and give him power of attorney over every bit of their financial lives. Aunt Ellen and Uncle Will had hired their own attorney to defend themselves against their son's attack. It wasn't a far stretch to think the drama from the last couple of months had played a significant role in Uncle Will's stress levels and subsequent near-stroke.

"No, he hasn't dropped the petition yet, but trust me, we're fighting the thing tooth and nail," Aunt Ellen replied. "Anyway, I wanted you to know he's on his way, so it doesn't come as a complete surprise to you when he shows up. Now, I want you both to be civil while he's here. We need to show a united front." She glanced between the two of us.

"Got it. We'll behave." I nodded, thankful I had scads of work waiting for me back at the farm to help keep my mind off the coming confrontation with Jim Haybeck.

Tristan closed his eyes and pinched the bridge of his nose. "Okay, Grandma. I'll do my best to get along with Dad, but for you and Grandpa. Not for his sake."

The door clicked open and Uncle Will shuffled out of the bathroom. Skip got him settled back in bed, then turned to Tristan. "My lunch break is coming up in a few minutes. Would you care to keep me company?"

Tristan's eyes lit up and he bounced on the balls of his feet. "Yeah. Sure. Sounds like a great plan."

Should I tell Tristan he reacted like an overeager puppy to Skip's suggestion?

Nah. I decided against teasing my cousin. This time. With his dad on the way, he could use the sweet diversion Nurse Skip was offering. I left them to their lunch plans and headed for the barn.

Chapter Eleven

I t's true hard work not only strengthens the muscles but also clears the mind. Three hours of raking up old straw and sheep nuggets from the sheep shed gave me a little clarity on a few things. Uncle Will's Great Pyrenees farm dog, Daisy, flopped down and kept me company as I gave my muscles a good workout. Between the Haybeck family drama and Lucy's murder, my brain muscle was also clicking overtime.

The first conclusion I arrived at was that I had absolutely no control over a single thing Jim said or did. Or Aunt Ellen and Uncle Will's actions, for that matter. If they wanted Jim here while Uncle Will recovered, then I'd better get okay with the whole scenario pretty darn quick. If he wanted to start any crap with me once he arrived, I'd march down the high road and leave him in the dust while his rancor rolled off my back like water off a duck. If I could manage to keep myself under control, he'd have no choice but to back off. It takes two to tango, and I wasn't planning on filling my dance card anytime soon. There were plenty of outside chores to keep me busy for the duration of his stay, and I could guarantee Jim wouldn't be tromping through the barn muck getting his shiny lawyer shoes dirty to lower his standards by helping out on the farm.

Second of all, I had a murder to solve. Okay, not me, per se, but unless Lucy rose from the dead and pointed a finger at her killer, I was positive Chief Barnhart still needed me to poke around and figure some things out. Sure, maybe he said to keep my eyes and ears open in case I heard anything as opposed to actively snooping, but didn't the two scenarios really boil down to the same thing in the long run?

And lastly, if Tristan wanted to fall in love with Skip, a gorgeous man with a solid job who lived in *Bobwhite Hollow* for crying out loud, who was I to stand in his way? I would give my left arm to have Tristan living here full-time. *Half a day, tops.* That's how long I figured it would take me to move out of my bedroom in the farmhouse and into the guest room so Tristan could have his childhood room back. It'd be an easy swap since I had yet to add my personal flair to the room anyway. My brain cycled through ways to throw Skip and Tristan together even more in the next few days.

With everything settled, in my mind at least, I scooped the last shovelful of old hay out of the barn and turned to toss it into the wheelbarrow.

"Bugsy! What in the love of Pete are you doing?"

The crazy goat sat in the middle of the wheelbarrow, blinking at me while contentedly chewing his cud.

"How did you get out again, you big silly goof? You can't stand it if you're not in the middle of whatever is going on, can you?" I glanced at Daisy, who was lounging on the ground a few feet away, ears perked and nose working the wind for any hint of danger. Normally, she barked at any little thing that dared to move, including falling leaves and butterflies, but this time she chose not to alert me to Bugsy's latest escapade. "Are you just going to lie there like a lump and put up with this bad behavior from one of your flock?" Daisy flopped over on her back for a belly rub, her tongue lolling out happily.

Instead of marching Bugsy back to the field with the other goats, I simply tugged him out of the wheelbarrow and gave him a quick scratch on the rump. His little tail wagged a million miles an hour like a flag in the wind. Content in the knowledge Bugsy would dog my footsteps as I worked instead of running off to get into trouble somewhere else, I let go of his collar. Daisy exploded off the ground with an ear-splitting deep bark.

"It's just me, Daisy. Settle down." Tristan strode across the field wearing jeans, a blue bulky sweatshirt, and leather work gloves.

Daisy hung her head, embarrassed, as she trotted to Tristan's side, her tail beating a rhythm as she leaned against him as an apology for her bad behavior.

Tristan stroked her fur while giving the big dog assurances that she wasn't in trouble for barking at him. "You were just doing your job. Good girl." He glanced up at me. "Let's get this party started. What's on the agenda?"

"Get the party started? Your timing is impeccable. The hardest part of the work is already done." I leaned on my shovel and eyed the clean floor of the sheep shed. "You can make yourself useful by carting off the last load of old gunk while I take a well-deserved break." I pointed to the full wheelbarrow. "Then we need to bring over a few bales of fresh straw." Prying open the lid on my lunchbox, I dug out the ham and Swiss sandwich I'd made earlier and bit in, washing the sandwich down with a swig of cool water.

Tristan dumped the wheelbarrow, then eyed the distance between the hay barn and the sheep shed while I finished my lunch. "What's the plan here? We're not going to carry those heavy bales the whole way over, are we?"

"Not we. You. My plan is to stand here and watch you lug the bales over." I placed a hand on my hip and raised an eyebrow. "Is that a problem?"

Tristan glared.

"Or I suppose we could use the tractor and trailer, if you think it might be easier."

"I vote for the last option."

Bugsy trotted along behind us like a loyal dog as Tristan and I made our way to the hay barn. Daisy chose to stay put.

"How was your romantic lunch with Skip?" I teased. "Figured you would be too googly-eyed to be of much use this afternoon."

"You must be talking about the hot nurse with the smoldering pools of black lava for eyes." Tristan grinned.

"So, did you hit it off? Tell me everything."

Tristan's green eyes sparkled as he nodded. "As much as you can hit it off in a hospital cafeteria over wilted salad and terrible coffee. If you can believe it, I didn't even care about the lack of atmosphere or edible food. We talked so much Skip was ten minutes late getting back to work."

"Sheesh. Don't get him fired right off the bat. Not a great way to start a new relationship."

"Maybe not, but it'd be a fun story to tell our grandkids."

"Grandkids? Aren't you getting a little ahead of yourself?" I smiled to myself. One evil plan was coming together nicely. "Am I hearing you're planning on seeing each other again? Away from the hospital, I hope?"

"For sure," Tristan replied. "As long as Dad doesn't fly in here like a wrecking ball and blow the entire show to smithereens."

"Fudge nuggets." For one joyful second, I'd forgotten all about Jim's impending arrival of doom. I blew a raspberry with my lips. "I hope he doesn't make everything worse than it already is."

"You and me both, cuz." Tristan hung his head and kicked at a rock.

From the sheep shed where we'd left her, Daisy let out a string of deep bellows and shot past us toward the house.

"Ugh. Don't tell me he's here already," Tristan groaned. "I thought we'd have more time."

We jogged up the hill until we had a view of the farmhouse and driveway. A white mid-size pickup sat idling in the driveway, steam flowing from the tailpipe into the chilly air.

"That doesn't look like a vehicle your dad would drive," I said with a smirk.

Tristan shook his head. "Absolutely not. Not even for a rental."

By this time, Daisy had made it to the truck, keeping up her barking the whole way, which meant the new arrivals weren't anyone she was familiar with. I picked up my pace. As I neared, I noticed two men sitting inside the pickup. I shushed the dog while the guy on the passenger side of the truck rolled down his window. I recognized him from the photography workshop.

"Can I help you with something?" I asked as Tristan and I approached the vehicle.

"The gal at Soul Dust Art Gallery directed us out here. She said you folks were allowing people to take pictures at Haybeck Farm during photography week. Did she steer us wrong?"

"Nope. Brittany gave you solid information. You're more than welcome to wander the farm and shoot pictures to your heart's content. All we ask is for you to be mindful that this is a working farm and make sure you close any gates behind you. We don't want the animals getting out onto the road or into places they shouldn't."

He nodded his chin at Daisy. "Is the dog going to be a problem?"

"Nope, not at all. This is Daisy. Come on out and meet her. Let her smell your hand and get to know you for a minute. She'll be just fine once we make introductions."

Once Daisy sniffed her approval, Tristan and I gave the men a quick snapshot of the topography of the farm, then left them to their photography.

We headed back to work, hooking up the small flat trailer to the green John Deere and loading five bales of clean yellow straw onto the trailer. Tristan and Bugsy hopped up and rode on the pile while I drove the tractor across the field.

Once we wrangled the straw into the sheep shed, I pulled my pocket knife out and cut the twine on the bales. I pulled the orange twine out of the straw and shoved the strings into my pocket. Tristan and I used pitchforks to spread the sweet-smelling straw over the floor. While we worked, my mind wrestled around with Lucy's murder. Before I knew it, I was diving into the pool of suspects.

"Spill the beans, Callie. Who do you think might have killed the photographer?" Tristan asked while we worked. "I know you've been coming up with a theory or two."

I nearly stabbed myself in the leg with the pitchfork as I whirled to face him. "What the heck? I was just thinking the same thing. Can you read my mind now?"

Tristan chuckled. "No, but I think I know you well enough by now to realize you're going to be spending every spare minute trying to figure out who killed her."

He was right. It already seemed like we'd known each other for years, but in reality, we'd only been acquainted since last winter when we'd both taken DNA tests through the same company. Once the results were in, the site matched us up as cousins. Tristan had been interested in his heritage, finding out what countries his ancestors originally came to the United States from, and I'd been searching for him. Well, not him exactly, since I didn't know he existed, but someone from his family—my dad's side of the family, who we knew very little about. When the website matched me with a second cousin,

I'd sent an email hoping to connect, then held my breath until Tristan replied nearly two weeks later. Since our first conversation, we'd gotten along like two peas in a pod. After a ton of phone calls and emails flew between Seattle and Boston, he'd invited me to New England where he introduced me to my great-uncle Will, who was my late grandfather's only brother.

"I don't know." I shook my head to clear the jumble of thoughts about Lucy's murder. "There were quite a few of us there, but nobody really knows what happened up on the mountain yesterday morning."

"Not true. Somebody definitely knows. They're just not talking. Does anybody stand out in your mind as acting weird that day?"

"It's hard to determine, since I don't know most of them, but yeah, there are a couple of people I think could use a closer look. I told Chief Barnhart my suspicions."

"So, tell me this time," Tristan prodded. "Let's see what we can work out together."

"Okay. Well, there were ten workshop participants, as well as Lucy, her assistant, Sunny, and Danae, the journalist writing a story on Lucy. You met Sunny and Danae at yoga this morning. They're the two staying in the guest cottage this week."

Tristan nodded. "Got it. And you and Brittany were there, too, sneaking in on the workshop while pretending you were doing yoga."

"Hey, we were doing yoga." I tossed a forkful of straw at him. "Don't give me that look. We were. So anyway, if the killer was someone who attended the workshop, in my uneducated opinion, there were two people who stood out for acting a bit odd. Of course, I don't really know them, so was their behavior really out of the norm for them? I can't say for sure." I shrugged and leaned against the shed wall.

"Alright. Who were they, and what about them got your radar up?" Tristan glanced around the farm. "Are either of them here right now?"

"No, not those guys. They were fine." I shook my head. "Alex Bell is the first one who comes to mind. He owns Golden Bell Photography in town. The guy has an ego the size of the Atlantic Ocean. According to Brittany, graduation and school photos are his bread and butter, but he fancies himself the best photographer in New England. Alex sent up a red flag because he made a few snarky comments about Lucy and how she was running the workshop. Alluded to the fact that he should've been leading it, then basically told the other photographers to not even bother entering the contest because he took the winning shots. Lucy's death hadn't been announced for two minutes before he was trying to wedge his way in there to make a buck by advertising his apparent skills at critiquing the other contestant's work. The whole thing totally gave me the icks."

Tristan chewed on his bottom lip. "What would be his motive, exactly? More business for his studio?"

"Yeah, maybe," I said hesitantly. "I mean, Lucy wasn't local, so Alex knocking her off to take her clients doesn't make a whole lot of sense. It seems far-fetched for him to think he could step into her shoes as the next big landscape photographer, though his ego is ginormous. In reality, it's highly unlikely, so gaining more business because of her death seems like a weak motive. Jealousy, maybe?"

"Could be. Who else had your spidey-sense tingling?"

I pushed off the wall and glanced around at the newly clean and fresh-smelling sheep shed. "Looks like we're done here, so come on. Let's walk the fence and check for any weak spots while we hash this out."

I grabbed the bucket of fencing supplies I'd put together earlier, and we set out, Bugsy and Daisy tagging along behind.

"The next person I have a strange feeling about is Jennifer Early. She goes by Jen. Fast talker, entitled, and a huge pain in the butt."

"Ah. I'm going to guess she was the blabbermouth at yoga this morning?" Tristan asked.

"The one and only." I told Tristan about Jen blocking me in with her van and not giving a flying frog about it. "She works as the receptionist or something at one of the churches in Bobwhite Hollow."

"Does she go to the same church Grandma attends?"

"Not sure. We'll need to ask." I shrugged. "Anyway, the only time Jen stopped running her mouth was when the group broke up to go out to take their own pictures. Even then, I bet she talked to the squirrels and trees the entire time. Anyway, when I told the group there had been an accident, Jen didn't appear at all concerned about what happened or who might be hurt; she was just concerned about getting back home so she could do her laundry and go grocery shopping."

"Some people just don't have any empathy. As long as the situation doesn't affect them personally, they don't care what happened to someone else. And even if it does affect them, they take the inconvenience as a personal affront. How did she react when the chief announced Lucy's death?"

"She'd already left to check on the bear damage to her van, so I don't know."

"Bear damage?" Tristan blinked in surprise, so I filled him in on the bear incident.

"Wow. That's wild. So do you have a possible motive for Jen offing Lucy?"

"Not really. On top of the lack of empathy thing you mentioned, she just rubs me the wrong way. This morning, I'm pretty sure the only reason she showed up for goat yoga was to scope out the latest gossip."

Tristan chuckled. "Being annoyed by someone isn't a good enough motive, Callie. Who's next on your list?"

"Well, the obvious suspect, I guess. Sunny, Lucy's assistant. She's the person who was closest to her, in Bobwhite Hollow at least, and this definitely doesn't seem to be a random murder."

"Right, the majority of murders are committed by someone the victim knew. Sunny was the one who found Lucy's body, right? The woman who was crying at yoga this morning?"

"Yeah. Brittany and I were helping Sunny search for Lucy, but you're correct. She is the one who actually found the body." I studied a section of sagging fence. "We need to fix this spot. Grab the wire pullers, please."

Tristan reached into the white pickle bucket and pulled out the tool. "Is this the ri—"

A terrified, high-pitched scream ripped through the air.

Blood rushed into my ears as Tristan and I gawked at each other for a split second before dropping our tools on the ground and charging toward the sound. We ate up the distance to the top of the hill in no time flat. Bugsy raced along with us, bucking and kicking up his heels. Once we crested the hill, the sight near the chicken coop stopped me in my tracks and sent me doubled over with laughter.

Rooster Cogburn, Aunt Ellen's gorgeous Rhode Island Red rooster, was in hot pursuit of the man who'd been riding shotgun when the two photographers had arrived at the farm. The man was screaming like a little schoolboy as his arms and legs pumped furiously, trying to stay ahead of the rampaging rooster. The man and bird raced around the barnyard, the rooster's wings keeping up a furious beating. The second photographer hid behind a large oak tree, snapping pictures of the debacle. Not wanting to be left out of the chaos, Bugsy screamed out a series of colossal bleats. Daisy loped up beside me, dropping her butt into the dirt and watching the spectacle with amusement. Apparently, the dog didn't consider the rooster or the rooster's intended victim to be her problem.

"Come on, Callie. Pull yourself together. We've got to help the poor guy out." Tristan nudged me with his elbow.

At the best of times, the rooster was a pure menace. Aunt Ellen assured me that if a person didn't panic and made sure the rooster knew who was boss, he'd leave you alone. So far, my personal strategy had been avoiding the mean old thing as much as possible. And wielding a big stick whenever I ventured into his territory. But if we didn't want Haybeck Farm to be sued within an inch of our lives, it looked like I was going to have to put myself directly in his path. And quickly.

I raced to the barn, frantically searching for anything to help me in my quest. The first thing I laid eyes on was Uncle Will's fishing net hanging on the wall next to his fishing poles. I grabbed the handle, hustled back to the scene of the crime, lifted the net over my head, and waited for the perfect opportunity. As the man and rooster passed by, I lined up the net and brought it crashing down over Rooster Cogburn's ornery head.

The big bird struggled for a moment, then stood still as if conceding his loss. Rotating my wrists, I scooped him up, holding the net high until he was swinging off the ground. The motion caused the rooster to be flipped upside down inside the net where he froze, unblinking.

"Everything's good. You're safe now," Tristan called to the screamer. "The rooster has been nabbed. He's under control."

The poor guy bent over, placing his hands on his knees as his breath came in raspy waves. His friend emerged from behind the tree, looking a little sheepish at his cowardice.

"Oh, no." The terrorized man lifted his head, his eyes wide and panicked as he pointed toward me. "You've gone and killed him. I was only trying to get a picture of him, but he determined I was a danger to his flock. He was trying to protect the hens and didn't deserve to die. You shouldn't have killed him."

"What are you talking about?" I glanced down at the comatose rooster in the bottom of my net and let out a scream of my own. The flipping rooster was dead. *I'm a murderer.* I had a love/hate, okay, let's just call it what it was, a hate/hate relationship with the bird, but killing him was a whole other matter. And now Aunt Ellen was going to kill *me.* Tears sprang to my eyes, and I wanted to throw up. "Holy buckets, he's dead!"

"Just flip him right side up again, Callie. He'll be fine," a deep voice chimed in. "Here, he's heavy. Let me do it for you."

Levi grabbed old Rooster Cogburn by each side and flipped the rotten bird upside right, then removed the net from around the rooster and tucked him underneath his arm. "See? All good. He'll be terrorizing the neighborhood again before you can say Jack Be Nimble." Levi grinned and chucked me under the chin with a finger while the rooster stretched his neck and peered at me through his mean, beady little eyes.

During all the rigamarole, I hadn't heard the veterinarian's truck pull into the driveway, but I shouldn't have been one bit surprised Levi had turned up when he did. The man was notorious for catching me in the most ridiculous of situations. The more humiliating for me, the better. I swear he must have an alarm clock that sends an alert—Callie's about to do something stupid—so he doesn't miss my blunders.

"See. All better." Levi turned to the horrified photographer as the rooster blinked and let out a sharp, irritated squawk. "You're right, though, it can harm them if you hold a chicken upside down too long, but a few seconds like Callie did is necessary sometimes."

"No harm, no fowl," Tristan interjected.

"Couldn't help yourself, could you?" I shook my head.

"Nope." My cousin laughed at his own joke while the rest of us stared at him unamused. "Seriously? Nothing? You have to admit that was a good one."

Ignoring him, Levi looked at me. "Do you want me to lock this guy up in the chicken coop for a bit?"

"Don't worry about it. We're done here and won't be back," one of the photographers said. "Just give us a few minutes to get in the truck before you let that terror loose."

"Should have known better than to come out here. My wife warned me no good would come of associating with folks who harbor murderers," the second guy muttered just loud enough for us to hear him.

Harbor murderers? What in the heck was he talking about?

I apologized profusely for the trouble the rooster caused and the role I played in causing even more trauma. As the men pulled out of the driveway, Lynyrd Skynyrd's "Gimme Three Steps" blared from their open windows.

Levi set the rooster on the ground and shooed him off toward the chicken coop. With his tail feathers flying in the wind, the bird couldn't get out of there fast enough. But how long of memories did chickens have? Did I just manage to gain a mortal enemy?

Chapter Twelve

Once Levi tired of laughing at my chicken shenanigans, he said he'd better get going. "Just stopped by to see if you needed help with any chores since Will's laid up, but looks like you're not letting anything slip through the net." He grinned, pleased with himself. "Call me if you need anything."

"Will do, but I'm not out here running around like a chicken with my head cut off, you know."

"Sorry. Didn't mean to ruffle your feathers."

I tried to not give Levi the satisfaction of laughing at his lame jokes, but a sharp-pitched squawk forced its way out from between my lips. We grinned at each other as I tapped my fingers on the hood of his truck and waved goodbye. "Thanks for undeading the rooster."

Back out in the field, Tristan fished the fencing tool out of the bucket one more time. "Okay, back to where we were going with the murder investigation. What are the chances Sunny found Lucy alive and killed her before you and Brittany got to her?"

I shook my head and shot new staples into the fence post as Tristan held the wire taut. "No way. The three of us had already been all the way up to the summit where the trail ends, calling for Lucy the whole time. If Lucy had been alive, she would've heard us calling and answered back if she was able. On our way back down to the lookout, the three of us split up to search the edge and cover more ground, but we weren't out of each other's sight for more than a minute at a time." I paused. "Except right before Sunny yelled that she'd found Lucy. That's when I almost fell over the cliff. It took me a few minutes to get myself back up to solid ground, and Brittany was with me the whole time, not Sunny. Still, only five minutes at the most." I tapped my chin and sucked in a sharp breath. "Though I suppose it's possible she may have had time to kill Lucy while we were distracted. It wouldn't have taken very long."

"Back up a minute, girlfriend." Tristan flung a dramatic hand in the air, palm out. "You almost fell over the cliff? Are you sure you fell, or were you pushed?"

"Definitely fell—slid—caused by my own clumsiness. But I didn't, and I'm fine. There wasn't any evil plan involved to distract me while somebody killed Lucy. But I don't think it happened that way. And Sunny was super distraught over Lucy's death. She said some things that made me think she idolized her boss, and talked about how much Lucy still had to teach her. Why would she want her dead?"

"Being super distraught over Lucy's death doesn't mean Sunny wasn't the one who caused it. Pretty sure if I killed someone, I'd be crazy emotional. Anyway, why she would want her dead is what we're going to have to find out."

I raised my eyebrows. "We? Are you saying you're in?"

Tristan huffed. "Reluctantly, but you know I've always got your back, so if you're going to insist on playing Nancy Drew, I guess I'll be your trusty sidekick again."

Sure, buddy. The fact Tristan wasn't meeting my eye led me to believe he wanted to jump into this mess as badly as I did. Earlier in the summer, we'd inadvertently gotten ourselves entangled in not one, but two, previous murder investigations. Tristan was already as addicted to ferreting out the truth as I was. We made a good team.

"The investigation could be a needed distraction from everything going on here at home." I pointed to another sagging portion of fence. "There's another spot right there. Give it a good, hard tug."

He frowned but set to work on the fence. "You mean because of Grandpa's near stroke?"

"Well, that too, but I was mostly talking about your dad arriving tonight."

"Ugh. Don't remind me." Tristan blew out a breath and pulled the wire so tight it snapped.

We focused on getting the fence fixed up, then I added another suspect to our pool. "We can't forget Danae. She's a journalist who works for a weekly feel-good TV program out of New York City. New York Vibrations. She told Brittany and me all about how she was recently up for a promotion but got passed over, and she admitted she's more than a little bitter about it. She was supposed to be doing what she called a fluff piece on Lucy, but she said she always has her eye open for a big breaking story that could catapult her career. She was irate when the police tried to keep her away from the crime scene. And she's already been reporting on Lucy's death, at least on the local news channels."

"Do you think she could have killed Lucy for a story? I mean, a story like this one might give Danae the big break she's been looking for," Tristan said.

"I've heard of flimsier motives, and she straight up hinted as much before we found Lucy's body." I shot more staples into the fencepost. "But when those two photographers were leaving, did you hear the comment the one guy made about us harboring murderers here at the farm?"

"Yeah, but I wouldn't put a whole lot of weight on anything those guys had to say."

"No, but it got me to thinking. Murderers, plural. Is it possible Sunny and Danae are in this together? Not sure what their connection would be, other than they're both being harbored at Haybeck Farm in our guest house."

"Which could have given them time together to plot murder. Hmm. Life insurance, maybe?" Tristan suggested.

I wobbled my head back and forth. "Doesn't insurance usually go to the next of kin? I suppose since Lucy isn't married and doesn't have any children, she could have a policy with her work associate, Sunny, as the beneficiary. Maybe to help keep her business going for a while after she's gone? Sunny could've hired Danae to help with the murder in exchange for a nice chunk of change after the insurance pays out."

"It's worth looking into, though I'm pretty sure you can select anyone you want to be your beneficiary for life insurance. It doesn't have to be the next of kin." Tristan counted the suspects off on his fingers. "So just to make sure I'm clear, we have Alex, Sunny, and Danae, who all have possible motives, and then Jen, who you've added to the list just because she irritates the heck out of you. Am I missing anyone?"

I bumped him with my hip as we walked back to the barn. "Hey, irritation seems like a perfectly reasonable reason to me." I laughed. "Oh, yeah, and let's not forget that Garrett guy."

"Who?"

"Garrett Rogers. He wasn't part of the workshop, but was at the trailhead before the photographers went out on their shoots. He stood back a ways watching Lucy. I didn't like how he was scowling at her. You should've seen her face when she noticed him. Lucy almost looked scared and made it clear she didn't want him to bother her, but when she went off to take her pictures, he took off on the trail in the same direction. He had a chocolate lab on a leash."

"And this is the first time you're mentioning this guy? He sounds totally sus. Seems like he should've been on the top of your list."

I shook my head. "From what I understand, everybody around here knows him, and they all claim he's an incredibly nice guy. I don't know. Maybe he just has a naturally scowly face. He works for the Forest Service and is the one who found the bear breaking into Jen's van, shooed it off, and then came back up the mountain to tell her. I don't remember seeing him go back down the trail, but he must've when the girls and I were doing our sun salutations. Chief Barnhart said he's known Garrett fifteen years and wouldn't even consider him as a possible suspect."

"Plot twist!" Tristan smacked me on the shoulder with the back of his hand. "This changes everything."

"What do you mean? How does it change anything?"

"Isn't the killer always the person law enforcement refuses to look at?"

"Sure. In the movies." I rolled my eyes. "And there's usually a dirty cop involved, which Dale Barnhart is most certainly not."

"But it sure sounds like something was going down between Lucy and this Garrett character."

I had to agree. I puffed out a breath of air. "You're right. We definitely need to look into Garrett, since the police won't be doing it."

"Of course I'm right." Tristan mimed polishing his fingernails on his chest. "I'm always right."

"Ha." I playfully glowered at him. "Oh, and did I mention Lucy had a black eye the morning of the workshop? And her camera seems to have been stolen from the crime scene?"

"Nope, you left those little details out. Both of those things add another layer to her death. Who did Lucy have an altercation with before she died, and who the heck stole her camera?" Tristan stared off into space. "How do we start? What are our next steps?"

"We need to jot our notes down when we get a chance, and then figure out exactly where each suspect was when Lucy was killed. Seems like a good place to start, but then we'll need to dig into their backgrounds and find out what makes each of them tick. Who had a reason to want Lucy dead?"

Chapter Thirteen

There wasn't time to dig into the suspect's history right now. We had a field of sheep needing to be moved to their winter pasture, which trumped our unofficial murder investigation.

Putting the bucket of fencing supplies back in the main barn, I slapped my hand against the side of my leg. "How about it, Daisy? Are you ready to earn your kibble?"

The big white dog burst off the ground in a fireball of energy, bouncing in excitement as if she knew exactly what I'd just said. Her main job was to be a guardian and companion, keeping the flock safe from predators. Great Pyrenees aren't traditionally herding dogs, but Uncle Will had trained Daisy to help him move the sheep around when he needed to get them from one pasture to another. She was always more than willing to lend a paw.

Tristan and I fired up the four-wheelers and each rode one out to the summer pasture. Between the two of us on the machines and Daisy picking up our slack, we had the flock of fifty sheep moved to their winter home in under an hour.

The sun was starting to set when we got back to the barn, and I was close to dead from hunger. It'd been a long day. Tristan went to gather eggs and feed the chickens while I took care of the goats, including leading Bugsy back into the field with the others. Finished with the goats, I threw half a bale of hay to Uncle Will's mules.

Next, Daisy got a well-deserved full bowl of kibble. "Daisy, come on, girl. Who's hungry?"

The dog usually came running when she heard the dry food hit her bowl, but this time she limped into the barn at a snail's pace, favoring her left front paw.

"What's the matter, girl? Did you hurt yourself?"

She looked at me with her saggy brown eyes and held up her paw for my inspection. I studied her foot, then ran my thumb over the pad, but didn't see or feel anything out of the ordinary. Daisy let out a heavy sigh and thumped down onto her butt, eyeing me with a disappointed expression.

"I know, girl. We'll go get you some help." I pulled my cell phone out of my pocket and checked the time. Twenty to five. If I hurried, I could get her into Levi's clinic before he closed for the day.

"Come on, Daisy. Load up." I held the passenger door of Old Rusty open for her. She landed on the seat in a cloud of white dog hair. "Tristan," I yelled. He was just mounting the steps to the front porch of the farmhouse. "Daisy has a hurt paw. I'm running her in to see Levi real quick. Be back in a bit."

Stonefield Veterinary Clinic sat on the edge of town in a Craftsman cottage Levi had converted into his clinic. Forest green shingles covered the building while river rock pillars held up the roof of the front porch. A cedar bench sat next to the front door with several terra cotta pots bursting with orange and bronze mums on a tiered stand flanking the other side of the door.

Levi's receptionist was flipping the open sign to closed when I ran up the steps.

"Is Dr. McClure still here? Daisy hurt her paw."

"Oh bummer! I'm sorry, but we're closing up for the day. If it's an emergency, you can take the dog over to…" The receptionist was interrupted by Levi opening the door from the treatment area.

"Dr. McClure?" Levi's deep voice held a hint of humor. His six-foot-two frame and wide shoulders filled the doorway. "It's Levi to you, young lady."

I grinned despite the heat rushing into my face. "I know it's last-minute, but do you have time to take a quick look at Daisy?"

"I always have time for Daisy. Bring her in."

I shot the receptionist an apologetic look on the way out to get the dog, but she good-naturedly shrugged and plopped into the chair behind her desk. "Don't worry about it. I still have some billing to catch up on anyway."

Daisy had been happy to take a ride in the truck, but she wasn't even a tiny bit pleased about being dragged, literally, into the vet clinic. She followed me as far as the porch just fine, but when I attempted to lead her through the door, she sat down on her big, hairy rump and refused to budge.

"Come on, girl. How would you like a biscuit?" Levi held out a dog treat, but it wasn't Daisy's first rodeo. She was well aware that inside that door was where those sharp metal needles lived and she wasn't about to have anything to do with that sort of nonsense.

"Well, shoot. Bribing dogs with treats is the only trick I have up my sleeve. I need better light than those give off to see what's wrong," Levi nodded to the two lantern-style porch lights mounted on each side of the door. He sighed. "Alright, Callie, let's get her inside. You pull. I'll push."

He got behind Daisy, and we slid her across the porch until she finally lumbered to her feet and allowed us to coax her the rest of the way into the lobby. Daisy was prone to dramatics so when she flopped down on the tile floor with a gigantic sigh, I laughed and rubbed her big head. "You're such a sensitive girl, aren't you? So mad." I glanced at Levi. "Do we need to take her into the back?"

He rubbed his trim beard. "Nah, this should work. No need to distress her any more than we already have. Which paw is giving her problems?"

"The left front."

Levi knelt beside the big dog and reached for her paw while talking gently to her the entire time. Daisy quickly sat up and sent worried glances between me and Levi, as if she was asking me if I saw what he was trying to do, and was I planning on rescuing her from the suspicious vet's clutches. When I didn't come to her rescue, she turned her head and growled at him.

"Daisy. No. Levi's trying to help you," I reprimanded.

"It's okay. She's allowed to be grumpy." He got up and went through the door to his exam room, coming back with a basket muzzle. "I'm going to strap this on to Daisy. It won't hurt her but will prevent any bites the old girl feels like handing out."

"Sounds like a good plan to me."

With the muzzle firmly in place, I was surprised how it immediately had a calming effect on the dog. Either that, or she'd resigned herself to her fate. Whatever the case, Levi was able to conduct a thorough investigation of her paw.

"Ah, here's the problem." He grabbed a pair of tweezers and pulled a thorn out from the soft spot between the pads of her foot. "Poor girl. Dang thing must've hurt, didn't it?" He cleansed the area with warm water, then added a dab of antiseptic gel. "There you go, Daisy. You should feel much better now." Levi wiped his hands on a towel, then gently removed the muzzle.

Daisy eyed the door like she was about to make a break for it.

"Can you just add it to our bill?" I asked.

"No worries," Levi replied. He turned to the receptionist, who was doing a fabulous job of pretending she wasn't just waiting to shut down her computer and go home for the day. "Got that, Kelsey?"

"Yep, but tell me which account, please." Kelsey scrunched up her nose and grimaced at me. "Sorry. I'm new here and not super familiar with all the accounts yet."

Levi was almost as new to town as I was. He'd been in Bobwhite Hollow about six months longer than me, and up until recently, he'd been a one-man band when it came to running his clinic. Almost a year after he'd opened his practice, he'd finally started to bring a small staff on board. Kelsey was his first hire, and he'd shared with me how he had started interviewing for a vet tech.

"Oh, gosh. No worries. Haybeck Farm. I'm Callie Haybeck."

Kelsey's chin-length strawberry-blonde hair swung around her heart-shaped face as she nodded and entered today's vet visit into the computer system. When she was finished, she looked up and smiled. "I'm Kelsey Bell. It's nice to finally meet you, Callie. You're the one Doc keeps talking about."

He does? I glanced back at Levi and watched as his Scottish complexion turned ruddy. Good. Nice for him to be the one embarrassed for a change.

"Did you say Bell?" I tilted my head, Kelsey's last name finally penetrating my thick brain. "Are you related to Alex, by any chance?"

Kelsey grinned even wider. "Yep, Alex is my big brother. How do you know him?"

"I don't really. We just met yesterday at the photography workshop."

Her eyes flared wide. "What a disaster. I feel so horrible about that poor woman getting killed. Alex has followed her career since he was, like, a little kid. She was his idol. It's so sad."

Interesting, since Alex had done nothing but talk crap about Lucy yesterday, to the point where I'd wondered why he'd even bothered to take the workshop at all. "I get it. My mom has always loved her work, too."

Which reminded me, I'd promised to send Mom pictures of Lucy. It was surprising she hadn't been blowing up my phone with demands for them, or shock over Lucy's demise. Had her death made national news yet?

Kelsey's voice penetrated my thoughts. "My brother is taking her death super hard. The police questioned him for a couple of hours yesterday. Poor guy." Kelsey sighed heavily. "This is the last thing he needs right now. I'm really worried about him."

"Is there something else going on?" It wasn't prying if the woman was giving the information freely, was it?

I glanced at Levi. He watched the exchange through narrowed emerald eyes and a disapproving frown wrinkling his forehead. I chose to ignore his judgy face and turned back to questioning…I mean chatting…with his receptionist.

Kelsey shook her head dramatically. "Alex is such a hard worker. He's put so much time and energy into his business, just like he did his photography degree."

It was a struggle to refrain from rolling my eyes. What was it with this family and their photography degrees?

Kelsey kept going while I tried to rein in my irritation. "It's not his fault that terrible professor took such a dislike to him. She wouldn't let Alex make up the assignments after he'd missed only a handful of classes, so he couldn't even finish his associate degree."

Wait. An AA? Alex had made it sound like he had a master's degree in photography.

"He was only four credits shy, but without that class, he couldn't graduate. The stupid thing was, it was like some general math class or something.

Didn't even have anything to do with photography. By then, he was on academic probation, and the college wouldn't let him enroll the next semester."

"Where did he go to college?" And I had news for Kelsey. Academic probation didn't stop someone from enrolling in classes, unless they'd been on it for more than one semester and didn't step up and do the work.

"At a community college up in New York City. He had to move out of his dorm and everything. My poor brother."

I raised my eyebrows, attempting to appear sympathetic. "That's too bad. Sounds like Alex got the short end of the stick." *Yeah, right. Maybe Alex should've just gone to class and done the assignments.*

"He tried his best, but there wasn't anything else he could do about it, so he came home, got married, and opened his studio. Golden Bell Photography?"

Kelsey said the name of Alex's studio as if it was a question, so I nodded.

"He's been working like a dog to make his business successful for five or six years now, but despite his best efforts, he's struggling to even pay the rent on his studio space. Alex is trying to find a second job so he can regroup. I think he has an interview at Max's Produce tomorrow."

No wonder Alex had been trying to solicit work from the other workshop participants and was hell-bent on winning the photography contest. The small cash prize would barely buy groceries for a week, but the recognition the photographer who got a photo included in Lucy's calendar could be huge for their career. Even winning first prize at the local level with Soul Dust's contest would've been big, seeing how the winner could rightfully claim Lucy Thorne judged their work to be the best. Well…would have judged the work if she hadn't wound up dead.

"I'm sure everything will work out for Alex just fine," Levi interrupted. He took Kelsey's arm and steered her toward the door. "Why don't you go on home now. It's been a long day. I'll see you tomorrow."

Kelsey threw a hand over her mouth, tears springing to her big blue eyes. "I'm so embarrassed. I've said too much. Alex is going to kill me."

Chapter Fourteen

Daisy and I drove home, her with her head stuck out the window and tongue slinging slobber down the side of the truck, and me with my head in the clouds. Before I left, Levi reiterated again how if I needed any help on the farm while Uncle Will was laid up, he was my guy. And then he'd asked me if I wanted to go with him to Fright Night at a pumpkin patch and corn maze. It was a stupid question, really. There was no way I wanted to go and get scared out of my mind in a haunted corn maze in the dark. After our trip through the funhouse at the carnival last summer, I was surprised Levi would even consider a haunted maze. What was wrong with going in the daylight and leisurely enjoying the maze while munching on caramel apples instead of being frightened out of our minds? But, then again, I wasn't about to turn my nose up at the offer and let my inner chicken shine through. What were a few jump scares between friends? Or were Levi and I finally moving out of the friend zone and into deeper water?

I was debating the merits of wearing a pair of Depends to the corn maze in case of loss of bladder control if Fright Night lived up to its name when I pulled into the driveway at the farm and immediately wanted to turn around. The black sedan parked in front of the porch could only mean one thing. James P. Haybeck, attorney at law and sharp-nosed disloyal rat, had arrived.

I glanced at Daisy, who was alert to the strange vehicle parked in her domain. "What do you think, girl? How long can we avoid going into the house?" Daisy studied me like I wasn't the brightest bulb in the socket. "Gotchya. It's only me who has to go in there. You get to go hang out with your sweet, fluffy sheep friends."

I sighed and slid out of the truck. Daisy shoved around me in her hurry to get on with her evening. With the thorn out of her paw, she wasn't limping at all, but her ears went up, and she swiveled her head, listening.

"What is it, girl?"

The sheep were putting up a racket, and Daisy took off like a bullet. Their protector was back on duty.

I frowned. "What are they so upset about?" I grabbed a spotlight out of the barn and followed the dog to the sheep's new winter pen.

As I moved the spotlight over the field, Daisy was already running the perimeter of the fence, but the sheep were clustered around the water tank. The empty water tank. My heart leapt into my throat. *I'm a complete idiot.* While I'd cleaned the sheep barn and Tristan and I had fixed the fence, brought the sheep to the winter pasture, and fed them, I'd failed miserably to provide them with drinking water, and they weren't happy about it. Neither would Uncle Will be if his sheep died from dehydration.

A frost-free hydrant was strategically placed beside the trough, so I hurried over and lifted the handle. Thankfully, cold water rushed out and began to fill the tank. Thirsty sheep thrust their noses in to suck up the refreshing water. During daylight tomorrow, I'd check the insulation on the pipe and do a test run on the stock tank heater to make sure it was in working order. We hadn't had freezing temperatures yet, but they could plummet any day.

My hands were ice cold, and shivers ran head to toe before the trough was full enough for my satisfaction. No sheep were going to kick the bucket from thirst on my watch.

"Guess I've put it off long enough. Time for a happy family reunion with Cousin Jim." I trudged as slowly as I could to the farmhouse, feeling like a half dozen fluttering bats were playing baseball in my belfry.

Jim met me at the door. "About time you showed up. Off galivanting around town when there's things we need to discuss." He didn't even give me time to take off my coat before tapping the face of his watch and starting in on me. "You've kept me waiting long enough; now come in and take a seat so we can get started." His pointy head disappeared into the front room

Aunt Ellen and Uncle Will called the library.

Reluctantly, I followed. "Nice to see you too, Jim. You're as charming as ever, I see. I would apologize for my tardiness, but I was unaware that I worked for you."

Jim's hostile greeting was on par with what I expected of the guy, which weirdly set me at ease. When he'd first started accusing me of trying to scam the farm from his parents and then filed a petition to attempt to have them declared incompetent, I'd been ready to pack my bags. The last thing I wanted was to make life harder for Uncle Will and Aunt Ellen. After lengthy conversations between myself, my great-aunt and uncle, and Tristan, I'd eventually come to realize Jim's problem with me was his alone. There wasn't any other family member but me helping out here on Haybeck Farm, so his accusations held no weight whatsoever. And Uncle Will and Aunt Ellen's lawyer assured them the petition would not get any traction in court.

Tristan shot me an apologetic look from the corner of the couch where he'd jammed himself. "Dad, Callie needs to get something to eat. She hasn't been out gallivanting. Like I told you, she had to take Daisy to the vet."

"And then fix the sheep's water trough once I got back home," I injected, glad Tristan had my back. "And Tristan's right. I'm going to go use the bathroom, change my clothes, and get something to eat." I swiveled on my stocking feet and left the room. With any luck, Jim would give up and go away before I returned.

Jim spluttered something uncomprehensible as I spun out of the room.

I took my time changing into a pair of comfy sweatpants and a warm sweatshirt. Slipping my feet into my wool slippers, I headed to the kitchen where I turned the kettle on to make a mug of tea, and rummaged through the fridge. In the back of the fridge, I found a container of butternut squash soup Aunt Ellen made a couple of days before. My mouth salivated. I fished a saucepan out of the cabinets and heated the soup slowly so as not to scorch the bottom, then sliced and toasted a piece of her homemade bread. When the soup was piping hot and the toast was golden brown, I filled a bowl with soup and slathered butter on the toast. Balancing my bowl and bread plate on my left arm, I grabbed my mug of steaming spiced tea and headed back to the library, settling into a leather armchair and placing my dinner on the walnut side table.

Jim tapped a pen on Uncle Will's desk and glared at me through dark-rimmed glasses. His pinched eyebrows, long nose, and pursed lips reminded me of Jafar from Aladdin. All he was missing was a pencil-thin mustache and goatee.

"Are you quite ready now, your highness?" Jafar…I mean, Jim…asked.

In response, I simply blinked at him as I loudly slurped a spoonful of soup. No way was I letting this cartoon villain get under my skin.

"And that's another thing," Jim started in, as if we'd already been discussing something. He made a wild gesture that encompassed my entire being. "You're living here free of charge, eating my parents' food, and doing nothing to help them out as far as I can tell. Do you even contribute to the grocery bill?"

"Hey," Tristan started to yell, but I shushed him.

"For your information, Mr. Haybeck, I pay your parents twenty-five percent of my profits from the Zen Goat. They get seventy-five percent of the money we make from the guest cottage rental, and I work on the farm beside Uncle Will nearly every day." I pronounced my words clearly so there would be no mistake about what I contributed to earn my keep around the farm.

"Not to mention all the time Callie spent with Grandma in the garden and helping her can the vegetables this fall," Tristan told him.

Jim appeared a bit taken aback, but cleared his throat and doubled down as if he hadn't heard a word. He leaned over and stretched his long, skinny arm across the room to hand me a sheet of paper. "I've prepared a list of all the chores needing done. Since you're the one living here and taking their hospitality for granted, it's on your shoulders to accomplish them. My dad will not be doing *any* chores for a good six weeks."

"You've prepared a list?" Tristan jumped up and snatched the paper out of my hand. "You haven't lived on this farm, or any farm, for forty years. Why do you possibly think you know what needs done around here? I've never lived here full-time and know way more than you do about it."

I wiggled my fingers at my cousin. "Give me back the list, and hand me a pen, please." I stared at the sheet and willed the rage welling up in my chest to go back where it came from.

As I suspected, Jim's list was ridiculously short and basic.

Adjust timer on chicken coop light to come on earlier. Check.

Bring sheep into winter pasture. Check.

Take lambs to auction. Oops. Uncle Will mentioned we needed to sell the spring lambs, but it was one task that had completely slipped my mind. Better get on it.

Preserve vegetables from garden. Yep, like Tristan already said—done. And Jim was a month too late on that one. If left up to his timeline, the veggies would all be rotting on the vines by now.

Cut firewood. Check.

I looked up. "Is this all you've got for me? These are already all done, except the auction which I'm scheduled to take the lambs to next Thursday."

I grabbed a magazine from the bottom shelf of the side table and placed it under the paper so I could expand the list.

Spread fertilizer over hay fields. Prune orchard and maple trees. Winterize the garden. Rake leaves. Roll up and store hoses. I added about twenty tasks before handing the sheet back to Jim.

"I'll have every single one of these tasks, plus a few more, done in the next few weeks." I pointed to my bowl. "Is it acceptable if I eat my soup now before it gets cold?"

Jim huffed and left the room. The next thing Tristan and I heard was the door to the spare room he was staying in snapping shut.

"Well done." Tristan high-fived me. "Were you really planning on taking the lambs to the auction next week?"

"Nope," I shrugged. "But I am now."

Chapter Fifteen

When I finished my dinner, Tristan pulled his laptop off the coffee table and patted the couch. "Come sit next to me."

"Why? You want to play a game?" Even though it was dark, and we'd scared Jim off to bed, it was only seven in the evening.

"Nope. I want to dig into the suspects we discussed today and see what kind of clues we can unearth."

I jumped up and plopped down beside him. "Good plan."

Two hours later, we'd gone down a warren of rabbit holes, but hadn't dug up any shattering news the police wouldn't have easily found in their first few hours of research.

"Welp, that was a waste of time." Tristan slapped his laptop closed and slid it onto the coffee table with a thunk. "If any of the people on our radar have deep dark secrets, we didn't find them."

"Everybody has secrets. We just have to figure out where to dig for them." I stared out the dark window, my legs jiggling in time with my jumbled thoughts. "How about a field trip to Golden Bell Photography Studio in the morning?"

"Don't you have a goat yoga session scheduled?"

"Well, yeah but early. It'll be finished at a quarter to nine, and most the shops downtown don't open until later. I bet its at least ten before Alex's studio opens."

"Really? Half the days gone by then." Tristan gave me an incredulous look.

"Welcome to small town life. You have to remember this is Bobwhite Hollow, not Boston. It took me awhile to get used to the slower pace, too, but now that I am, I have to admit, I like it."

"When in Rome. Count me in." Tristan shrugged. "Are you up for a game of Scrabble?"

* * *

Sunday morning goat yoga brought people out in droves. With Sunny's short commute walking from the guest cottage to the barn, she was the first to arrive. She flung her arms over the top rail as I was fluffing up the straw and getting the Zen Pen ready for the session. After the way she'd left in tears during yesterday's session, I hadn't expected to see her this morning. Dark circles rimmed her eyes while her hair stuck out every which way. It reminded me of the times my sister and I would rub leftover birthday party balloons all over our heads when we were kids to achieve a similar look.

"Girl, you look exhausted," I said. "You know, you can skip yoga. It's not a requirement."

She stretched her neck and ran a hand down her long hair, smoothing out a tiny bit of the static electricity. "I haven't been sleeping well at all and thought maybe goat yoga would get my mind off Lucy's death for a few minutes and help me relax."

"It won't hurt," I agreed. "If you want to just sit and cuddle a goat, that's fine, too. Whatever works for you. Although stretching and moving your muscles might feel good. Yoga isn't going to solve any problems, but if it gives your brain a rest for a little bit, it's worth the effort."

"My thoughts exactly." Sunny pulled her sweatshirt sleeves down and tucked her hands inside. "Thanks for dropping off the basket of muffins and fruit. Those apple cinnamon muffins are addictive. I ate all four of them before Danae woke up, so let's not mention them to her."

I laughed. "My lips are sealed. Good thing I put the pumpkin muffins in the basket today, too. Or did you eat those ones as well?"

Sunny's smile almost reached her eyes. She shook her head. "Only one of them."

Ten minutes later, Tristan shuffled out of the house rubbing sleep from his eyes just in time to collect the fees from the arriving yoga students. The crowd was basically the same as the morning before, minus Danae and Brittany's husband.

"Did we scare Chris off?" I asked Brittany.

She scooped her hair into a high ponytail. "No, he legitimately loved the whole thing. He thought the goats were hysterical, but he had to work today. I only rubbed it in a little bit that I got to play with goats while he's out delivering vegetables."

To give Sunny extra help calming her mind, I shifted my routine to include my favorite stress relieving poses, knowing the goats would aide in helping her, and the rest of us, find some peace this morning.

"Everybody, please grab a mat," I indicated the tub of rolled up yoga mats sitting next to the gate. "We're going to start in the child pose today. Kneel on your mat, sitting back and resting your rump on your heels to start. Reach your arms all the way forward, lower your head between your shoulders, stretch your fingers as far as you can, and relax."

"Relax? With a goat on my back?" Brittany laughed. "They're already playing King of the Mountain."

Giggles and full out belly laughs rang throughout the barn. I lifted my head to peek at Sunny. Instead of jumping on her back, a brown goat had wedged her way into the triangle created between Sunny's head and stretched out arms. Sunny wrapped her arms around the goat and sat back, pulling the goat into a hug on her lap.

"Let's roll up to the cat-cow position now." I moved the class into the new pose. From there, we hit downward dog before transitioning into a high lunge where the goats ran underneath outstretched legs as if they were racing through tunnels in an obstacle course.

"How's everybody doing? Are you feeling a good stretch?" After a chorus of yesses, I requested the students to sit on their mats. "Legs stretched out in front of you. Now lean forward, reaching for your toes the best you can." After the forward fold, we moved into the butterfly pose, finishing the sequence with the knees-to-chest pose.

"Lay back, tuck your hands behind your knees and bring them to your chest. Gently rock side to side. Good. Now bring your arms around your knees and hug them to your chest. I will warn you, in this pose…"

Before I finished my instructions, a small explosion rocketed through the Zen Pen.

"…you might accidentally pass gas," I finished up.

Nancy, her face as red as a ripe apple, sputtered, "That was Queenie!" She pointed to an adorable black goat with brown spots who looked as startled as Nancy.

"Don't worry. I think it was me," Jen loudly confided to Nancy. "Whoopsie. Shouldn't have indulged in that extra breakfast sausage."

The class dissolved in a sea of laughter. Even Nancy joined in after a few seconds of mortal embarrassment. Not to be outdone, the goats bleated and raced around the pen, kicking up their heels as if they were in on the joke.

Once the yoga session wound up, Nancy sidled over to me. "Loved the session today, Callie, even if I wanted to sink through the floor there for a minute."

"Glad to hear it, and happy you joined us again this morning. We need to catch up soon."

Nancy nodded. "I was thinking the same thing. In the meantime, you won't believe what I'm about to tell you." She lowered her voice and leaned closer to me, "Rumor has it that Alex Bell was fired from Sugar Rush Bakery when he was a teenager for eating donuts on the job. Without paying for them. Can you believe it?"

"Uh. Okay." I wasn't sure what kind of a response Nancy expected from me.

She huffed and pursed her lips. "Don't you see how stealing donuts led to Lucy Thorne's murder?"

I crossed my arms and shook my head. "I'm sorry, I don't see the connection."

"Well, stealing started the Bell boy down the wrong path, right into a life of crime, obviously. Stealing is a gateway offense, you know. If, even as a young boy, he could steal pastries from his employer, as a man he most certainly would be capable of murder."

It was all I could do to keep a straight face.

Chapter Sixteen

If everything went according to plan, Uncle Will should be released from the hospital soon and he and Aunt Ellen would be home by this afternoon. The only thing we'd seen of Jim this morning was his car leaving the driveway as he headed into town while I waved goodbye to today's yoga students, and that was perfectly all right by me. The less Jim in my face, the better the day would go.

Tristan and I committed a high-speed neatness on the house, making sure not to leave any dirty dishes in the sink, crumbs on the floors, or unmade beds. By the time we finished, everything was spic and span and in its rightful place. We wanted Uncle Will and Aunt Ellen to be able to relax once they got home instead of Aunt Ellen feeling like she needed to buzz around like a bee, setting things to right we'd neglected in her absence.

Tristan shoved the vacuum into the broom closet and brushed off his hands. "I think we've got it handled. Are you about ready to conduct our recon mission at the photo studio?"

"Yep." I hung the dishtowel on the oven handle to dry. "I just need to grab my bag."

"Girl, no. The only thing you need to grab is a shower. Change out of those yoga clothes, and redo your hair. You'll feel way more confident and relaxed when you don't look like a hot mess." My cousin blinked and shook his head like I was a lost cause. "Have I taught you nothing after all these months?"

"I showered earlier. I'm fine," I started to argue.

"And then you fed the animals, taught a goat yoga class, and cleaned the house. You smell a little rank." He pointed to the ceiling. "Shower upstairs. I'm going to use my grandparents' bathroom to freshen up."

Half an hour later, I felt refreshed and much more presentable, albeit a little grumpy about Tristan always being right. Downtown, I directed my cousin to turn his green Mini Cooper onto Webster Street.

"There's his studio." The words "Golden Bell Photography" stood out in painted gold lettering across a plate-glass window. The studio was in the same brick building as Whimsical Willow, my favorite Bobwhite Hollow clothing shop. But where Whimsical Willow faced Main Street, Golden Bell Photography's storefront looked out onto Webster.

Tristan pulled to the curb directly in front of the studio. A dry red leaf skittered down the sidewalk, coming to rest against a light pole. Lights from inside the studio glowed on the overcast day. Before we could exit the car, the front door of the studio swung open and a dark-skinned woman with corkscrew curls rushed out. Danae.

"See? I swear that woman is everywhere." I pointed the reporter out to Tristan as Danae's retreating form disappeared around the corner.

Tristan shrugged. "Looks to me like she's doing her due diligence on this story. If she's trying to break into serious journalism, she needs to make sure all her Is are dotted and Ts are crossed."

"True enough. There's nothing nefarious about getting the facts straight."

We got out of the car as the church bell down the street pealed delicate notes throughout town. I stopped to listen and to admire a set of mugs in the window of Fire & Rain Pottery next door to Alex's studio. Leaves were engraved into the sides with a gorgeous rusty red glaze covering the lip and inside of the stoneware mugs.

"I'm going to need to come back for those," I said as Tristan tugged me through the door of Golden Bell Photography.

Alex sat at a small desk, his back to a dark blue display wall where a dozen portraits of various people hung. He jumped to his feet as we pushed through the door.

"Welcome to Golden Bell Photography." Alex greeted us. "You came at a good time. I'm usually not open on Sundays, but I thought with the photographers in town, I should make myself available. Seems I was right." He pointed to me. "You're the yoga gal who was up on the mountain with Brittany from Soul Dust the other morning. Callie, if I'm not mistaken?"

I nodded. "Yep, you caught me. And this is Tristan." I pointed to my cousin. "Speaking of the workshop, it's absolutely terrible what happened to poor Lucy. More than a bit traumatic for all of us who were there." I hoped forging a bond with Alex over our shared trauma would get him to open up with me. I touched his arm lightly with my fingertips. "How are you doing with everything?"

"You sound like the reporter who was just in here asking me all kinds of questions." Alex shook off my hand. "Like I told her, I'm fine, and I didn't have a single thing to do with her murder. Lucy Thorne was nothing to me, and to top it off, she didn't even know how to conduct a helpful workshop."

"You made your opinion of her clear that morning." His attitude was over the top, so I had a hard time containing my own. The rancor in his words didn't align with the hero worship his sister said he harbored for Lucy. What had happened to cause his idol to fall off her pedestal so hard?

Alex blinked, maybe realizing how callous he sounded. "I mean, you're right. Her death is terrible, and I hope the police arrest her killer soon. Nobody deserves to die that way. We'll all sleep easier once they have someone behind bars."

I dove into the opening he provided. "It's so disconcerting to think the person who murdered her had to have been someone who was at the workshop, don't you think? Or at least someone we would have seen on the trail. Do you remember anything that stands out to you as strange?"

"Nope. I was off taking my own pictures, not worried about what everyone else was doing. Trust me, I barely noticed who the other participants were. Not one of them is a professional, so they aren't really my peers. I was hoping a workshop taught by the great Lucy Thorne would've attracted some actual talent so I could rub elbows with other photographers. I hoped to network and build some professional rapport. Too bad only the local riff raff came out." Alex's phone rang, and he held up a finger. "I need to get that. Give me one second."

Tristan wandered over to the rack of photo props, and I took the opportunity to take a better look around the studio while Alex was distracted. The space was one large room with a door I assumed led to a storage closet but could have as easily been a restroom. Besides the dark blue display wall, the rest of the studio was painted bright white. Light grey faux wood flooring covered the floors. Rolls of photography backdrops were mounted high on the back wall with a couple of large, umbrella-shaped lights standing nearby. Various small wooden chairs and a couple of neutral-colored poufs were shoved into the corner. I assumed they were props for photo sessions. A shabby couch, throw rug, and artificial fiddle leaf fig tree made up the small waiting area near the front window.

A few minutes later, Alex disconnected from his call. "Now, what can I do for you? Are you two looking at an engagement package? I offer great packages for any budget." His tone of voice had flipped from irritated snob to used car salesman.

Tristan and I gaped at each other in horror. "No," we yelled in unison.

I waved my hands in front of myself. "Let's clear this up right now. Tris and I are cousins, not romantic partners."

Alex changed gears in the blink of an eye. "Great. There's just as many options for family portraits. Let's get started, shall we? You've come to the right place. I have the best ratings in New England. My clients rave about my work. I'm not even lying when I say I've never had an unhappy customer."

I tried to hide my snort by clearing my throat. If we were ten, I'd bet my last dollar his fingers were crossed behind his back.

Alex moved at a frantic pace, pulling down a grey brick backdrop and placing a small wooden chair in front of it. He chattered the entire time about the price of his packages and how he'd give us a special deal with a free eight-by-ten thrown in. Tristan and I looked at each other, but every time I attempted to speak and tell Alex we weren't interested in getting our pictures taken today, he raised his voice and bulldozed over me with his sales pitch.

Before we knew what was happening, Tristan was seated in the chair, and I was standing behind him with a fake grin plastered on my face and lightbulbs flashing in my eyeballs. Alex told us to swap positions, so we blindly followed orders. At one point, I swiveled around, looked at Tristan, and threw my arms out in an exaggerated shrug. The next thing we knew, we were hamming it up with some crazy poses. Tristan rummaged around in Alex's props and found a sailor hat for himself and a cowboy hat for me.

"Look. We're the Village People!" I stood and formed a Y while Tristan made the C.

"Minus a few members. We're missing our M and A."

Alex gamely snapped the shot but then huffed and placed a hand on his hip. "Come on. Be serious now."

A bell tinkled as the front door to the studio swung open and Jen Earley entered with a burst of chilly air. Her long hair fell loose around her shoulders and was held away from her face with sparkly pink clips secured above each ear. A tote bag the size of a small suitcase hung from one of her shoulders. A pink flamingo above the words "I Don't Give a Flock" decorated the front of the bag.

"Glad I caught you open for a change." Jen placed a hand over her heart as she panted.

A smarmy smile played across Alex's features as he rubbed his hands together. "Well, Jen. Fancy you showing up here. I knew you wouldn't be able to resist my offer to critique your work at the discounted rate I offered the other participants. Guess it would be rude not to extend the same courtesy to you, despite our past grievances with each other. Time to put that behind us. I'm surprised you didn't rush in yesterday afternoon. Most of the others have already come and gone."

Jen's face registered surprise. Her nose wrinkled as she asked, "They have?"

"Of course. It would be stupid to pass up such a great deal. You're the last one to take advantage of my offer."

Or the first one, if I was to venture a guess. And what was this about trouble between these two? I glanced at Tristan to see if he'd caught the comment. His furrowed brow screamed a big fat yes.

"Well, great for them, but you can count me out." Jen flapped a dismissive hand. "The only reason I'm here is because my daughter insists on getting her senior portraits taken by none other than you since all of her friends have. I was planning on running her down to my friend's studio in Hanover, but you know teenagers. Raising them is equivalent to being pecked to death by chickens." Jen paused to laugh at her own joke. "Anyway, I told Rae I'd already gotten her senior pictures appointment made with you, just to get the girl off my back. She's relentless when she wants something and won't stop nagging me about it until I get it done. I swear the girl only shuts her mouth when she's sleeping."

Like mother, like daughter.

"Anyway, I need to get her on your schedule asap. What does your schedule look like this coming week? The forecast shows this drizzle clearing up on Tuesday. What times do you have available then? After school would be preferable. Say three?" Jen stopped talking for a second and finally noticed Alex was in the middle of a photo shoot with Tristan and me. "Oh, goodness. I didn't see the two of you standing there. You're so quiet." She pressed a dramatic hand to her heart again. "I'm sorry. Did I interrupt something?"

"A few more shots and we'll be done here, then I'll be right with you," Alex told her. "While you wait, take a look at the information in the brochure about the various senior portrait packages I offer." He nodded toward the brochures on his desk.

Jen grabbed one, then stepped behind his desk to study the display of portraits on the wall.

Alex turned his attention back to our shoot. "Alright. Lose the hats and let's get a couple more serious shots taken."

I tossed the cowboy hat back into his basket of props, and Tristan and I attempted to school our features into appropriate expressions. All I could think about was the stern old-timey photographs where the subjects appeared pained by the experience. One look at Tristan with my pursed lips and furrowed brow, and he followed suit. We both stared at Alex with matching glum expressions.

Alex huffed. "Are you two ever serious? This is ridiculous."

Tristan and I both burst out laughing, and Alex snapped a few more shots.

"We have plenty of pictures to choose from, especially since this was completely impromptu," I said. "I think we can be done."

"Impromptu?" Alex repeated, surprised. "You came in here for portraits today, did you not?"

"No, we did not. We dropped in to inquire about your services and prices, but didn't expect to have pictures taken today. I assumed your schedule would be full and we'd have to make an appointment for our sitting." Which I hadn't had any intention of doing.

"Oh, oh, well…" Alex stuttered and hurried to explain. "You're right. My services are in high demand, and for most sessions, I do have to schedule several weeks, months even, in advance. You two were lucky today, since, like I mentioned, I'm not usually open on Sundays, so I had time on my books this morning and could squeeze you in."

Sure, buddy. If what Kelsey said the other day was correct, Golden Bell Photography was hanging on by its fingernails. And judging by how eager Alex had been to rush us into a sitting, it sure looked like his sister knew what she was talking about.

"Are you ready for me, now?" Jen spoke up. "I'm in a bit of a hurry here. Time is of the essence."

Alex glanced at me. "This will just take a second. Do you mind? Then we'll get your package choice locked down."

I held up my hands. "Go ahead."

Alex made a show of flipping through his schedule book, but from where I stood, I had a clear shot, and those pages reflected a handful of appointments, at best. He'd probably also forgotten about the electricity bill he'd left on his desk, clearly marked by a giant red "Overdue" stamp. Could he have killed Lucy and taken her camera to sell in order to pay a bill or two? The need for money made people do strange things. Sunny said the camera wasn't worth a lot, but what was a lot when it came to the value of a professional camera? Even a couple hundred dollars could make a difference if you were sinking in quicksand. Not to mention the SIM card in the camera would contain Lucy's last photographs. Whoever stole the camera could claim the photos as their own and make a decent profit off of them. If Alex had her SIM card, it might explain why he was so confident that he had the best photos of the session and was going to win the contest.

Alex loudly cleared his throat, bringing my attention back to the two photographers standing at the desk. "Three o'clock Tuesday afternoon. Let's see. I may be able to move the Knickerbocker family. They mentioned they had a flexible timeline." He ran a hand through his gelled hair, causing spikes to stand up like a blue jay.

The Knickerbocker family? Did he just make that name up?

He puffed up his cheeks and blew out a breath. "Rick and Morty were coming up from Concord for senior photos, but I could possibly..." his voice trailed off.

Tristan laughed out loud when Alex mumbled the names Rick and Morty. He leaned over and whispered in my ear, "Who's next? Bert and Ernie? Maybe Pebbles and Bamm-Bamm have wedding pictures scheduled?"

I jabbed him with my elbow and attempted to shut him up with my best stink eye, but looking at my cousin right then was the exact wrong thing to do. Instead of reprimanding Tristan, my own mouth shot open, and I brayed like a donkey. Tristan lost his bananas. Both Alex and Jen turned and stared at us as we doubled over in uncontrollable laughter.

It took a minute, but once I composed myself and stomped on Tristan's foot to get him to calm down, I apologized. "Sorry about the outburst. I just got to thinking about our Village People pose and it cracked me up, then Trist got going, too." I fanned my face. "Whew. I think I need a drink of water."

Wordlessly, Alex pointed to a water dispenser next to a small coffee station. I tugged Tristan with me and left Jen and Alex alone to finish conducting their business.

Since they were still haggling over time and place, I slipped behind Alex and crept behind his desk to take a closer look at the portrait display. A diploma was attached to the wall underneath the row of professional photographs. Leaning in, I studied the degree, reading it quietly under my breath. "New Englund College has conferred on Alexander T. Bell the degree of Bachelor of Fine Arts."

Weird. Maybe Kelsey was wrong about her big brother not finishing his degree? The document appeared to be legit. I studied it more closely and felt like a complete fool when I noticed the spelling error. My mouth dropped open. E-N-G-L-U-N-D. No way would New England College spell their own name wrong. Not only had Alex faked his diploma, he had the nerve to display it loud and proud, confident no one would take a close enough look. I waved Tristan over and quietly pointed out the phony degree. I whipped out my phone and snapped a picture a second before Alex turned around, almost catching me in the act.

"These are great, aren't they? I had some wonderful subjects." The photographer turned his attention away from Jen for a second, thinking I'd been admiring his focal wall.

I slipped my phone back in my pocket and turned to acknowledge him with a nod. It was then I noticed the bottom drawer of his desk hung wide open. Alex followed my gaze and swiftly kicked the drawer shut with a thunk, but not before I caught a quick glimpse of the Nikon camera stowed in the compartment. *No way. Is that Lucy's missing camera?* I had no idea if it was the same model or not, but Alex hadn't wasted a second hiding it from my view. I needed to get a good look into that drawer, but if the opportunity didn't present itself, I knew someone who could get in with no problem. Chief Barnhart.

I tore my attention away from the drawer as Alex and Jen finished up their business.

"Great. Three o'clock Tuesday afternoon it is." Jen beamed as she slapped the appointment card against the palm of her hand. "Nice to see you again, Callie. Tristan, you too. Oh, by the way, if you're bored later, come on down to the high school and watch my baby play in the final soccer game of her high school career. Our team needs all the support we can get. Don't forget to bring your lawn chairs."

I mumbled something noncommittal and grinned back at her. Once she left the studio, I turned my attention to Alex.

"Alrighty then, let's get you two settled up here." Alex pulled out the chair and sat behind his desk. "The sitting fee for today is three hundred bucks, and then…"

I choked on the price as Alex wrestled my debit card out of my white-knuckled grip to pay for the photo session we'd been wrangled into.

Alex swiped my card through his card reader, then glanced up as we waited for it to process. "Hey, I'm glad Jen stopped in while you were here. It reminded me of something."

"Yeah?"

"Were you at the lookout the other morning when Jen came back from shooting pictures?"

I nodded. "Yep. I was amazed when she climbed up to the lookout from over the cliff edge."

Alex agreed. "And do you remember later her saying that she'd been down to the trailhead to use the outhouse?"

I did remember. Something about it didn't sit right with me. If Jen had been down at the trailhead, how did she miss all the commotion about the bear breaking into her van? Instead of voicing my concern, I waited to hear what Alex had to say.

"Well, I didn't just stay in one spot to take my pictures. I walked around and found various vantage points to shoot from. Several times as I was moving around throughout the morning, I ran into Jen. There's no way she would have had time to go to the trailhead and get back to all the places I saw her." He raised his eyebrows at me. "Plus, about ten minutes before she came up from over the cliff edge, I'd seen her in the woods above the lookout. I didn't know Lucy was dead at that point, but it couldn't have been far from where she was killed, yet Jen said she'd found a great ledge below the lookout where she'd been camped out taking pictures for a while." Alex shook his head. "It doesn't add up. She was lying."

Chapter Seventeen

As we left Golden Bell Photography, I paid special attention to the lock on the front door. Perfect. It was a simple, everyday doorknob and lock. Shouldn't be too hard to pick if push came to shove. There didn't appear to be any security cameras inside Alex's business, either. Not that I planned to break and enter, but if Chief Barnhart chose not to show concern about the Nikon in Alex's desk drawer, what choice would I have?

"How do you feel about going to a soccer game later?" I slid my gaze to Tristan once we were standing on the sidewalk in front of Golden Bell Photography.

"Works for me. With what Alex just told us about Jen, it seems like a logical next step. Good thing she came in, since we didn't learn anything else worthwhile."

"Of course we did." I stepped aside to let a couple pass, then lowered my voice. "There were tons of empty appointment slots on his calendar, overdue bills lying on his desk, and a Nikon camera in the bottom drawer that he obviously didn't want me to see."

"Whoa." Tristan's eyes flared, and his mouth dropped open. "I didn't pick up on any of those things."

"You're going to have to hone your observation skills, Watson, if you're going to hang with me." I grinned at my cousin. "It'll be interesting to see what we can find out from Jen, but I have the distinct feeling Alex threw her under the bus to take the heat off of himself."

Tristan frowned. "I thought it was a little suspicious he didn't have anything to tell us until Jen came in. Do you think he made it all up?"

I shrugged. "I don't know. Possibly. But that's what we're going to find out."

As I reached for the handle on the car door, Brittany's husband, Chris, blazed past us.

"Hey, Chris." I raised a hand in greeting, but he didn't so much as turn his head in my direction.

Chris ripped open the door of Alex's studio and started yelling before he was even inside the building. "We had an understanding."

The door closed behind him, and while both Chris's and Alex's angry voices reached us, I couldn't make out the actual words being flung around. Tristan and I froze in place as we stared at the closed door until Chris emerged again half a minute later.

"...or I'm coming after you," he threatened as he slammed the door shut. In a full-blown temper tantrum, Chris reached up and jerked down a strip of decorative lights strung around the front window of Golden Bell Photography. The bulbs shattered on the sidewalk. Chris stalked off, his face a mask of rage.

"Wow. That was wild!" Tristan opened his driver's side door.

I pointed to the photography studio. "Should we check on Alex before we leave?"

"Why? It's not like he's your buddy. Let's just get out of here."

My mouth was still gaping open like a cave when Alex himself opened the door to his studio and stepped out onto the sidewalk with a broom. He flung his hand out to shoo us off. "Nothing to see here," he called in an irritated tone. "Might as well move along."

I shot Chief Barnhart a text about the camera in Alex's drawer as Tristan slid the car away from the curb. We'd been held hostage in the photography studio for an hour and a half. If things had gone well this morning at the hospital, Uncle Will and Aunt Ellen might make it back to the farm before we did.

"Want to go grab lunch at Mustard Stains?" Tristan asked.

"I kind of want to go home and fix lunch for your grandparents, in case they get back soon, but I'll take a rain check on Mustard Stains." My mouth watered at the thought of the juicy hot dogs the small hole-in-the-wall café was known for.

"You can cook?" Tristan stared at me with a blank expression.

I smacked him on the arm with the back of my hand. "Don't act so surprised. I'm no Aunt Ellen, but I've been puttering around the kitchen since I was a preteen, and am pretty decent at it, if I do say so myself."

Tristan looked skeptical but shrugged after a few seconds. "Okay then, let's find out what Grandma and Grandpa's ETA is." Tristan pulled out his phone and had a quick conversation with Aunt Ellen. "Grandma said they're waiting on Skip to come back in with the final paperwork to release Pop-Pop right now."

Back at the farm, I whipped up a kettle of chicken rice soup and made a quick batch of buttermilk biscuits. The timer for the biscuits went off just as the front door opened and Jim guided Uncle Will through the door, Aunt Ellen at their heels.

"Ah, there's nothing better than home." Uncle Will smiled and took a deep breath. "What smells so gosh darn good? I'm famished!"

"Welcome home. There's fresh soup and biscuits for lunch. It's not Aunt Ellen's cooking, but hopefully it'll be edible."

Aunt Ellen bustled into the kitchen and swatted at me. "Oh, now stop that. Lunch will be delightful, I'm sure. It's quite the treat to come home to a home-cooked meal that I didn't make myself. I was planning to heat up some leftovers, so this is a wonderful surprise." She set to work right away, pulling bowls out of the cupboard and setting them on the counter next to the stovetop.

Uncle Will brushed off Jim's hovering hand and settled into one of the hard chairs at the kitchen table.

"Wouldn't you be more comfortable in your recliner?" Tristan asked. "We can set you up in the library and bring your soup in there."

"No, grandson. Thanks for the concern, but I'm going to eat lunch right here at the table with my family." His tone of voice made it clear he wouldn't brook any argument.

"Stubborn as always." Jim wandered to the stove and lifted the lid on the kettle. His sharp nose flexed as he sniffed at the soup. "You made this?" He looked at me with a frown.

"Yep. Should I ladle you up a serving?" *With a nice, tasty dollop of rat poison?* I took a bowl over and set it down in front of Uncle Will, sans rat poison.

"Sure. I'll give it a try, I guess," Jim answered.

"Don't let me twist your arm. There are some leftovers you're welcome to heat up instead." I attempted to keep the irritation out of my voice.

"No, no." Jim waved his hands. "Your soup will do just fine."

Aunt Ellen had tumbled the hot biscuits into a basket and placed a red and white checkered towel on top before taking them to the table and settling into her chair beside Uncle Will. I brought her a steaming bowl of soup, then ladled up bowls for Jim, Tristan, and myself before placing butter and honey on the table and bringing each of us a small bread plate.

"What are you waiting for? Dig in while it's hot," I said. I blew on a spoonful of soup, then tucked it into my mouth. I scrunched up my nose. "Needs salt."

Tristan reached for the salt shaker and gave his soup a couple of good shakes, then passed the salt to Uncle Will. Aunt Ellen ripped it out of his hand before he had a chance to add any to his meal.

"The soup has good flavor, ladybug. You made it just right." Aunt Ellen smiled at me, then glowered at Uncle Will. "Did you not hear what Doctor Luo said? No added salt, old man."

Uncle Will harrumphed while the rest of us feigned sudden interest in our lunches. Aunt Ellen filled us in on the instructions from the doctor and Uncle Will's expected recovery time.

"He'll have weekly checkups for the next several weeks, but the doctor expects him to be back to his normal charming self in a month to six weeks. He's to take it easy until then," Aunt Ellen spoke as if she was already scolding Uncle Will for bad behavior. "And mainly, he needs to cut back on stress." Her eyes threw daggers as she turned them on Jim, who avoided the interaction by getting up to refill his soup bowl.

"And I will follow Doctor Luo's instructions to the T, my dear." Uncle Will patted his wife's hand, then turned to me. "Not to be a nag, but were you able to make any progress on the sheep shed yet, Callie?"

I slurped up my last spoonful of soup and wiped my chin with a cloth napkin. "Sure did. I got the shed cleaned out, then Trist helped me bring in fresh straw and move the sheep into the winter field."

Uncle Will narrowed his eyes and studied me. "Surely it isn't all done? Water tank filled and fence checked? You shouldn't have moved the sheep until everything was taken care of."

"It's all done, Pop-Pop," Tristan jumped in. "There was a couple of places the fence was loose, but Callie and I got it tightened back up, no problem."

I chose not to mention that I'd forgotten the water tank for several hours. The sheep were safe and healthy, and I certainly wouldn't make the same mistake again. Other mistakes for sure, but not that particular one.

"Well, I'll be hanged. Two strong young sprouts are better than one dusty old codger, it seems. It usually takes me two full days to get the sheep field winterized the last few years." Uncle Will shook his head as if amazed. "Did you hear that, Jimbo? What do you think about my great-niece pulling her weight, now that you're here to witness it for yourself?"

Jim's mouth was too full of my buttermilk biscuits to answer.

Chapter Eighteen

At quarter to three in the afternoon, Tristan and I pulled on our coats and warm boots, and stuffed our pockets full of gloves and hats just in case it got cold sitting outside at the high school soccer game. Uncle Will had finally agreed to go lie down in his bedroom, and I made my great-aunt promise not to do any farm chores while we were gone.

"We won't be late. I'll take care of all the animals when we get back, even if it's dark. That's what barn lights and flashlights were made for. You rest and don't worry about anything except taking care of Uncle Will."

Aunt Ellen agreed while Jim silently eyed me over the top of the local newspaper he was reading.

When we arrived at the high school soccer fields, the game had gotten underway.

"Jen's over there." Recognizing her by the coat she'd worn during the photography workshop, I pointed to a group of people on the sidelines.

Tristan and I wound our way through the spectators, managing to squeeze our camp chairs into a gap right next to Jen.

Before I had a chance to say hello, she jumped up and cupped her hands around her mouth, yelling at her daughter. "Come on, Rae. Step it up. You can do better than that. Show them what you've got." She clapped her hands together. "Don't let me down!"

It didn't surprise me one tiny bit that Jen was *that* parent. Had her own dreams of being a star player been shattered so she had to live vicariously through her daughter? I shook my head. I'd never understood parents who yelled at and berated their kids over sports. Not my cup of tea, and I was thankful my own parents had been far less aggressive spectators during my gymnastic years.

With her eyes glued to the game, Jen stepped backwards to her chair and plopped down. As the players thundered down the field, she turned her head to watch and finally noticed Tristan and me sitting beside her. A welcoming smile lit up her face. "Oh, hey. Glad you two could make it." She placed a hand over her heart and batted her eyes. "I'm such a proud mama. You'll have to excuse me, I tend to get loud at these games. You know, cheering on my baby and all."

Her supposed cheering had sounded more like criticizing her baby than cheering to me, but I kept my opinion to myself and tried to focus on the game for a few minutes. The ref threw a yellow card to one of the Bobwhite Hollow Whistlers who had blatantly tripped a player on the opposing team. Jen exploded to her feet, throwing finger jabs at the ref and screaming about him needing to get his eyes checked and how he was playing favorites to the other team. The enraged woman reminded me of a furious wolf, and it wasn't even her kid who had been carded.

Tristan leaned over. "Holy bananas. Didn't you say this lady works at a church? She's pure mental."

I shifted my eyes back and forth between him and Jen. "I'm pretty sure that's what Brittany said."

The girls' soccer coach sprinted up. "Mrs. Earley, calm down. You're this close to getting booted out." She indicated an inch with her fingers. "You know I'll do it. It wouldn't be the first time."

Jen threw her hands up in surrender. "Fine, fine. I'm done." When she turned to me, her clicking canines morphed back into a wholesome smile. "Now, isn't this fun? I'm sure glad you came."

The woman was so focused on the game, it was hard to talk to her about the other morning on the mountain. Between halves, Tristan went to the concession stand to get us cups of hot chocolate, and I was finally able to squeeze in a question.

"Oh, hey, I've been wondering about the damage the bear did to your van the other day. How bad was it?"

Jen's eyes flared wide, and she grabbed my arm, her nails digging in despite my thick coat. "Listen. Never leave a sardine salad sandwich in your vehicle."

Sure thing. For about a thousand more reasons than only providing bear bait. I wrinkled my nose and nodded while wresting my arm out of her intense grip.

"My poor van. That bear got her claws in the window somehow and ripped the door right off the hinges. She shredded up the back of the front passenger seat while she was at it. The body shop was able to get my door back on, but between ordering parts and matching the paint color, it's going to be a couple of weeks before the van is fully restored. Good thing we have decent car insurance." She huffed out a breath. "My husband was not happy with me."

"I bet, but did the bear get to eat the sandwich after all her hard work to get it?"

"She did. And I hope it was worth it." Jen chuckled. "It'll be a funny story later."

"For sure," I agreed. "Do you mind if I ask you something else?"

She shrugged. "Shoot."

"You mentioned you'd gone down to the trailhead to use the outhouse, but you didn't know about the bear when I told you. Without throwing anyone under the bus, another witness told me they saw you coming out of the woods from above the lookout, not from the direction of the trailhead."

Jen threw both hands in the air, then stared at me straight on. "Okay. Fine. I didn't go to the outhouse. I relieved myself in the woods. Is that a crime?"

"Not last I checked, but why did you say you went to the outhouse then? Why not just tell the truth?"

She pressed a dramatic hand to her heart, which I'd come to understand was Jen's signature move. "Because it's embarrassing," she whispered. "I shouldn't have indulged in so much coffee before the workshop, and then I wouldn't have had to relieve myself so often. I know better."

Jen was embarrassed about peeing in the woods, but considered it perfectly acceptable to scream at a high school soccer referee like a lunatic? Okay, then.

"You know," Jen turned to me just as the players were returning to the field, "if you're wanting to be nosy about this whole unfortunate situation, take a good long look at Alex. Did you hear all the nasty things he was spewing about Lucy during the workshop? That guy's got some anger issues." She raised one eyebrow and nodded her head vigorously before turning her attention back to the game.

Tristan bumped my shoulder and handed me a paper cup of hot chocolate. The ref was setting up the ball for the first play. Jen swiveled in her chair and held up a hand in greeting to someone behind me.

"Hey there, Garrett. Avery's on top of her game today," Jen called out.

I twisted around in my seat. Garrett Rogers stood ten feet behind us.

"Garrett's daughter plays on the same team as Rae?" I asked Jen.

"Sure does. That's her right there." Jen pointed to the dark-haired girl who had received the yellow card earlier. "She's nearly as good as Rae." Jen turned her laser focus back to the game as the ref blew his whistle.

"She looks super familiar," I mumbled.

"Who are you talking about?" Tristan asked.

I pointed out Garrett's daughter, but shook my head slightly. "I don't know why. It's not like I've been hanging out with high school kids."

"Has she come to one of your goat yoga sessions?"

"Oh, I bet you're right. I had a lot of teenagers come out for yoga this summer, especially after the fair." I nodded. "That's got to be it."

I wedged my hot chocolate into the drink holder on the arm of my chair, then patted Tristan's leg and stood. "Be right back."

With Garrett at the game, I couldn't pass up the opportunity to have a little chat with him. Three steps into my mission and four away from my target, another woman swooped in and filled the spot beside Garrett I'd been aiming for.

The brunette rubbed her mittened hands together. "Sorry I'm late. The store was busy today. How's our girl doing?" she asked Garrett.

He chuckled and smirked at the woman. "*Your* daughter got a yellow card for tripping the winger on the other team."

The woman, whom I assumed was Garrett's wife, gave him a solid side-eye.

"She gets her bad behavior from you, not from me." She turned to the game and cheered for the Whistlers.

I swiveled around and stood where I was for a second, pretending to watch the game and trying to act like I meant to be standing there by myself.

"Hey," Garrett's wife said to him in a stage whisper. "Any new news on Lucy yet?"

I covertly glanced over my shoulder in time to see Garrett shake his head slightly. Slowly, I took two steps backward so I wouldn't miss anything they were saying.

"I'm telling you, this whole thing is going to come back to bite you in the butt. You really need to come clean with Chief Barnhart."

"Heather," Garrett growled, "Until two days ago, I hadn't seen the woman for twenty-five years. And I certainly didn't kill her. Drop it, please."

"Eeep." I covered my mouth in a vain attempt to hide the squeak that jumped out, then hurried back to my chair between Tristan and Jen.

Dang, I'm glad neither one of the Rogers knows how to whisper. The looks shot between Lucy and Garrett the other morning had made it clear, at least to me, that they had known each other. Chief Barnhart had brushed my concerns about Garrett under the rug. I pumped my fist with the validation I'd been correct.

Tristan scrunched up his face. "What are you celebrating? The visiting team scored, not us."

"Oops." Hopefully nobody else had seen my blunder. I leaned over and whispered to Tristan what I'd overheard.

He pursed his lips. "Okay. Gives me something to dig into."

Only a few minutes remained of the game. The Bobwhite Hollow Whistlers were down three to one when sirens cut through the air.

Jen grimaced as she glanced around and pressed her hand to her heart. "Sounds like something's happening downtown. I pray it's nothing too terrible. We've had enough bad news recently."

Chapter Nineteen

To get home to the farm from the high school, Tristan and I didn't need to go through downtown Bobwhite Hollow, so we were able to bypass any chaos happening from whatever problem was causing all the siren activity. Aunt Ellen sprang off the couch and rushed forward as soon as we opened the front door.

"Where have you two been? I was so worried." She wrung her age-spotted hands, then wrapped us both in hugs.

"Grandma, we told you we were going to the high school soccer game. Remember?" Tristan wrinkled his brow and peered into her face. "Is everything okay?"

My heart leapt into my throat. "Has something happened to Uncle Will?"

Aunt Ellen straightened to her full height of five-foot-nothing. "He's sleeping. No, we're good here at the farm; it's what's going on in town that has me uptight."

Tristan shrugged and shook his head. "We heard a bunch of sirens, but not sure why. Whatever it is, it didn't have anything to do with me and Callie."

"It's the young man you went to see this morning, the photographer?" she said as if it were a question.

"Alex? What about him?" I asked.

"He's been murdered." Aunt Ellen's blue eyes flared wide behind her wire-rimmed glasses.

I yelped and Tristan gasped.

"Are you kidding me? Alex is dead?" I asked.

"No way!" Tristan exclaimed as he and I exchanged startled glances.

"Get your coats off and come sit. Let me round you up some hot tea and cookies." As soon as Aunt Ellen ascertained we were safe, she flipped into her normal food-makes-everything-better mode.

She ushered us into the library, where Tristan and I sank into opposite ends of the comfy couch while Aunt Ellen bustled away to fetch our treats.

"If someone killed Alex, then it stands to reason he isn't the person responsible for Lucy's death." I kicked off my shoes and pulled my feet up underneath myself on the couch.

"Probably not, but are you thinking what I'm thinking?" Tristan eyed me.

"Chris Shields," we said in unison.

Tristan rapidly nodded his head and leaned in. "Right? I mean, we don't know what they were screaming at each other about, but we definitely both heard Chris threaten Alex."

I nodded. "And what? Not even eight hours later, Alex is dead? I can't wrap my head around it."

As soon as Aunt Ellen returned with mugs of vanilla rooibos tea and a stack of snickerdoodle cookies for each of us, we bombarded her with questions.

"Who told you Alex is dead?" "How do you know he was murdered?" "How was he killed?"

"Your dad," Aunt Ellen looked at Tristan, "and Joe Harris are in town catching up over drinks at The Fox Hole. Jim called to check in on you kids. The news of the murder is already all over town." She shrugged with the palms of her hands held upward. "And I don't have any idea how the young man was killed, just that he was."

Inwardly, I huffed. First of all, if Jim called to check on us "kids," then I was a trapeze artist. He might've been checking on Tristan, maybe, but they didn't have the best father/son relationship, and he could've called Tristan directly, or even sent him a text. Secondly, Joseph Harris made my eyes squint. He was the local pharmacist and a childhood friend of Jim's. The second I came to town, Joe had made it abundantly clear he was on Jim's side. Before I even knew Jim and I were fighting and there were sides to take.

"So, not the most reliable source from two guys chugging beer at the bar,"

Tristan said drolly.

"And getting their information from the Bobwhite Hollow grapevine," I added. "I'm going to call Chief Barnhart and get the real scoop."

"Callie, I don't think it's the right time to bother him," Aunt Ellen scolded. "No doubt Dale's busy with the murder."

But my fingers moved too fast. The other end of the line was already ringing. If Alex truly had been murdered, I needed to tell the chief about the argument between him and Chris.

"Not now, Miss Haybeck," Chief Barnhart's gruff voice came over the line. "I'm in the middle of a murder investigation."

"I might have some useful information for you," I rushed to say before he could hang up.

A heavy sigh. "What does it involve?"

"Not what. Who. Chris Shields."

"We'll talk in the morning." He disconnected the call.

A twinge of guilt for having betrayed a friend by not talking to Brittany before mentioning her husband's name to the police made my stomach roll. I instantly regretted my impulsiveness and wished I could pull the words back.

I took a deep breath and looked at my family. "Sounds like Jim was right. Alex was murdered." Feeling like I weighed a thousand pounds, I pushed myself off the couch. "I better get the barn chores done before Bugsy starts a mutiny."

Chapter Twenty

It turns out that giving goat scritches behind their floppy ears is every bit as good as therapy. The goats didn't ask any probing questions or attempt to get me to bring all my feelers out. They simply smiled, burped up their cud, and chewed happily as long as I kept doling out the scratches.

After everyone was fed and watered, I eased onto my rump in a corner of Bugsy's enclosure. He lowered himself to his knees, then lay beside me with a grunt and stretched his head into my lap.

"Gotta admit, Bugs, I'm shook over this whole thing. First Lucy and now Alex? What is going on in our little cozy village? Hmm? Any thoughts?"

Bugsy was listening to me drone on about my theories over Lucy's death and how Alex had been one of my top suspects when the creak of the barn door alerted us to someone else coming to barge in on our party of two. Expecting the intruder to be Tristan, I called out, "Back here."

I was surprised when a female voice tentatively answered, "Back here where?"

Scrambling to my feet, I brushed straw off my butt and peered over the top of the stall. Sunny's dark hair swung loose around her shoulders as she tipped her head to look into various nooks and crannies of the barn. Her wide jade green eyes reminded me of a frightened child. I quickly surveyed Bugsy's stall, looking for anything I could use as a weapon if the need arose. Sunny seemed genuinely distraught over Lucy's death, but I hadn't spent enough time with her to get a good feel for her true personality. The obsession she had with her boss was still a bit sus, if you asked me.

I wonder how a water bucket to the head would feel? There was nothing else in the stall to help me in a fight for my life if it came to that. Except Bugsy and his horns. "You got my back, Bugs, right?"

I swear the goat winked.

"Sunny, down here." I hung my head over the gate and waved. "Come on in."

She shot me a tight smile and broke into a trot. "I saw a light on in here and hoped it might be you."

"You know what they say, don't you?" I asked.

She tilted her head and frowned. "No, I guess not. What?"

"Never work for a man who has lights in his barn."

Sunny shifted her eyes back and forth a couple of times, then shrugged. "Sorry, I don't get it. Don't lights make it easier to see what you're doing?"

"Exactly! Which is why he'll expect you to work after dark. If there's no lights in the barn, you get to go home once the sun goes down."

Sunny roared in laughter, similar to what I'd done the first time Uncle Will got me with the same joke. The twentieth time, it wasn't quite so funny, but here I was, cracking his farmer jokes as if they were my own.

While Sunny laughed, Bugsy wandered over, leaned against her leg, and tugged on the hem of her jacket. I eyed him suspiciously, but if my best goat liked the woman, who was I to argue? His apparent approval put me at ease.

"Is there something you needed help with?" I asked.

Sunny's gaze found my face. "No, I just thought maybe you wouldn't mind chatting. Danae's off in town, chasing after another story. It's been a tough few days, and it gets a little lonely sitting in the cottage by myself."

"Yeah, of course." My eyes widened. "Have you been stuck at the farm this whole time? I forgot you don't have your own car out here and had to rely on Danae to get you around. Oh no, you poor thing. I'm sorry I haven't done a better job of making sure you were taken care of." I felt like a complete heel. "Let's go sit on the haystack to talk. It'll be more comfortable."

"It's been okay. Danae has made sure I have food and snacks. Not sure where I would go anyway," Sunny said as she followed me to the end of the barn where the hay was stacked.

Bugsy screamed his distress at being left behind.

"They haven't released Lucy's car to you, then?" I climbed up a level on the stack and took a seat on a bale of hay.

Sunny climbed up beside me, shaking her head. "No, the police will only release her possessions to her next of kin. Lucy has a sister in Idaho. She's who will have to take care of all the arrangements. It's kind of what I wanted to talk to you about. I need some advice and don't really have anyone to help me talk things out."

"Danae's not a good listener?" I asked.

Sunny grimaced. "I mean…yeah, probably, but she's all about getting her big break by busting open a big story. If I'm honest, I don't know how much I trust her. It's not like we knew each other before this trip."

I nodded. "I get that. Not sure how much I'll be able to help, but I'm all ears."

Sunny chewed on her bottom lip and folded her hands together in her lap. After a minute, she cocked her head and studied me. "Your family seems super nice. Did you have a good childhood?"

"Um, yeah. I grew up in Seattle. My parents and older sister still live there. Where did you grow up?" I was surprised Sunny wanted to make small talk, but whatever she needed to work through her grief was fine by me.

"Alaska."

"Oh, I bet Alaska was a great place to grow up. Are your parents still up there?"

Sunny shook her head and swiped at a tear. "No. They died in a plane wreck when I was twelve. They'd been out at a remote cabin with some friends, and the small plane they were on went down when they were on their way home. Nobody survived. After my parents died, I was shuffled around in the foster care system until I turned eighteen and got booted out onto the street."

I gasped.

"As if it isn't tragic enough for a young girl to suddenly be an orphan, the day after my parents died is when I found out I'd been adopted as a baby. A case worker spit it out like it was no big deal. I was already devastated over losing my parents, and the news that I was adopted was nearly more than I could take. I was really angry for a few years, which made me hard to place in foster homes."

"Oh, Sunny. I can't even imagine how horrible it all must have been for you." I wanted to hug her, but her body language screamed no.

"Not going to lie, it was pretty rough." She nodded. "As soon as I was old enough, I took a DNA test hoping to find my biological parents. Do you know anything about those kits you can get in the mail?"

"Yeah, in fact, that's how I found the Haybecks. Will is my dad's uncle, but Dad never knew this side of his family. His parents divorced when he was small, and my grandmother took my dad and moved to Seattle. He doesn't remember ever knowing them at all." I motioned toward the farmhouse as if she could see my great uncle and aunt sitting inside. I wanted to say more, but now was not the time for my story. "Did you have any luck with your DNA results?"

Sunny pressed her lips together for a second before she spoke. "I did. I found a maternal aunt."

"That's great news! Did you contact her?"

"No, I was too scared. Instead, I paid for a background search and found out my aunt only has one sister."

I threw my hands out excitedly. "The sister must be your mother! Please tell me you contacted her."

This time, Sunny nodded. "Yep, but I didn't tell her who I was. Instead, I went to work for her."

"Went to work for her?" Sometimes I'm not the fastest horse on the track. I stared at Sunny, blinking rapidly for what felt like a full two minutes while my cogs turned. "Are you telling me Lucy Thorne was your birth mother?"

"Yep." Sunny squeezed her shoulders together and wrapped her arms protectively around herself.

"And you never told her you were her daughter?" Tears welled in my eyes when she shook her head.

There'd been so much tragedy in Sunny's life. It was a small wonder she looked like a lost child. But holy cow. Did this revelation mean my off-the-wall life insurance theory could be right? As Lucy's biological daughter, would that make Sunny the next of kin even though she'd been put up for adoption at birth? I hadn't given any more thought to the possibility Sunny and Danae might have been working together to kill Lucy, but it was going to bear looking at again. For now, I needed to gather as much information as I could while Sunny felt like talking.

"Do you mind my asking how old you are?"

"Twenty-four," she replied.

Only three years younger than me, but she'd had a lifetime of harder life experiences. "So, you've been on your own for half your life at this point."

"Yeah, basically."

"You said you were hoping for some advice. What are you looking for?"

"The biggest thing I regret right now is not coming clean with Lucy and telling her who I am. Now it's too late to really get to know her. I wish I could figure out how to get into her room at the inn."

"What are you hoping to find?" I asked.

Sunny shrugged. "I'm not sure. I feel like there might be something in her possessions that would help me get to know her better. A diary, maybe, or family photos. Anything, really. I just want to know her."

It must've been tough on Sunny all those years after her adoptive parents died, missing them and not knowing who her biological mother was. Even after finding her, she never really got to know her and definitely didn't have a mother-daughter relationship with her. It was hard for me to fathom. My parents were my rock. I knew I could count on them for anything, and it made me sad for Sunny that she didn't have a parental connection to lean on. As I contemplated Sunny's life, it suddenly occurred to me that my dad could most likely relate to her circumstances better than I could. He'd never known his own dad and had always believed his father didn't want him. It was only recently we'd discovered the story grandma had him believe about his father abandoning them was an entirely different version of the truth than what Aunt Ellen and Uncle Will regaled me with. To top it off, the records my sister uncovered in the Seattle court system backed up their claim that Grandpa Orville hadn't wanted the divorce and had tried to get shared custody of my dad. Family dynamics were always a complicated animal, and it had become crystal clear to me even trusted grandmas were capable of lying in order to cover up hard truths.

I steepled my hands while I tried to think of ways to help Sunny with her quest. "Have you been to The Bobwhite Inn at all?"

"No, I've barely been anywhere since we checked in, except to the workshop on Weaver Mountain the morning Lucy died. Why?"

"I have an idea." I jumped off the haystack and paced the wooden floor of the barn.

"What are you thinking?" Sunny asked.

"What if we go to the inn, simply tell them you're Lucy's daughter, and you need to get something from her room?"

Sunny frowned. "Do you think it would work?"

I shrugged. "It's worth a shot."

Sunny went to the guest cottage to freshen up while I went to tell my family I was running her into town. Jim's car was back in the driveway. My stomach lurched. *Too bad I didn't get out of here quicker.*

Aunt Ellen sat alone in the front room watching a Rick Steves' documentary about traveling around Italy.

"Is Uncle Will still sleeping?" I whispered to her.

She stretched and yawned. "He is, and hopefully he's down for the night. I know it's early yet, but I'm not far behind."

"You need to get some sleep. I'm sure you didn't sleep well at the hospital."

"Not a wink." She yawned again.

"What's going on up there?" I pointed to the ceiling, where the tenor of subdued but angry voices could be heard.

"Jim and Tristan are having a father-son talk."

"At least they're communicating," I said with a grimace.

"I couldn't agree more, ladybug." My aunt eyeballed me as I took the keys for the truck off the hook. "Where are you going this time of night?"

I glanced at the clock. "It's only eight and Sunny needs to...well, get something from town, so I told her I'd drive her in."

"You're a sweet girl. Drive carefully. I won't be up when you get back, but

I'll see you in the morning. Have a good night," Aunt Ellen replied.

Something banged on the floor overhead, and I glanced at the ceiling. Tristan would likely be as mad as a wet hen when he discovered I'd left him behind, but I wasn't about to interrupt whatever was going on between him and his dad. I'd ask for forgiveness later.

Chapter Twenty-One

Bobwhite Hollow glimmered in the autumn evening. Many of the downtown shops were closed for the day, but most of the restaurants and a handful of shops remained open and lit up from within. Streetlights illuminated Main Street with a cozy glow. Crispy leaves lined the sidewalks and the edge of the street, while orange twinkle lights wound artfully around tree trunks. Pumpkins stood guard in front of every door. The Bobwhite Inn was on the opposite end of Main Street from the direction we'd entered town, and I wasn't mad about dragging Main to show Sunny our magical little village.

Magical except for the murder a few hours ago. Well, and the one a couple of days before that. Thankfully, all the police activity from Alex's death earlier today was gone, except for the yellow crime scene tape I'd spotted flapping in the breeze when I'd glanced down Webster Street.

"I'm nervous. What do I say?" Sunny ran her fingers through her long, dark hair as I wheeled Old Rusty into a parking spot beside the historic inn.

"Just be natural. You aren't lying. You really are Lucy's daughter, and you need to get something from her room," I coached. *Not to mention getting in with a key is a whole lot better than breaking and entering.* "Do you know what room she was staying in?"

"Room fourteen. You're going with me, right?" Sunny asked.

"Just try to leave me behind." I chuckled.

The inn was bustling with out-of-state leaf peepers enjoying a late dinner at the in-house restaurant called Hearthstone Grille, a glass of wine at Pie-Eyed Cellars, or warming themselves by the crackling fireplace in the lobby.

Several couples and one large family stood in line, suitcases at their feet, to check into their rooms.

Sunny straightened her spine and made a beeline for the reception desk with me close on her heels. Once we made it to the front of the line, Sunny delivered her plea to enter Lucy's room. "Hi. I understand my mother was staying here. Lucy Thorne?"

"Yes, she was. We're so sorry for your loss." The clerk wore a white Bobwhite Inn tag with her name, Greer, engraved in burgundy lettering, pinned to the front of her burgundy vest. "What can I help you with, Miss Thorne?"

Sunny didn't correct Greer's misassumption. "I'd like to get into my mother's room, please."

I was impressed. Sunny hadn't lied once in her request, and her voice remained steady.

The harried lone front desk clerk didn't even blink an eye before handing Sunny a key to the room. "Here you go. I'm really glad you're here to collect your mother's possessions. It's been a joke trying to figure out who can come and go, outside of the police, and I'll be happy to have that decision taken out of my hands. The room needs a revolving door on it."

"Oh, I'm not collecting her stuff yet. The police haven't…" Sunny started to say.

"Shh." I nudged Sunny with my elbow before turning to Greer with a frown. "A revolving door? Who's been in Lucy's room besides the police?"

Greer flapped her hands and shook her head. "Nobody to worry about." She pointed up the staircase as she considered my questions. "Just the reporter earlier today who had been traveling with Miss Thorne, and then her assistant. In fact, you just missed the assistant by half an hour, at the most."

"Her assistant?" Sunny pointed to her own chest. "I'm her only assistant."

The clerk blinked as if flustered by the news. "But you said you were her daughter."

Sunny nodded, her eyes flaring. "Yeah, her daughter and her assistant. One and the same."

Greer sucked in a sharp breath and tucked a strand of dark hair behind her ear. "Then who was the other lady? The same person had gone up to Miss Thorne's room the first night she stayed with us. Which is why when she told me she was her assistant, I believed her."

"You believed wrong. And when exactly was the reporter here?" I asked.

"A few hours ago, I guess. She said she had permission from the police."

I highly doubt that. Apparently, Danae could lie with the best of us. Except for Sunny, who skirted around the truth like a professional.

Sunny and I glanced at each other, then took off at a run for Lucy's room on the third floor of the inn. We sounded like a herd of elk thundering down the old, wide-plank wooden floors. At room fourteen, we came to a screeching halt where Sunny fumbled with the key in the lock. It took a couple of tries, but she managed to get the door unlocked and flung it open.

The room looked like a tornado had swirled through. The drawers of the dresser hung open, even though they were empty. Bedding was torn off and the mattress rested on the frame at an odd angle. Clothes were scattered across the floor, and a black suitcase sat empty and upended beside the closet. Lucy's room had been ransacked.

I snapped a few pictures to send to the police. Sunny bent to righten the suitcase and reached for some of the clothing on the floor.

"Wait." I grabbed her arm to stop her and whipped disposable gloves out of my coat pocket.

"Whoa. You came prepared," Sunny exclaimed as I handed her a pair.

"Let's just say this isn't my first time around the block."

Sunny reared back and looked at me with horror. "Are you a criminal?"

I laughed. "No, nothing that exciting. I've just helped the police with a couple of cases and know not to touch anything in a crime scene." Okay. Helping the police might be a stretch, but I did know to keep my fingerprints off stuff. "We really shouldn't move anything until we report that the room has been tossed."

"Unless the police are the ones who did it," Sunny said.

I looked around and shook my head. "I know Chief Barnhart, and this does not look like his work."

"It's probably a long shot, but I'm still going to see if I can find anything personal of Lucy's. I'll be careful to not move things around too much." Sunny got on her hands and knees and felt through the scattered clothing. "Lucy never put her clothes into the dresser when she was traveling. She didn't like to waste time packing and unpacking when she would only be in one spot for a few days."

I flipped on the flashlight app on my cell phone and checked behind the dresser and nightstand. Nothing. "The inn should have security cameras, so it shouldn't be too hard to find out who was posing as Lucy's assistant." I shook out the bedding and dropped it back onto the floor where we'd found it.

A business card fluttered out of the bottom sheet like a leaf drifting from a tree. I bent to pick it up. Garrett Rogers—New Hampshire Forest & Lands. The card had the official yellow and green seal for the Forest & Lands division, then listed a phone number and email address for Garrett. I turned the card over in my hand. Written on the back in neat print was, "Lucy, call me. We need to talk." It was signed simply "G."

"More proof they knew each other." And this time it wasn't only an overheard conversation. I turned to show the card to Sunny. "Take a look at this."

"What is it? What did you find?" She stepped over a pair of jeans still sprawled on the floor.

"It's Garrett Rogers business card. He's a local forest ranger and was up at the lookout the morning of the workshop. Do you know him?" I showed Sunny the card and pointed out the personal note on the back.

She shook her head. "Nope. Never heard of him."

I shrugged and slipped the card into the pocket of my hoodie. "I don't think this room has any more secrets to give up. What do you say we get out of here? Pie-Eyed Cellars has a fabulous chicken pesto pizza, if you're hungry." A good meal might take Sunny's mind off her troubles for a few minutes, and I hadn't eaten anything besides tea and cookies since lunch.

"That sounds amazing," Sunny agreed, glancing around the room a final time while tears welled, unshed, in her eyes. "I was really hoping to find something personal, and can't help but wonder what Danae was looking for, and who the mystery assistant was."

"You and me both," I said.

We locked the door to Lucy's room and made our way down to the inn's wine bar.

On the way past the reception area, I stopped and leaned across the desk. "Do not let anybody else in that room, outside of the police. Somebody trashed it." I used my bossiest voice.

Greer's face drained of color when I showed her the pictures I'd taken.

"You can guarantee I'll be passing these photos on to Chief Barnhart, and somebody's going to have some explaining to do."

But first, pizza. Not to mention the fact the Chief basically told me earlier not to bother him anymore tonight.

Chapter Twenty-Two

Weather moved in overnight, and it was pouring buckets by morning. Only a handful of stalwart individuals showed up on the dismal, grey day for goat yoga. When I tried to pry Tristan out of bed like he'd requested, he'd groaned and pulled his quilt over his head, so I gave up after a couple of minutes. To this native Seattleite, the dark skies and rain beating on the roof felt cathartic and cozy. By the conversation swirling around from my students, it was clear I was the only true pluviophile in the group.

"Man, I hate being soggy," Jen announced as she entered the barn, shaking water droplets off her navy-blue rain jacket. "It's so depressing."

"Did you see the forecast? We probably won't see the sun again for a week," MJ grumbled.

"They're expecting the river to reach flood stages by this afternoon. The mountains are getting hammered hard, so we're going to see the results of all that water soon. Remember the big log jam a couple of years ago that flooded The Bottoms?" Brittany asked.

The Bottoms was a low-lying area of Bobwhite Hollow on the east side of the river where an older neighborhood of small homes resided.

"Oh, those poor people," Jen said. "Our church provided meals and a dry place for them to sleep until the waters receded. Let's all pray that doesn't happen again."

"Were their houses livable after the flood?" Sunny asked.

Jen sputtered a raspberry sound. "They barely were livable before, if you ask me. But yes, all the families moved back in once they dried out their carpets. Can you imagine the mold growing behind those walls?" She wrinkled her nose and shuddered.

MJ shot her friend a funny look I couldn't interpret.

Once the talk of the weather and the historic flooding withered out, I got the session started. "Take a seat on your mat, then cross your legs, with each foot under the opposite knee. Or as close to under as you can get. Now sit up straight, and rest your hands on your knees, palms facing up. Close your eyes and listen to the rain. Allow it to center and relax you."

We'd been in the pose for only a few seconds before a little goat climbed into my lap and settled down. I opened my eyes. All four of my students sported laps overflowing with goat. I held the pose for an extra minute, letting them soak up the calm and joy the rain and goats provided.

The mood outside and in made me want to keep the session quiet and restorative for the day. What better way to do that than some relaxing stretches, so I moved everyone into an extended child pose. The goats picked up on the tempo, and instead of jumping from one rounded back to another, they climbed up, curled their own legs under themselves, and settled down. When it was time to get out of the pose, I went around to each person and removed the goat that was lounging on their backs.

The session continued in the same vein, with everyone seeming to benefit from the calm pace. At the end of class, they each appeared more relaxed than when they had arrived.

As everyone was leaving, I approached Brittany. "Hey, can you stay behind for a minute? There's something I need to talk to you about." My stomach rolled with anxiety.

"Sure, I have a few minutes."

We waved goodbye to Jen and her friend, then watched Sunny sprint across the lawn to the guest cottage.

When it was just the two of us left, I turned to Brittany. "Um…I'm not sure…" I stuttered around. "Well, you heard about Alex Bell, right?"

"Yeah." Brittany sighed. "I wasn't super fond of him, but didn't wish him dead. It's terrible."

"Well, so that's what I needed to talk to you about." I wrung my hands.

Brittany frowned and touched my arm. "You look really worried, Callie. What's the matter?" She sucked in a sharp breath and pulled her hand back. "You didn't have anything to do with his death, did you?"

"Me? No!" My eyes flared in surprise as a hand flew to cover my mouth.

"What is it then?" Her eyes narrowed. "You know something."

I hung my head. "My cousin Tristan and I were in Alex's studio yesterday. When we were leaving, Chris went storming in. He was yelling and seemed super mad at Alex over something."

Brittany blinked. "Chris? My husband, Chris?"

I nodded.

"That man and his temper. I keep telling him it's going to get him in hot water one of these days."

She closed her eyes and took a deep breath. I let out my own breath, glad my friend was taking this better than I'd expected she might.

Brittany snapped her eyes open and grabbed my upper arm. "Listen. Do me a favor and keep this to yourself for now, okay?"

I grimaced and sucked in a sharp breath between my teeth. "Well...I may have accidentally already mentioned the argument to Chief Barnhart."

"You did what?" Her voice rose three octaves. "Karma on a cracker. I've got to go. I'll deal with you later."

Brittany spun on her heel and sprinted out of the barn. Mud from the rain puddles splattered up the sides of her black Jeep as she tore down the driveway.

Did Brittany just threaten me? I watched her leave, my heart heavy with regret. I'd only made a handful of friends since coming to Bobwhite Hollow, and now I'd already managed to lose one.

Chapter Twenty-Three

"Oh, are you heading back to Chicago already?" I was startled, and a bit ecstatic, if truth be told, to run into Jim coming down the stairs with his suitcase in hand when I was headed up to my room after yoga.

Jim's caterpillar eyebrows drew together in his perpetual scowl. "My dad is home and mending. Nothing more I can do here." He squeezed past me on the narrow staircase and mumbled, "Looks like you've got the farm work under control."

I nearly choked. "Excuse me, what?" Had I heard him correctly?

Jim cleared his throat. "You're doing…you know, okay. I never thought you'd be able to step up to the task, being such a flighty city girl, but you seem to be handling things well enough to get by."

"Go me." I raised a wimpy fist in the air to show my lack of enthusiasm for Jim's backhanded compliment.

"For your information, I'll be dropping the petition against my parents' competency, for the time being. You have my son to thank for that. I will, however, still be keeping a close eye on you. You may have proved your mettle as a hard worker, but I still have my reservations about your intentions being fully above board." Clearly not expecting an answer, Jim turned away from me and bellowed down the stairs, "Mother! I'm heading out now."

Good riddance. Would it have killed the guy to admit he'd been wrong about me? Probably. My whole body felt lighter as I danced the rest of the way up the stairs. His change in attitude didn't make losing Brittany's friendship any easier, but Jim dropping the competency petition was no small victory. I'd take what I could get, and the rest would work itself out.

Showered and dressed in black leggings, a tan turtleneck, and a super cute plaid shacket in brown, cream, and black I'd found at Whimsical Willow recently, I joined my family in the kitchen. Aunt Ellen and Uncle Will had already eaten breakfast, but sat with us nursing mugs of hot tea while Tristan and I filled our plates with the maple bacon sweet potato hash and scrambled eggs Aunt Ellen had whipped up for us.

"Don't forget to help yourself to a piece of the pumpkin spice coffee cake." Aunt Ellen flipped a green-and-white checkered kitchen towel back that was covering a square serving dish to reveal the crumb-topped treat. "I delivered a basket of coffee cake and plums to the girls in the guest cottage earlier, so this is all ours."

"Don't mind if I do." Uncle Will reached for a slice, and for a second, I thought Aunt Ellen was going to smack his hand, but she smiled indulgently at him and scooted the serving dish into easier reach. I was glad to see he had more color in his cheeks than he'd sported the afternoon before.

After taking a couple bites of my delicious breakfast and downing half a mug of coffee, I came up for air. "I ran into Jim as he was leaving. He told me he's dropping the petition." I glanced around the table at my family.

"He gave us the news this morning, as well." Uncle Will nodded as his blue eyes sparkled. He reached over and clamped a hand on my shoulder. "My son was impressed by our girl here when he finally had the chance to see her in action. It takes a lot to change that kid's opinion once he sets his mind on something. He's stubborn as an old mule, but you proved yourself."

Heat crept into my cheeks, and I shook my head. "Believe me, it wasn't anything I did. Jim is nowhere near a Callie fan." I swiveled my head to Tristan. "What did you say to your dad to get him to change his mind?"

"Beats me. I just didn't get fired up when he tried to push my buttons and raised his voice like I normally would. I told him we all want the same thing here, and that is to make sure Grandma and Grandpa are healthy and strong and aren't being taken advantage of. It's the common ground we all share, including Callie." My cousin pointed his fork at me. "We went back and forth, but in the end, even Dad couldn't come up with any more arguments."

"I guess you proved the old adage about attracting more bees with honey than with vinegar. Well done, grandson." Uncle Will beamed at Tristan. "Now we can all get back to living our lives and put this ugly chapter behind us."

"Thank goodness. Maybe now we can all get along," Aunt Ellen said with gusto. "All this family turmoil has had me tied up in knots. With the old man here healing and my son coming to his senses, I'm going to spend some quality time in my kitchen." She stood and rinsed her tea mug in the sink while peering out the window. "A stormy day like today calls for beef stew and a loaf of homemade bread for dinner, don't you think?"

Aunt Ellen pulled a clean apron out of a drawer and tied it on in one quick movement while Uncle Will cunningly slipped his hand under the cloth and retrieved another helping of pumpkin spice coffee cake.

"What kind of plans do you young ones have for today?" he asked, brushing crumbs out of his snow-white mustache.

"I have an appointment with Chief Barnhart this morning," I said. "Well, not really an appointment, but I'm supposed to touch base with him. I was going to start spreading fertilizer in the hay fields today, but with this rain, it looks like that will have to wait a few days." I tapped my finger on my chin while I considered the day's options. "I can still get all the garden and flower hoses rolled up and stowed away in the garden shed. A little rain never hurt anybody. Then I'll muck out the barn. Should keep me busy enough."

Uncle Will elbowed Tristan. "My strong grandson would be delighted to give you a hand."

"Ugh. The rain is going to spoil my hair, and it was looking so good today." Tristan rolled his eyes but shot me a grin. "Town before chores?"

"Yep. Let's roll."

Chapter Twenty-Four

On the way into Bobwhite Hollow, I caught Tristan up on what he'd missed while he'd been having his productive come-to-Jesus meeting with his dad, and I'd been snooping through Lucy's room with Sunny.

"Did Brittany and Chris come to yoga this morning?" he asked.

My stomach flopped. "Just Brittany."

"Did you say anything to her about Chris and Alex yelling at each other?" Tristan prodded.

"Yeah. She didn't take it well when I told her I'd already mentioned the argument to the police."

"Was she mad?" Tristan gave me a concerned look.

Only if threatening me counts as mad. Not wanting to talk about it, I shook my head, hoping Tristan would drop it.

As soon as we arrived at the police station, Chief Barnhart escorted us back to his office. "Take a seat." He indicated the chairs on the opposite side of his desk as he slid into his own. "What do you have for me? Last night you mentioned something about Chris Shields?"

Tristan and I made eye contact before I answered. "Yeah, so yesterday Trist and I had a photo session at Alex's studio. We were there for about an hour and a half, but we'd finally finished and left. We were just getting into the car to leave when Chris walked past us and went into the studio."

"Walked? He blew past us at Mach five with his hair on fire. The guy was furious and on a mission," Tristan added.

"True," I said. "Anyway, he went inside—"

"No, you're wrong. He started yelling as soon as he opened the door. He wasn't even inside yet," Tristan interrupted.

"What was he yelling about?" Chief Barnhart asked.

I shook my head. "I don't know. Something about some deal he'd made with Alex."

"Actually," Tristan held up his index finger, "Chris yelled, 'we had an understanding,' then the door slammed behind him, and we couldn't hear what they were saying anymore."

I glared at my cousin. "Do you want to tell this story?"

"Sure." He nodded, obviously not picking up on my sarcasm. "The mad guy, Chris, went into Golden Bell Photography. We could still hear him yelling, and Alex yelling back, but we couldn't make out what they were saying. He came back out after a couple of seconds and that was about it."

My mouth gaped open. "Seriously? I thought you were telling the story." I shook my head. "When Chris came out of the studio, he was still yelling. He said something to Alex about coming back for him if Alex didn't do whatever it was he was mad about. Then he pulled down and broke all the outside lights around the studio's front window."

"Ah, so that's what happened to the lights." Chief Barnhart made notes on a pad of paper before looking up. "What happened after Chris broke the lights?"

"Nothing more, that we saw anyway. Alex came out with a broom and told us to move along," I answered. "I think he was embarrassed we'd witnessed the argument."

"So, we left." Tristan nudged me with his elbow. "You need to tell him about Brittany's reaction this morning."

Thanks a lot, jerk face. I hadn't wanted to bring it up.

"Brittany Shields?" Chief Barnhart enquired.

Since Tristan had thrown me under the bus, I had to be honest with the chief. "Yes. Brittany came to yoga this morning, so I told her what Tristan and I witnessed between her husband and Alex. She asked me to keep it to myself, but when I said I'd already mentioned it to you, she got upset and stormed out of there."

"Alright. Thanks for this information. I'll follow up with the Shields. Did you see anyone else while you were at Golden Bell Photography yesterday?" Chief Barnhart tapped his pen against the notepad.

"The only other person who came in while we were having our photo session was Jen Earley," I answered.

"Do you know what her business was with Alex?"

"Yeah, she was making an appointment for her daughter's senior portraits."

The chief stood and stretched, indicating it was time to wrap this up.

Tristan and I stood to go, but then I snapped my fingers. "Were you able to follow up on the camera thing? Remember, I'd sent you a message about seeing a Nikon in the bottom drawer of Alex's desk yesterday?"

The chief nodded solemnly. "We did find the camera. Thanks for the solid tip."

"I'm guessing it wasn't anything, though, right? Just one of Alex's cameras? My guess is he probably shut the drawer so fast so nobody would accidentally trip over it."

"That's need-to-know information, and you don't need to know," Chief Barnhart responded.

"Please, Chief. You're the one who asked me to keep my eye out for anything out of place, and I did provide you with the tip. What could it hurt now to share a little information with me?" I wasn't above pleading to get my way.

"Fine, but this goes nowhere else. You two have to promise to keep it to yourselves."

When Tristan and I both nodded our agreement, the chief continued. "You were right to call it in, Callie. The camera belonged to Lucy Thorne."

Tristan and I both gasped as if it were our jobs.

"But the SD card was missing," Chief Barnhart continued. "We're still searching Alex's shop and home in hopes of finding it."

"How was Alex killed, if you don't mind my asking?"

"Oh, you can ask all you want." Chief Barnhart hitched up his britches. "Doesn't mean I'm going to tell you."

"This old song and dance again," I groused. "How can I keep my eyes and ears open if I don't know what I'm looking for?"

"She has a point," Tristan added.

"You're both a pain in my neck." The chief sighed. "If you must know, early indications are looking like Alex was poisoned."

"Poisoned how?"

"We believe the poison was stirred into a cup of coffee. We'll know more when the crime team gets the toxicology results back, but that'll take time." He thumbed through his phone, then showed us a picture. "The coffee was in this cup. Do you recall seeing it on his desk while you were in the studio?"

It was a tan-colored disposable paper cup, the kind with a built-on rippled sleeve.

I shook my head. "That's a super generic cup. Definitely not what Cranky Bear serves their coffee in."

"Maybe one of the gas stations around here uses those kind of cups," Tristan suggested.

"Hey, would you mind sending me the picture? Tristan and I can keep our eyes open for someplace using the same type," I asked the chief.

"Sure thing."

My phone pinged with the received text.

"Well, I'd better get to it. Thanks for the info, and please let me know if you run across a similar coffee cup." Chief Barnhart slipped his phone back into his pocket. "And Callie, be careful."

"Will do."

As we left the police station, I grinned at Tristan. "Can you believe the chief trusts me? It's so cool."

It wasn't until we were standing in the parking lot that I realized I hadn't breathed a word to the chief about the adventure Sunny and I went on inside Lucy's room at the Bobwhite Inn the night before. Or mentioned the other visitors who had been in her room before us. I turned to go back inside the police station when a Bronco with Chief Barnhart behind the wheel flew by us from the parking lot behind the station. He was halfway down the street while I was still raising my arm in a vain attempt to get his attention.

My next revelation for the chief was going to have to wait until later.

Chapter Twenty-Five

"What time is it?" I asked Tristan as I slid behind Old Rusty's steering wheel.

He thumbed open his phone. "Ten-thirty."

"In your professional opinion, is ten-thirty in the morning too early to eat ice cream?"

Tristan scoffed. "And they say there are no stupid questions."

I pulled out onto the street, turning in the direction of Sweet Pete's Ice Cream Shoppe.

When we entered the sky-blue gingerbread cottage on the riverwalk, Pete himself greeted us with a hearty wave from behind the ice cream counter. He sported his trademark Hawaiian shirt, this time with black palm tree silhouettes and grinning alligators frolicking against a sunset orange background. With the chilly October weather, Pete wore a black long-sleeved T-shirt underneath his iconic Hawaiian shirt, the sleeves pushed up to his elbows.

"Good to see you, kids. I heard you were in town, Tristan, and wondered when you were planning on coming by to say hello." Apparently not expecting an answer, Pete continued. "How's Will doing now that he's home? That near stroke was a scary thing, but glad to hear he's out of the woods and home. What can I get you two today?"

I laughed. "Hello to you, too, Pete. Yep, Uncle Will's doing great, better than expected, but it sounds like you already have all the intel."

Pete shrugged with a wry smile. "Hey, what can I say? I hear things."

Tristan and I glanced at each other before answering in unison, "We know."

"How about a maple creemee, Callie? I just made fresh waffle cones." Pete wiggled his eyebrows, his shiny bald head flexing with the movement.

"My answer is yes. You always know exactly what I'm craving. How about you, Trist?"

My cousin studied the menu board hanging on the wall behind the counter. "Give me a hot fudge and peanut butter sundae, please. With chopped nuts and a cherry."

His order sounded so good I was tempted to change my mind. Instead, I decided I'd just steal a bite or two of Tristan's sundae.

While Pete made our soft serve treats, we chatted about the crazy events of the last few days with the murders of both Lucy and Alex.

"Well, you know Alex and Jen Earley were huge photography rivals, don't you?" Pete asked.

I shook my head. "Not really, no. I mean, I knew they both took Lucy's workshop and entered the contest at Soul Dust. Alex owned a studio and was a professional photographer, but Jen works as a secretary at a church, so how would they possibly be rivals?"

Pete handed me my maple creemee.

"Wow! This is so pretty." The ice cream was covered in crystallized maple sugar, making the whole thing sparkle. I didn't waste one second before taking the first lick.

"It's my October special." Pete grinned, pleased at my reaction. He topped Tristan's sundae with a maraschino cherry and handed it across the counter.

With our ice creams in hand, Tristan and I picked a lime green table near a side window. Neil Young's mellow "Harvest" crooned from the overhead speakers. Since we were the only early customers, Pete poured himself a steaming mug of black coffee and joined us.

He settled back in his chair and stretched out his long legs, crossing them at the ankles. "Anywho, like I was saying, Alex and Jen's squabbling is why the Bobwhite Hollow Photography Club shut down."

"Seriously? I didn't know there was a photography club." I licked maple soft serve off my fingers.

"Oh yeah. It was going strong for a solid ten years or more," Pete replied.

"Until about two years ago, if I'm remembering correctly. Alex was elected president and Jen vice president, but it took only a couple of months under their contentious leadership before all the members got fed up with the arguing and stopped going to the meetings."

"What was there to argue about? Clubs like that are supposed to be fun." I pointed at Pete. "Like your UFO group."

Last summer, Tristan and I found out our Sweet Pete was a card-carrying member of a local group of UFO chasers. Until then, it was a hobby he kept under his hat, but now with it out in the open, he was embracing his quirky hobby with a few fun metal alien signs on the wall. He'd even added a purple and pink swirled galaxy ice cream to the menu.

Pete pursed his lips and shrugged. "Techniques, equipment, how the meetings should be handled, the color of the sky. I don't think it mattered; those two would argue about anything."

"Were you a member?" Tristan asked.

"No, but Claire was. She was one of the first to stop attending."

Claire was Pete's wife. Most days, you could find her in the back of the shop, either making waffle cones or with a pencil tucked behind her ear as she balanced the shop's accounting books.

"Where is Claire today? I wouldn't mind getting her opinion on Alex and Jen's relationship, since she witnessed their bickering firsthand," I said.

"Aha, I knew you'd be poking around in this mess." Pete rubbed his fingers together in the shame-on-you gesture.

"Just so you know, Chief Barnhart asked for my help this time."

Pete grinned. "He's a smart man." He took a sip of his coffee. "Claire's over in Stonehaven visiting her sister today. Would you like me to ask her to give you a call when she gets home?"

"That'd be great." I chomped on my cone. "Have you heard anything about tension between Alex and Chris Shields?"

Pete pushed his lips out like a duck and slowly shook his head. "Not that I can think of. Both those guys have a temper, but they weren't ever friends, as far as I know. Why?"

Tristan and I filled him in on the argument we'd witnessed between Alex and Chris.

"Interesting. My guess would be their squabble may have had something to do with Alex behaving badly at Soul Dust. Chris definitely can get confrontational if someone messes with his family, and I know Alex was talking crap about not winning the photo competition the other day. Said it was all just a popularity contest."

"Back up a minute. I didn't realize the winners had been announced." I blinked. "Lucy died before the judging was scheduled to take place."

Pete nodded. "True enough, but the show had to go on, so Brittany decided as the owner of the gallery holding the contest, she had the authority to decide the winners herself."

I snapped my fingers. "That's right. She did promise the photographers the contest would still be held. I'd forgotten."

"Don't leave me in suspense here. Who won?" Tristan asked.

"Not sure." Pete shrugged. "You'll have to stop by Soul Dust to find out."

I buried my face in my ice cream, not wanting to admit that I didn't think I'd be welcome at the art gallery today. Not to mention, with my throwing Chris under the bus, I might need to watch my back with both him and Brittany. If Chris killed Alex for acting like a jerk to his wife, I might be next.

Something else Pete had said caused me to straighten my spine. "What did you mean about Alex having a temper, too? The guy was prickly, for sure, but I didn't see him flying into a rage over anything."

"Maybe he's matured some, but when Alex was about nineteen or so, he took a baseball bat to his best friend's truck for thinking his buddy was flirting with Alex's girlfriend."

"Ex best friend, I'd guess," Tristan quipped.

"Indeed," Pete confirmed. "Alex got a 'malicious destruction of property' conviction for that little stunt."

"Up at the workshop on Weaver Mountain, Alex kept making all kinds of snide comments about Lucy. He made it super clear he didn't like her one little bit. With what you've just told us about his temper, it's possible he's the one who killed her."

"Could be. Alex has always been petty and trying to be the top dog around town. My guess is he would have been fairly jealous of a well-known photographer coming to town and horning in on what he thought of as his territory," Pete said.

Tristan frowned and shook his head. "But now Alex is dead, too, so that blows your whole theory out of the water."

"Not necessarily." I scrunched up my face. "What are the odds that these two murders are completely separate incidents?"

"I think there's a low chance, but not zero. Definitely something to consider." Pete was quiet for a few seconds. "You know someone else who is tangled up in this whole thing, don't you?"

"Several people I haven't been able to tie the right knots together yet," I replied. "Who are you thinking about?"

"Danae Mutasa."

"The reporter?" Tristan asked incredulously.

"How do you know Danae?" I questioned Pete.

Pete smiled and sipped his coffee. "I don't know her personally, but I've been following her career since the beginning. The woman has talent and is going to break out one of these days and make it big. Mark my words. Unless she winds up in prison for murder."

"Noted," I said around a mouthful of soft ice cream and crunchy cone. "Sure, Danae's in town because she came here with Lucy, but what makes you think she might be involved with the murders?"

"Well, that's not exactly what I said, but she does have connections to both victims."

"She was following Lucy around for a story she was assigned by her network, and was at the workshop along with Alex and the other photographers, but I was with her most of the time, and am fairly confident Danae and Alex never spoke a single word to each other."

"Not surprising. That's how I would expect them to act," Pete replied.

Tristan plopped his spoon into his sundae. "Okay, you're losing us here, Pete. You're saying you would expect complete strangers to act like complete strangers. What's weird about that?"

Pete held up an index finger. "Ah, but Danae and our boy Alex were not complete strangers."

I huffed. "Stop beating around the bush and spill what you know."

Pete was a good friend, but the man had the ability to exasperate me to no end. He loved to drag his tidbits of gossip out like a slow, rainy afternoon. I had neither the time nor the patience for his nonsense today.

"Like I said, I've been following Danae's career from the beginning. Claire and I love her spots on New York Live, and she posts all kinds of entertaining content on her YouTube channel. Her Instagram feed is more personal stuff, family and friends, you know?"

I swirled my hand in the air for him to get on with it while I finished my cone.

"A handful of years ago, Danae's new boyfriend started showing up in her personal photos. Claire and I both recognized him right away."

I choked on the last bite of my waffle cone. "No way. Alex?"

"Yep." Pete chortled, pleased with himself. "The one and only Alex 'Golden-Boy' Bell." He leaned in across the table and lowered his voice as the door opened and two women came into the ice cream parlor. "Before I go, let me just say, their breakup after a year or so of dating was ugly. Not two months later, Alex was back in town and engaged to his high school girlfriend. Do what you want with that information."

I whipped out my phone and pulled up Instagram.

"You won't find anything. Danae scrubbed out all the pictures of the two of them together after the breakup." He raised his hands, stood, and strode behind the counter to greet his newest customers.

Tristan frowned at me. "The plot thickens."

"Indeed, it does."

In case Danae had missed one, I scrolled through her feed but didn't find any mention of Alex. I was still scrolling when Tristan's phone rang.

He jumped up. "I'm going to take this outside."

A handful more customers came in and lined up at the counter. The first two women had received their ice cream and settled at the table right next to mine.

"I shouldn't indulge, but after the morning I've had, I deserve this," one of the women said.

Her friend patted her hand. "You absolutely do. Taking our pets to the vet is always traumatic for everyone involved."

"My sweet Mischief. He gets frantic the minute he sees me get out his cat carrier. The poor boy is twelve now, so I have him on a six-month checkup schedule so we don't miss anything important. You know you can't be too careful with your pets. They're part of the family and should be treated as such. Look at this new scratch he inflicted this morning. Of course, he didn't mean to hurt me; he was just so frightened. I won't hold it against him." She pushed up the sleeve of her sweater to show her friend.

Out of the corner of my eye, I could make out a six-inch-long red scratch running down the center of the woman's forearm.

She licked her ice cream cone before continuing. "Mischief and I weren't the only ones having a rough time. The vet clinic was a disaster this morning."

"Busy?" Her friend finally managed to get a word in edgewise.

"The phone was ringing off the hook, people were lined up a mile deep for their appointments, dogs were putting up an unholy ruckus, cats were hissing, and someone's poor rabbit managed to escape from its cage. Boy, if that wasn't a mess with all the dogs straining at their leashes trying to murder the poor scared little fellow. That handsome young vet of ours was beside himself, trying to do everything at once. He said his schedule was booked solid, but his receptionist was out of the office with a family emergency. I felt almost as bad for him as I did for my little Mischief."

Stonefield Veterinary Clinic was the only vet office in Bobwhite Hollow, so the woman had to be talking about Levi. It made sense Kelsey would be out for who knows how long because of her brother's sudden death.

"Hey," Tristan said, interrupting my musings as he slid back into his seat. "So, that was Skip. It's his day off today, and he was wondering if I could go for a drive with him to look at the fall foliage. Do you mind? I know I'd promised to help you with farm chores."

I stood and grabbed my bag. "Not at all. There's nothing that can't wait. You should go, it'll be fun for the two of you to get to know each other better. Where should I drop you off?"

"Skip's already waiting for me over by the park." He shot me a crooked smile.

"Oh, really?" I teased. "It wouldn't have mattered if I cared or not, huh? Why'd you even bother to ask?"

Tristan bumped my shoulder as we left Sweet Pete's. "It was a courtesy question."

Skip waited on the sidewalk in front of a midsize white SUV, his hands tucked into the front pockets of slim blue jeans. He broke out with a wide, white smile when he caught sight of Tristan. My cousin let loose with a small, excited hop before he got himself under control. He gave me a cool backhanded wave as he split off to join Skip while I turned in the opposite direction to find my truck.

Chapter Twenty-Six

Even before I pushed open the door at Stonefield Veterinary Clinic, it was obvious the woman at Sweet Pete's hadn't been exaggerating. The parking lot was jam-packed, and every chair lining the walls of the small waiting room was occupied. The humans sitting in the chairs either had a death grip on a dog's leash, their lap full of dog, or a pet carrier in front of them. Glancing into the carriers, I saw a few cats, a rabbit, a guinea pig, and what appeared to be a hedgehog. I wrinkled my nose at the overpowering smell of wet dog.

The telephone on the desk jangled loudly as Levi escorted a man and a giant black Newfoundland dog out of the back of the clinic. The dog wore a white plastic cone around his neck. "Sherman should recover well. We'll see you in two weeks for his follow-up."

"What do I do about payment, Doc?" the man asked.

Levi glanced around the room as if confused, then his eyes fell on me and lit up. "Uh, Callie will be glad to take your payment." He strode over to me and whispered an amount in my ear. Levi grabbed a clipboard off the desk, studied it for a second, then called out, "Chewie?"

A young woman with a concerned-looking dachshund in her arms stood up. "Here we are."

Levi held the door into the examination area open, then turned to me. "Callie, could you please answer that blasted phone?"

"Uh, okay." I scurried behind the desk and fumbled with the greeting. "Um, Levi McClure's office?"

"Well, I should hope so. I'm trying to reach Stonefield Veterinary Clinic.

Is that you?" a gruff voice replied.

I took a deep breath. "It is. What can I help you with?"

"Got a horse with a cough. I need Doc McClure out here pronto. When can I expect to see him?"

"And who is this, please?"

"Mel Palmer, like I said. Doc knows me."

"You didn't say, sir." I knew better than to argue with customers, but the words fell out before I could bite my tongue.

"Well, I most certainly did, young lady. Now I'm not going to take any guff from the likes of you. Put Doc on the phone."

"I apologize, Mr. Palmer, but Dr. McClure is tied up with patients at the moment. I'll have him call you the minute he's free. May I have your phone number, please?"

"It's in his records. Look it up."

The dial tone rang in my ear.

Alrighty then.

Instead of slamming the receiver back into the cradle like I wanted to do, I replaced it gently and smiled at the much nicer and more patient man waiting to pay his bill. His dog, Sherman, sat on his haunches and grinned at me, his enormous tongue dripping drool all over the floor. The man handed me his debit card while I stared stupidly at the card reader. The machine wasn't a type I was familiar with.

"I'm sorry, but I don't actually work here and have no idea how to tell the card reader the amount of your bill." I was confident I could figure it out if given a few minutes, but I didn't want to keep the nice man waiting any longer than he already had.

He chuckled. "No worries. I'll take Sherman here out to the truck and grab my checkbook. Will that work?"

"Yes, a check would be perfect." I nodded like I knew what I was doing, completely unaware if Levi accepted checks or not. Didn't matter. He did today.

After Sherman's owner settled up, I studied the paper on the clipboard Levi had used when he called in the last patient. It appeared to be a sign-in sheet, so when the door opened and a teenage boy came in with a blue parakeet in a cage, I had him sign in and take the seat Chewie's human had vacated.

The next time Levi poked his head out to change patients, I asked for the password to the computer. I was able to locate the daily schedule and give myself a quick overview of the billing program. Thankfully, his system seemed fairly simple and straightforward. In order to make sure I didn't royally screw anything up, I scribbled down the phone requests for appointments with promises to call the worried pet owners and farmers back as soon as I had a chance to check with the vet.

An hour later, Levi asked me to phone in a delivery order for sandwiches for the two of us, which we hurriedly ate in his office with the phone on Do Not Disturb. The lobby was still full of patients waiting to be seen. While we gobbled down turkey sandwiches, Levi gave me a quick rundown on how his schedule worked—small animal clinic three days a week, and farm visits the other two.

By the time five o'clock rolled around and Levi had seen his last patient for the day, I had a decent handle on how things worked around the vet clinic and could take payments like a pro.

"Thanks, Callie. You saved my hide today." Levi propped his elbow on the front counter and let out a heavy sigh. "I was about to call it quits."

"My pleasure. You probably don't have any idea when Kelsey will be back yet, right?"

He shook his head. "At this point, her leave is indefinite. She won't be back until after Alex's funeral, and maybe not even until the murder investigation is wrapped up. Hard to tell, really. I told her it didn't matter. She needs to take all the time she needs. Her job will be waiting for her when she's ready to return."

"Yikes. What are you going to do in the meantime?"

Levi looked a little lost. He glanced around his clinic, then directly at me. "Not sure. You're not looking for a part-time job, are you?"

"Uh, maybe. Are you serious?" This could be the answer to my winter unemployment problem.

"Deadly serious. Like I said, though, it could be two weeks or two months.

I really don't know at this point, but I do know there's no doubt I need somebody manning the office on my clinic days. This morning was a complete train wreck."

"It just so happens, with the weather changing, I don't have any more goat yoga sessions scheduled. It'll be spring before I start them back up again. I'll take the job!"

Levi's emerald eyes sparkled, and he pumped a fist in the air. "Fantastic. Now I don't have to pack my bags and slink out of town with my tail between my legs."

"Nope." I beamed a smile back at him. "So, Monday, Wednesday, and Fridays are clinic days, right?"

"Yeah, except only mornings on Fridays. I save the afternoon for emergency farm visits."

"Oh, which reminds me." I held up a finger and shuffled around the desk for the pink sticky note. "A crotchety farmer called about his horse earlier."

"Let me guess. Mel Palmer?" Levi asked.

"The one and only." I located the note and handed it to him.

"I'll run out and see Mel when we're done here. So, those days of the week will work for you?"

I nodded. "Absolutely. And it'll still leave me with plenty of time to get work done at the farm, since we're headed into a slower season. It's perfect, really."

Levi clapped his hands together once. "Great. Would you be willing to have dinner with me after I get back from the Palmers' place? As a thank you for saving my skin today?"

I couldn't think of anything I'd like more.

Levi gave me a set of keys to the clinic before he grabbed his medical bag. "How does the Hearthstone Grille sound? Should I pick you up at the farm?"

"The Hearthstone is great, but no, how about I meet you there? I've got a few errands to run. Text me when you're on your way back."

"Sounds good. I guess I better go see a man about a horse." Levi chuckled at himself as he walked out the door.

Before I left for the day, I rummaged around until I found a file folder with

Kelsey's employee paperwork inside. Guilt bit at my heart, but I was only looking for one piece of information. Once I located Kelsey's home address, I scribbled it down on another pink sticky note and slapped the file closed. I shot Aunt Ellen a quick text to let her know where I'd been all day and to not wait on me for dinner, grabbed my bag, and locked the front door of my new place of employment.

Chapter Twenty-Seven

The Bells lived in an older neighborhood west of downtown Bobwhite Hollow and up the hill a little ways. The three-story, butter-yellow house with white trim was likely built in the early 1900s and featured a wraparound porch and a detached garage. The driveway was lined with red brick, and an oak tree stood majestically in the front yard, some of its golden autumn leaves scattered across the green lawn.

When I rang the doorbell, quick footsteps thudded my way before the door was pulled open. Kelsey's red-rimmed eyes held confusion as she stared at me. "Hello?"

"Hi. You may not remember me, but I met you at Stonefield Veterinary Clinic the other day when I brought our dog in. I'm Callie Haybeck, and I wanted to stop by and extend my family's condolences on the terrible loss of your brother." I held out the small vase of white roses and blue hydrangea blossoms I'd picked up at Mountain Daisy Floral on my way over.

"Of course, I remember you." Kelsey reached for the vase. "I'm sorry. My mind doesn't seem to be functioning at normal speed right now." She stood aside and invited me in.

"No need to apologize. It's perfectly understandable with everything you have going on." I stepped around Kelsey into a rich and warm living room.

A tan stone fireplace with a crackling fire and a gleaming cherry wood mantel took up a large portion of one wall, while matching floor-to-ceiling bookshelves lined both sides of what appeared to be the doorway to the dining room. A ginormous Oriental rug in sage green with a design in creams and reds covered the honey-gold hardwood floors. Kelsey placed the flowers on a coffee table and sank into one corner of the beige couch, so I took the other corner. Hushed voices reached us from another room.

"I'm sorry to barge in on you and your family at such a horrible time, but I couldn't get you off my mind and wanted to tell you how sorry we all are for your loss." When she continued to stare at me as if not seeing me or hearing a word I said, I blabbered on. "And I wanted to let you know not to worry about the vet clinic. I'm going to help out and take up your slack while you're out. Not that I think you're slacking. That's not what I meant. I only meant for you not to worry because I've got it covered and took your job when Levi offered it. Oh, shoot, I don't mean I took your job, only that I'm going to be *doing* your job until you get back. Your position is perfectly safe and still yours as soon as this whole mess is behind you. Not to say that I think your brother's death isn't a tragedy, it totally is, or that you should get over it soon. Oh, for crying out loud. I'm just making everything worse. I'm going to stop talking now." I clamped my jaws shut.

Kelsey shook her head as if to clear out cobwebs. "I'm sorry, I'm having a hard time concentrating. What were you saying?"

Whew. It was one time I was relieved to have someone completely tune me out. "Just how sorry I am about your brother."

She turned her attention to me for the first time since I'd arrived. "Thank you, Callie. I can't wrap my mind around his death. Alex is such…was such an amazing person. Everyone loved him. Who would do this to him?"

Who indeed.

"Did Alex have any enemies that you knew of?" I asked.

Tears streamed silently down Kelsey's face as she shook her head. "No, like I said, he was the most popular guy in town."

It seemed Kelsey held her brother up on a pedestal. The most popular guy in town badge wasn't the picture I'd gotten of Alex from anybody else I'd talked with. Not knowing what to say, I simply nodded.

"Except for his ex-girlfriend, maybe. Danae. She's a reporter and weirdly is in town right now." Kelsey sucked in a sharp breath and straightened her spine. "I bet you're right. That jealous woman killed my brother."

I held up my hands in protest. "Now hold your horses. I didn't say anything of the sort. But why do you think Danae might have hurt him?" Now, here was the true reason I'd stopped by.

"Alex and Danae dated in college. They'd even talked about marriage, but then Danae started getting super competitive with Alex. Like, she would be furious with him when he got recognition for his stellar grades and she didn't. He made the dean's list and she was barely squeaking by. What was he supposed to do, flunk out so his girlfriend would feel better about herself? I don't think so."

"Is that why they broke up?" And I'd bet my last dollar you could flip that whole scenario on its head.

Kelsey nodded emphatically. "Oh, yeah. While they were together, Alex gushed about how wonderful she was but after they broke up, the truth finally came out. He even caught her copying his papers and trying to turn them in as her own. How she has made it as far as she has with her career is beyond me. Probably by crushing her coworkers under her sharp, pointy heels."

The front door opened, and a woman carrying a toddler and holding the hand of a small girl entered, kicking the door closed behind her.

Kelsey opened her arms for the little girl, who ran into them for a snuggle. "Oh, my sweet Addie. I'm so sorry about your daddy."

I took the arrival of Alex's wife and children as my cue to leave.

* * *

When I'd arrived at the Bell's house, I'd purposely left my phone in the truck. While I'd been inside, Levi had texted that he was on his way back to town. I shot him a quick response, telling him I was done with my errands and ready to grab dinner whenever he was.

Give me 15 minutes, came his reply.

Two minutes later, I was at the Bobwhite Inn. I took advantage of an empty seat near the big stone fireplace while I waited for Levi. When Chief Barnhart strolled through the door and up to the reception desk, I hopped up and tagged behind him. He'd just greeted Greer, the woman working the desk, when I stepped up beside him and said hello.

"What in tarnation are you doing here?" Chief Barnhart looked at me in surprise.

"Waiting for my dinner date." *Is it a date? Nah, just a thank you for helping out today.* I shook my head to clear out the annoying chatter. My relationship, or non-relationship, with Levi was a whole different topic and not appropriate to discuss with the Chief of Police. "But seeing you reminded me there is something I needed to talk to you about that I forgot to mention when Tristan and I stopped by your office this morning."

"Could you possibly be talking about your little adventure into Lucy's room with Sunny last night?"

"Yeah, how did you know?" I asked as my eyes flicked to Greer.

Her face was pale as a sheet, most likely feeling guilty about the people she'd let coerce her into getting into Lucy's room.

"I have my ways." The chief turned back to Greer, who plastered a public service required smile onto her face. "Greer, I was hoping you could help me out with a little something."

"I'm happy to help with anything I can, sir." Her voice wavered nervously.

"I need to review your CCTV footage from the times when the reporter and supposed assistant were at the desk asking for access to Lucy Thorne's room."

Greer bowed her head slightly. "Yes, sir, please follow me."

She called out to another employee, asking them to watch the desk in her absence, then led the chief into a closed office. I slipped in behind them.

Levi would be arriving any minute, so I shot him another text:

I'm here but with Chief Barnhart. Give me half an hour?

My phone binged with the notification of a thumbs-up emoji. Ugh. I hoped he wasn't as irritated as I usually was when I sent someone the same emoji.

Sorry, I texted back.

Greer pulled out a chair and sat behind a desktop computer. I crowded in beside Chief Barnhart, who sent me a scowl but didn't tell me to get out. She pulled up footage showing twelve different angles, including two frames in the parking lot and other various angles around the public areas of the inn. She scrolled back until stopping on a set of frames marked with yesterday's date and a timestamp of fourteen hundred hours.

"The reporter came in shortly after two, so this should be a good place to start," Greer said as she slowly started moving forward through the frames.

"There she is." Chief Barnhart pointed to a shot of the front door, clearly showing Danae entering the inn.

As we followed the frames, she walked across the lobby and approached the front desk, where a past version of Greer greeted Danae with a large smile. The two of them held an animated conversation before Greer winked and handed Danae a room key. Present-day Greer blushed a deep red before flipping to a screen of a mostly empty hallway where we watched Danae unlock the door and enter Lucy's room.

"Go ahead and pause there for a minute, if you will," Chief Barnhart directed. When Greer did, he questioned her. "I realize there's audio we can access along with the footage, but I'd like to hear the story in your own words. Why did you deem it reasonable to give this woman access to the room the police had specifically instructed the staff to not let *anyone* enter?"

Greer rolled her shoulders and cleared her throat. "I knew Danae had been traveling with Miss Thorne for a segment for her show. She was really nice and told me part of her notes were in the room and promised me she had permission from the police to go in and get them."

Chief Barnhart leveled Greer with a look that I was more than happy wasn't directed at me this time. "And you just took her word for it? You didn't think to pick up the phone and find out if her story checked out."

Greer's voice was tiny as she answered, "No. She swore on her mother's grave."

"I'm going to go out on a limb and bet her mother is alive and well," the chief quipped.

The time stamp showed Danae was in the room for twenty minutes before exiting.

"Alright. Let's get to this so-called assistant." Chief Barnhart swirled his right hand in the air to speed things up.

Greer glanced up at me. "She came in about a half an hour before you and the daughter arrived."

"Daughter? Whose daughter?" The Chief sent me a questioning look.

I grimaced. "Another thing I failed to mention. Turns out that Sunny is Lucy's biological daughter."

He pinched the bridge of his nose and sighed heavily. "You've got to be kidding me."

I kept quiet.

Greer sped through the frames until she located the correct time. The chief and I both leaned in when Greer pointed to a woman with dark hair in a shoulder-length bob entering the Bobwhite Inn. The mystery woman wore a long nondescript gray coat and a brimmed black cloche. She kept her head down, even as she approached the desk. During her conversation with Greer, the woman used the hat to keep her face shielded from the camera, as if she knew exactly where the security cameras were mounted.

When Greer flipped to the hallway shots outside of Lucy's room, we watched the woman look both ways down the hallway before inserting the key and entering the room. Ten minutes later, she rushed out of the room, down the stairs, and out the front door, never once letting the cameras see her face.

Knowing it was a dumb question, I asked anyway, "Anybody recognize the hat?"

Chief Barnhart frowned at me. Again.

"I don't know her name, but the same woman was in here shortly after Miss Thorne checked in. She asked for Lucy's room number then and told me she was the assistant. That's why I didn't think twice when she came in again and said she'd left some of her equipment in the room."

"Show me the footage from that night," Chief Barnhart demanded.

When Greer pulled it up, it was like déjà vu. The same woman, wearing the same outfit, kept her head down and approached the desk. After a short conversation, the woman headed for the staircase. In the hallway frames, we watched her knock on Lucy's door. When Lucy opened it, her face was clear on the security camera and showed irritation at the interruption. Lucy tried to close the door, but the woman stuck her foot in. She didn't push her way into the room, but Lucy opened the door wider again.

It looked like the two had a short but heated conversation. All three of us gasped when the mystery woman hauled back her fist and punched Lucy in the eye. She then stormed off, and Lucy slammed the door.

"Well, that explains one part of the mystery," Chief Barnhart said.

"Lucy's black eye," I answered.

Chapter Twenty-Eight

Greer went back to her duties at the reception desk of the Bobwhite Inn, and Chief Barnhart and I parted with a promise that I'd stop withholding information I ran across.

"In my defense, none of it was willful withholding. I just forgot to tell you a couple of little things." I pleaded my case.

"More like a couple of key pieces of information." He pulled off his hat and ran a hand through his thinning hair while muttering something unintelligible under his breath. "If you're going to insist on being involved in this thing, you're going to need to do better. If you have a memory problem, take notes."

I studied my shoes and remained silent, feeling like I was being scolded by my middle school basketball coach.

As he walked away, Chief Barnhart pulled out his cell phone. I heard the beginning of his conversation. "Danae Mutasa? Chief Dale Barnhart here. I need you to meet me at the station, pronto."

Levi was waiting for me in the lobby, looking like a dream. His dark blue jeans, button-up deep plum shirt, and suede jacket left me wishing I'd taken the time to run home and freshen up. Or recombed my hair, at the very least. Too late now.

"Ready?" Levi placed a hand on the small of my back. "They have a table waiting for us."

The Hearthstone Grille was warm and inviting. We were seated at a dark walnut table, the perfect size for an intimate meal. A small amber vase filled with a gorgeous autumn bouquet next to a flickering votive decorated the table. Red and gold flames danced in the fireplace while soft acoustic music filtered down from overhead speakers. Our waiter placed a fragrant basket filled with a variety of warm breads and rolls in the center of the table before leaving us alone to make our dinner selections.

Over his ribeye steak and my jumbo prawns, we both chattered so much I don't know how either of us managed to eat our dinners. We touched on everything from our favorite childhood TV shows, family, pets, travel destinations, and worst dates. The time flew by, and the next thing we knew, we were the last holdouts in the place. Our dinner plates had been cleared eons ago, and our wine glasses remained empty. The candle on our table had burned down to a nub by the time I tore my gaze away from Levi's dreamy emerald eyes and glanced around the dimly lit restaurant, noticing all the other diners had left. Waitstaff quietly huddled together around a table against the far wall, tapping fingers on the wooden tabletop and throwing disdainful glances our way.

"Whoops. Looks like we've outstayed our welcome." Embarrassed, I hurried to rise and smashed my knee painfully against the leg of the table as I attempted to shove my chair back.

"Are you okay?" Levi asked.

"Yep, just clumsy." I did my best to hide my limp as we strolled through the dark, rainy parking lot.

When we reached my truck, I turned to Levi. He leaned in, a romantic smile on his face. I stood on tiptoes to reach his lips for a sweet goodbye kiss, only to have my puckered lips whoosh by his ear as he pulled me in for a ten-second-long, one-armed hug.

My mouth hung open as Levi winked, clicked his tongue, and shot me with a finger pistol. "See you at the clinic."

Wait a minute. What just happened? During our handful of dates in the past two months, Levi and I had gotten way past the awkward hug phase. Or so I thought. Tonight, I'd expected the sweet, lingering goodnight kiss our dates typically ended with.

Not caring that I was getting drenched, I stood in the rain and watched the taillights of his pickup pull out of the parking lot. It was the first time

Levi hadn't waited to make sure Old Rusty started and to wave as I drove off first. I wanted to blame the abruptness of his departure on the weather, but another thought niggled at the back of my brain. What if he was acting weird and standoffish because I was his newest employee? If that was the case, I just might need to continue my job search.

* * *

Tristan had rolled in from his extended date with Skip only a few minutes after I finally made it back to the farmhouse. Aunt Ellen and Uncle Will's bedroom door was closed without any light shining from underneath, so I dried my hair and slipped into flannel pajamas before the two of us lounged on the bed in my room to talk about our respective days. Tristan gushed about his time with Skip while I held back most of my thoughts about my time spent with Levi until I had time to savor the sweet and mull over the weird by myself.

"Now that Uncle Will's home, do you need to get back to Boston soon?" I asked once Tristan's Skip gushing died down to a slow trickle.

He blew a raspberry. "Not if I can help it. I'm going to milk this family emergency thing as long as I can."

Tristan's response took me by surprise. "You love Boston. What's going on?"

He hemmed and hawed until the story finally started to spill out. "Remember how I told you the salon sold a month or so ago?"

I shook my head. "Vaguely, I guess. You said your job was safe and you were sure you were going to like the new owner."

"Well, I was wrong. My new boss is a complete chowderhead. He is super unprofessional and has no idea how to behave around clients. Our salon is now a toxic work environment."

"Like what kind of things is he doing? I want examples."

"He's catty and competitive, always trying to steal clients from me and the other stylists. Say I have someone in my chair and my next appointment comes in a few minutes early, my boss will swoop in, telling my next client they don't have to wait and offering them a twenty-percent discount if they sit in his chair. It's so underhanded."

"Not to mention unethical," I added.

"Exactly. He can't manage to keep his own books full, so he doesn't see anything wrong with stealing our clients. I can't tell you how many cuts and colors I've had to fix because he's screwed them up. And the other day, he reeked of old vodka. Like it was radiating out of his pores."

"Gross. How did this guy get the funds together to buy the salon?"

Tristan shook his head. "No idea, but I'm not sure how much longer I can take it. When I get back, I'm going to start looking for a chair in another salon."

"And take your clients with you."

"Oh, yeah, my clientele comes with me."

"Or, and I'm just putting this out there as food for thought, you could take a look at this adorable empty storefront downtown I noticed the other day. It's right on Main Street and would make a perfect salon." I held my palms up to indicate no pressure.

"In Bobwhite Hollow, Callie?"

"Why not?" I shrugged.

"It's just so…provincial. I'm a modern guy, not traditional at all. I don't think I'd fit in very well here. It's all so vanilla."

"So bring your own flair and add some strawberry to the mix." I bit my lip, trying to be careful with my wording. This was the first time Tristan hadn't immediately shut down any mention of him relocating to Bobwhite Hollow. "I think you'd be surprised at how accepting this town is. And honestly, there's a bigger LGBTQ+ community here than you would imagine. And you'd have me. That's a huge bonus, right?"

Tristan flopped back on my bed and stared at the ceiling. "I don't know."

I smacked him over the head with a pillow. "It wouldn't hurt to look at the space, would it?"

He shrugged. "Maybe. We'll see. The idea of being my own boss does hold a certain level of appeal."

We talked about it until we finally talked ourselves out, then Tristan stumbled to his room. The last time I looked at the clock, it read two in the morning.

* * *

The animals didn't care that I was barely existing on four hours of sleep. They still wanted their breakfast. I managed to get everyone fed and watered before grabbing a mug the size of a cereal bowl and filling it to the rim with hot coffee and vanilla creamer. Once I felt somewhat human, I pulled on a fleece jacket, topped it with a raincoat, and tugged my feet into my rubber work boots. It was time to tackle the chores I'd managed to avoid the day before.

All the garden hoses and equipment were rolled up and stowed away and the outside faucets winterized by the time Tristan joined me to muck out the barn. He grabbed a shovel and wheelbarrow and set to work. The two of us had the barn shipshape by lunchtime.

"Do you want to go to town with me after lunch?" I asked. "I need to apologize to Brittany for throwing Chris under the bus. It's been eating at me, and I don't want to wait any longer to try to talk to her about the whole thing."

Tristan agreed, and we trooped into the house for steaming bowls of Aunt Ellen's homemade tomato soup and grilled cheese sandwiches. Her soup hit the spot on the chilly autumn day.

An hour later, after cleaning up the kitchen so Aunt Ellen could relax with Uncle Will, I hopped out of the truck and slammed the door, trying to swallow back the nervousness bubbling up in my throat.

"Do you want to go in alone?" Tristan asked.

"No, come on." I grabbed him by the sleeve and pulled him along with me. "But try not to hover."

"Hey, am I just your emotional support cousin?" He brushed off his sleeve but slipped an arm over my shoulder. "I deserve more respect than that."

"I'll treat you to a coffee after."

"Deal."

A soft chime sounded as Tristan and I stepped into Soul Dust Art Gallery. One wall was dedicated to the photographs that had been entered in this week's landscape competition. The soft white walls showcased the art beautifully, as folks gathered around, oohing and aahing over the entries. Low instrumental music set a peaceful tone.

Brittany was behind the counter, wrapping a painting for a customer while two others waited patiently in line. Danae was in the gallery, taking her own photos of three of the people I recognized from Lucy's workshop on Weaver Mountain. Jen beamed from the middle, holding a large, framed photograph of lonesome railroad tracks disappearing around a bend and surrounded by gorgeous fall foliage with blue-tinted mountain peaks in the distance. Her friend MJ stood next to her with a photo of an arched stone bridge with the river under the bridge appearing to flow off one corner of the frame. The man Alex had berated at the workshop for using subpar equipment stood on the other side of Jen. His photo showed a clear mountain lake with spectacular fall foliage reflected in the water. I'd be delighted to hang any one of them on my walls.

When Danae finished with her photo shoot, I asked, "Are you three the winners?"

"We are," Jen answered immediately. "My 'Mountain Rails' took first. I'm beyond thrilled. MJ got second place with her stone bridge, and Manuel here scored third on his mountain lake shot. Isn't that exciting? My work is finally getting the recognition it deserves."

"Congratulations to all three of you. Your photos are stunning." I paused to admire their work, then glanced at Jen. "You said your photography is finally getting recognition. Have you been entering your photos in competitions for long?"

"Ages." Jen's voice rose an octave in her excitement. "And I've had some terrible experiences entering various contests, one in particular, but because of this win, Brittany is going to feature my work in an exclusive exhibition. And my winning photo will be front and center in a local calendar. It makes all the turmoil worthwhile."

"Don't forget I'll be doing a story spotlighting the three of you winners on

New York Vibrations," Danae said.

Jen blushed and grinned so wide she was in danger of her face splitting in two. "How could I forget? I'm so excited I can't see straight. I'm already planning to have a watch party at my house when the episode airs. But shoot, now that I think about it, my house isn't going to be big enough to hold everyone who will want to come. I'll need to talk to the pastor about using the church meeting space instead. What a great idea. We can serve coffee and cookies, and the whole town can squeeze in. It'll be a big celebration."

It was clear Jen wasn't talking to anyone but herself now, so I quietly stepped away. Brittany was finishing with a customer, so I stood in line to wait my turn to talk with her.

When the customer left with her purchases, I stepped up to the counter. Brittany looked up, blew up her cheeks, and let out a puff of air. My stomach rolled.

"Look, Brittany…"

"Callie, I need to…"

We both started talking at once.

"Go ahead," I said.

Brittany took a deep breath and tried again. "I've been meaning to call you to apologize for storming out of yoga the other morning. I was worried about my husband. His temper can get him in trouble sometimes."

I reached out and took her hand. "You don't need to apologize. I do. It was wrong of me to talk to Chief Barnhart before giving you a heads-up. I'm sorry."

Brittany shook her head. "No, you were right to do what you did. Two people have been killed, and we all need to tell the police what we know if something seems even a bit off. I'm not mad at you." She called out to an employee. "Tracey, will you take over here for a few minutes? I'm going to take a break."

"No problem," Tracey agreed. "Take your time, but be back in two minutes." The woman chuckled at her own joke.

"Come on." Brittany motioned for me to follow her into her small office. I glanced around for Tristan, but he appeared to be deep in conversation with Danae, so I followed Brittany. She clicked the door shut behind us and cocked a hip onto the top of her paper-laden desk.

"It's busy today, so I do need to get back out there pretty quickly, but I wanted to ease your mind about my husband being a murderer." She paused, and I blinked. "Let me rephrase that to add him *not* being a murderer."

"Thank goodness for that. Do you know what Chris and Alex were squabbling about then?"

Brittany nodded. "Back in June, Chris got a new pickup and sold his old one to Alex. Or sort of sold it, I guess."

"What do you mean, sort of sold it?"

"Alex gave him a thousand dollars down and was supposed to make monthly payments on the balance."

"Let me guess, he didn't." My mind produced the image of the overdue bills lying on top of Alex's desk.

Brittany shook her head. "We haven't seen a dime."

I wiggled my fingers, doing a quick count. "Holy buckets. That was four months ago. He hasn't paid anything?"

"Nope. Chris doesn't like to be confrontational, so he hadn't said a word, trying to give Alex the benefit of the doubt, but then…" she paused.

"Then what?" I prodded. "He snapped?"

"Chris overheard Danae talking on the phone. She was telling someone how Alex had blown a gasket when he found out he didn't win the gallery's photography contest. Apparently, he told her I'd rigged it."

"Rigged it how?"

"By promoting the contest as having a star judge and then playing favorites with the contestants when Lucy was no longer available to judge. By Alex's account, the only reason he didn't take top honors was because I didn't like him because of his business dealings with Chris."

I narrowed my eyes. "But you said Chris hadn't said a word to him about his late, or nonexistent, payments."

"He hadn't."

"Sounds to me like Alex had a guilty conscience."

"Agreed. He apparently told Danae I'd planned the whole thing in order to slap him in the face, and he was going to report me to the Better Business Bureau for false advertising."

"Oh, like you killed Lucy so you could judge the contest yourself to make sure Alex didn't win?"

Brittany nodded. "You nailed it. That's exactly what it felt like he was saying. Which makes zero sense, seeing how I own Soul Dust and make the rules for the contest. It was such a ridiculous accusation."

"And that's when Chris finally lost it?"

"Oh, yeah. He would've let the nonpayment go on forever, but the minute Alex started badmouthing me and messing with my business, Chris was all over him. He stormed out of here before I even knew what was going on." She gestured wildly with her hands as she talked. "But I promise you, Chris did not kill Alex. He doesn't have a violent bone in his body."

Tearing down the lights around Golden Bell Photography in a fit of anger could be construed as vandalism, so I wasn't sure I'd agree. On the other hand, Alex was poisoned, which led me to believe his death was premeditated and not a spontaneous act of violence by an irate husband. Still, he was going to stay on my radar until I gathered more evidence.

"Thanks for your candor, Brittany. I'm really glad we talked and worked this out. I like you and want to remain friends, if you'll have me." *Even if I am still suspicious of your husband.*

"Absolutely. I like you too and want to stay friends. But right now, I better get back out there before I'm in trouble with Tracey."

"It's good to see the gallery so busy."

"We've been swamped since Lucy died. Everyone wants a piece of her work now. It's terrible to say, but her death has been great for my business. Good thing I'd ordered a fair amount of her prints in anticipation of selling extra since she was supposed to be in town," Brittany said over her shoulder as she walked out of the tiny office.

My treacherous brain immediately wondered if my friend would have killed the famous photographer to drive more business to Soul Dust. *Stop it, Callie. Brittany is innocent.* She'd been with me the entire time during the workshop. It wasn't even a remote possibility that Brittany was the killer.

Chapter Twenty-Nine

"If I was the police, I'd be taking a close look at Garrett Rogers," Jen was saying to Tristan and a rapt MJ. She glanced at me as I joined the circle, raised an eyebrow, and lowered her voice while each of us leaned in. "Mark my words."

"Why Garrett?" I whispered.

Jen shook her head dramatically. "The whole thing is so scandalous. I heard all about it in church, so this goes nowhere." She mimed zipping her lips and looked at each of us in turn for our agreement. Satisfied, she continued, "It seems Garrett had a beef with Alex, because Alex had been hitting on Heather, Garrett's wife. Are you following me?"

I frowned. "I saw Heather at the soccer game the other afternoon. She's a pretty woman, but she must be a good decade older than Alex."

Jen snickered. "Believe me. Some young men are enamored by older women. We have all the experience and all the moves." She shimmied her hips, then looked me up and down. "You wouldn't know that yet."

I squeezed my eyes shut and shuddered. Way too much information. Eww. "Still, Alex's wife is gorgeous. Are you sure there's truth behind this so-called scandal, or is it just a vicious rumor?"

Jen shrugged. "Generally, I find where there's smoke, there's fire." She straightened her posture and looked at MJ. "Ready to head out?"

Tristan nudged me with his shoulder. "Speaking of ready, where's the coffee you promised me?"

"Do you want to grab one to go, or sit in the coffee shop and enjoy it?"

"Do you even have to ask? Of course, I want to sit and enjoy my coffee like a civilized human being."

When we stepped out onto the sidewalk, Jen and MJ were gathered around Jen's van with two other women.

"See right there? Those are puncture wounds in my car. I'm not sure if they're teeth marks or claw marks." Jen pointed to part of the frame around a window.

Curiosity got the better of me, so I edged closer to see for myself. "Punctures the bear made?"

Jen looked back at me and nodded. "Yeah, come and take a look."

Tristan and I both moved in and peered at the puncture marks.

"She got her paws or nose under the window and managed to get enough leverage to jerk the door right off. Thankfully there wasn't too much damage, and the garage was able to put the door back on with only a few minor adjustments," Jen explained as we all oohed and aahed over the story of the hungry bear.

Jen slid the van door open to show us the damage the bear had done inside. While she talked about how long it was going to take the garage to get the correct seat in stock to replace the torn-up one, I glanced around the interior of the van. No wonder the bear peeled the door off like a can opener when she smelled a snack. Jen had struck me as a tidy person, but her car told a different tale. Discarded clothing items, scrunched-up fast food bags, and other pieces of trash littered the floor and backseats. A stack of Amazon boxes sat on the seat beside a tote with a box of tissues, a roll of toilet paper, and the floppy dark hair of a doll's head poking out of the top of the bag.

"Anyway, it's nothing that can't be fixed, and it makes for a great story to tell." Jen closed the door. "MJ and I have to get to the church, so the show's over. We've got a lot to organize for our Harvest Craft Fair for the downtown associations' Second Saturday this upcoming weekend." She sent a friendly wave our way as the two friends got into the van.

Arm in arm, Tristan and I strolled down Main Street to Cranky Bear Coffee Company.

"Mmm." Tristan fairly groaned as the decadent, warm scent of good coffee washed over us when we entered the shop.

The red brick walls and hardwood floors of the coffee shop added to the cozy warmth. I studied the fall menu and finally settled on the toasted coconut mocha, while Tristan chose the pumpkin spice latte. We grabbed a small table tucked against the wall.

"Back at the gallery, I noticed you were talking to Danae at one point. Did you get any info out of her?" I asked.

Tristan shook his head. "Not much. That woman keeps her secrets close. I tried flattering her by gushing about how much I enjoy her show and how it's been nice to see her covering Lucy's high-profile death. Mostly she just accepted my praise. She did flash a sly smile, though, when she mentioned we'd be seeing a lot more of her on the nightly news from here on out. It looks like her dreams of fame are coming to fruition."

I pulled a small notebook out of my bag and flipped it to a blank page. "Let's jot down what we know at this point. Or what we think we know, anyway. Starting with Danae. Go."

"Alright," Tristan rubbed his forehead. "We know Lucy's death has elevated Danae's career, at least to the point where her network left her in town and sent a camera crew to film her reporting on the murder. She's gone from being a small journalist on a weekend magazine show to a face on the nightly news in a short time span."

"At least while Lucy's death is still breaking news," I added. "It seems like this could create momentum for her career, and she hinted as much to you." I made some notes. "We also know Danae unlawfully entered Lucy's room at the Bobwhite Inn, though we don't know what she was looking for." I thought for a minute, then shrugged. "I might just have to ask her point-blank."

Tristan eyed me over his coffee but didn't argue. "What else?"

"We know Danae has, or had, a tie to Alex, too. His sister verified that Pete was right about the two of them dating. And remember Alex said Danae had been in Golden Bell Photography the other morning, but he didn't admit to knowing her other than as a reporter."

Tristan shrugged. "Yeah, but that was hours before he was killed."

"Doesn't mean she didn't sneak back later with a cup full of poisoned coffee."

"Anybody could have." Tristan blew my speculation off. "Who else is on the list?"

"Sunny should be next."

"Agreed."

"Let's start with the facts. We know Sunny is Lucy's biological daughter, since she told me so herself. According to Sunny, she wormed her way into the job but had never worked up the courage to reveal her true identity to Lucy. After spending time with her, I honestly don't think she murdered her own mother. She wanted to get to know her, not kill her."

"Let me play devil's advocate for a moment, then," Tristan said.

"Go ahead."

"Let's say Sunny lied to you about not confronting Lucy. What if she did, but Lucy wasn't the warm, fuzzy mother Sunny was hoping for? Maybe Lucy even denied being her mother at all. People lie to protect themselves all the time. You said yourself there was tension between the two of them when they first arrived at the guest cottage."

I fiddled with the miniature pumpkin decorating the table. "So, you're saying Sunny may have killed Lucy because Lucy rejected her? If you're right, maybe Sunny was upset Lucy wasn't staying at the farm because she'd planned to kill her in her sleep, not because she wanted to spend more time with her like she said."

"I think it's as good a possibility as anything. Can you imagine how horrible it would be to have your parents deny they were your parents?"

"Good point. And up on the mountain that morning, Lucy directed Sunny to take the extra gear back to her car, then Lucy went out on her shoot, and Sunny disappeared. I assumed she'd gone to the parking lot, but when Sunny resurfaced later, she still had the same bag of equipment with her."

"Meaning she never took it back to the car, which gives her plenty of unaccounted for time where she could have snuck away and murdered Lucy. Plus, we have the theory that has Sunny and Danae working together for some sort of monetary payout, like life insurance, for instance. And now that we know Sunny was Lucy's next of kin, it makes it more plausible."

"Except we haven't found any evidence of either a life insurance policy or the two of them working together whatsoever. From what I can tell, the only thing Danae and Sunny share is separate rooms in our guest cottage. I think they're like roommates who don't really speak to each other."

Tristan blew out a breath. "We're getting nowhere fast. Do we know of any ties Sunny had to Alex?"

I shook my head. "Nothing I know about, except for Alex attending Lucy's workshop, which is a thin thread at most." I wrote a few more notes. "Let's move on to Jen."

"Where was Jen the morning Lucy was killed?"

"At the workshop with everyone else. All the photographers split up, so any one of them had the time to murder Lucy. I remember Jen going off in the opposite direction from the way Lucy took. She admitted to lying about going down to the trailhead to use the outhouse, so Jen doesn't have any more of an alibi than any of the other photographers who were on the mountain that morning."

Tristan sighed. "That's not much to go on. Anything else?"

I sipped my coffee and stared at the ceiling, trying to remember. When the photo shoot time was over and everyone was back at the lookout, they were all scrolling through their photos and showing each other their shots, but Jen refused when MJ asked to see hers."

"She was probably just protecting her shots. Can't say I blame her there."

"Makes sense. She said she's had problems before, so I imagine she was being cautious." I tapped my pen against the page. "Let's see. What else?"

"We witnessed Jen's dark side at the soccer game, but I still don't know why she'd kill Lucy. There doesn't seem to be a motive there at all," Tristan said.

"Not that I can come up with. Alex maybe, since Pete said their spatting was the reason the photography club broke up. Pete said he'd have Claire call me, but I still haven't heard from her," I said. "But if Jen hated Alex so much, why was she scheduling her daughter's senior portraits with him?"

"Because her daughter insisted, remember? She told Alex she wanted to take her somewhere else, but the daughter threw a hissy fit."

"Oh, yeah. Like mother, like daughter." I grabbed the sides of my head. "There's too much nonsense rattling around in here. I can't keep it all straight."

"Speaking of nonsense, Jen has been pretty quick to throw around names as possible suspects," Tristan said.

I scrunched up my nose. "You mean like we're doing right now?"

Tristan shot me with a gun finger. "Exactly like what we're doing right now. The difference is, we're trying to suss out a murderer, and Jen seems to be trying to stir up drama."

"Some people thrive on drama, and I think Jen fits firmly in that demographic." I wrote "drama queen" next to her name. "Moving on. How about Chris?"

"You and Brittany were sequestered in her office today. Did you learn anything from her?"

"According to Britt, Chris was selling Alex a pickup, but Alex hadn't made the agreed-upon payments for like, four months." I filled Tristan in on what Brittany had told me. "She's insistent that Chris doesn't have a violent bone in his body."

Tristan wobbled his head back and forth. "I suppose him shattering the lights on Alex's studio could've been a one-off, but the jury's still out."

"My thoughts exactly. Though poisoning someone is premeditated, and I don't know if Chris would go that far. He had a temper tantrum, not a diabolical plan to kill someone. There's a difference."

"Not to mention him not having a motive to kill Lucy," Tristan added. "And did he have the opportunity? Did anyone see Chris on Weaver Mountain the morning of her death?"

I pursed my lips and shook my head. "Not that I'm aware of, no."

"So, the last person on our list is the forest ranger guy, right?"

I nodded. "Garrett Rogers. He was on the mountain that morning. He took off in the same direction Lucy did. There was definitely a look passed between the two of them…"

"But then he was down in the parking lot dealing with the bear a little bit later," Tristan interrupted.

I sighed. "True. And back up to the lookout to find Jen, and then back down to the trailhead. Not sure he had the time to commit murder in his busy schedule."

Tristan tilted his head. "Honestly, the murder part couldn't have taken very long."

"Agreed. And we know at some point, Garrett left Lucy a note saying they needed to talk. Then I overheard Garrett's wife telling him he needed to come clean with Chief Barnhart."

"Not to mention Jen's accusations that Alex was making a play for Garrett's wife." Tristan ran a hand through his curls. "Where does that leave us?"

"Beats me. And we can't forget about Lucy's camera being found in Alex's desk."

"Which muddies the water even more. Are the two deaths even related?"

I blew out a tired breath as I studied my notes. "I'm more confused than ever."

Chapter Thirty

Back at the farm, Tristan went inside to check on his grandparents while I headed straight for the guest cottage. It was time to find out more about both of our guests. Unfortunately, Danae's car wasn't in the driveway, and she was really the one I wanted to talk with the most. Oh, well. With any luck, I could pry a little more information out of Sunny.

My knocking didn't produce any results, and I was about to give up and try again later when Danae's car rolled to a stop in front of the cottage.

"Hey there," she said as she slammed the car door. "What's up?"

"Just checking in. Is Sunny around?"

"She texted earlier to say she was going for a walk and would probably be gone a few hours. Can I help with something?"

"Is everything still good with the cottage? Do you need fresh towels or toiletries? I'm happy to come in and clean, if you'd like me to."

Danae shook her head. "No, I think we're all good. The cottage is so well-appointed, we really don't need anything. Sunny threw a load of towels in the wash yesterday. It's really nice to have a washer and dryer to use, and with the pastries and fruit you guys provide every morning, I could live here full-time. This place is seriously great."

"I'm glad to hear it. Let me know if anything changes." I turned to go without getting a single thing I came for, but steeled my spine and turned back around. "There is something I've been wondering about, though. Do you have a second?"

"Sure." Danae held the door wide for me to follow her in. "I wouldn't mind picking your brain for a few minutes, either. Why don't you come in for a bit?"

We both wiped our feet on the mat in the front entryway before each taking a seat in the small, cozy swivel chairs near the window. Danae pulled a box of chocolates from a local store out of a shopping bag. She took off the lid and deposited the candy onto the walnut end table between the two of us.

"These looked too good to pass up. Help yourself," she offered.

"Tempting, but I'm good for now. Thank you."

"What is it you were curious about?" Danae broke the ice.

"Please don't take this wrong, but I heard you wormed your way into Lucy's room at the Bobwhite Inn the other afternoon, and I wondered why."

"Wormed my way in?" Danae's sleek eyebrows shot sky high.

"Maybe wormed is a little harsh, but given how you told the front desk employee you had permission from the police, which wasn't true, I think it is a valid description." *Geesh. Back it up, Callie.* From the time I'd spent with Danae the morning of the murder, I legitimately liked her, so I wasn't quite sure where my aggressive attitude was coming from. Too much coffee and not enough sleep? "Anyway, I know you're just doing your job, but would you mind telling me what you were searching for?"

"Hey, a worm isn't the worst thing I've ever been called." Danae chuckled. "I was looking for the same thing everyone else is after—clues the police may have overlooked that could help solve Lucy's murder."

"And did you find anything?"

Danae pursed her lips and stayed silent, a muscle ticking in her cheek. She was hiding something.

"Or were you looking for something specific you needed to remove from the room? Something that would make you look guilty if it was found?"

"Don't be ridiculous. What reason would I have for killing Lucy?"

"Maybe to further your career. You said yourself you needed a sensational story to get yourself seen and taken seriously." I hadn't meant to confront the reporter so blatantly, but my mouth had a terrible habit of running away with itself. I'd gone too far, but there was no turning back now.

Danae's eyes flashed with anger, but to her credit, she simply took a deep breath and remained calm. "I don't imagine you'll take my word for it, but I had nothing to do with Lucy's death. You and I were together nearly the whole morning, or at least within eyesight of each other, so I don't understand where this accusation is coming from."

"Except when you went to use the outhouse." I bit my lower lip. "I know I'm coming on strong, and I apologize, but you seem to be everywhere, and have definitely taken advantage of pumping up your television presence with the coverage of Lucy's murder."

Danae widened her eyes and leaned forward. "Any reporter worth her salt would be doing the same thing if they were in my shoes. The story literally dropped into my lap. And the fact that I'm all over town, reporting and attending all of the functions, is just another part of the job. I'm trying to do my best to cover all the bases and get all the facts out to the public that I can."

"And covering all your bases includes uncovering information however you can, even if it's obtaining access to Lucy's room illegally?"

"Please. I'm pretty sure I could ask the same question of you. Seems like you and your cousin are embroiled in your own unofficial investigation." She stared at me with a challenging gleam in her eyes. "From what I understand from the community, you're a regular little Nancy Drew. You know, we really should pool our resources and work together, instead of you not so subtly accusing me of murder. We're both after the same thing in the long run." Danae flipped her hair over her shoulder and leaned back against the couch as she waited for my response.

She wasn't wrong. I jiggled my foot rapidly as I considered her proposition. "Okay. If we were to work together, are you prepared to share what you've learned with me? Because I have a sneaking suspicion you're hiding something."

"Absolutely. Tit for tat."

For me, there were a few things I would be keeping close to my chest, so I was under no delusion a professional reporter like Danae wouldn't be keeping her own secrets, but it was possible we could help each other out, like she'd suggested. I nodded my agreement. "Fine. We have a deal. You go first. What did you find in Lucy's room."

"Nothing." Danae clicked her tongue on the roof of her mouth. "Nada. Zero. Zip."

"Nothing?" I sighed heavily. If she was willing to share exactly nothing with me, I'd reciprocate in kind. I shrugged. "Me neither."

I leaned forward to stand when Danae coyly said, "It wasn't Lucy's room where I found the intriguing information."

I plopped my butt back into the chair. "But you did find something?"

She grinned as she dug a small laptop out of her messenger bag. "Yep. Take a look at this."

I moved to kneel beside Danae and leaned over the arm of her chair as she clicked through her documents to a folder marked with Lucy's name. When she opened a document, a divorce decree filled the screen. The Supreme Court of the State of New York declared Lucille Agnes Rogers, plaintiff, and Garrett Charles Rogers, defendant, officially divorced with an uncontested filing. A judge and both parties signed the document over twenty-five years ago.

"This is the secret Garrett's wife wanted him to come clean about," I whispered while reading through the document and simultaneously kicking myself for not putting two and two together sooner.

"I don't know what you're talking about, but here's the next filing." Danae clicked through to a second document.

The next form was a petition for a name change. It had been filed on the same day as the divorce and effectively changed Lucy's surname from Rogers back to her maiden name of Thorne.

"You're up now. I've unveiled my secrets, now it's your turn to tell me what you meant about Garrett, his wife, and a secret," Danae insisted.

"At the soccer game the other day, I overheard his wife telling him he needed to come clean with the police about Lucy." I gestured to the laptop screen. "Now it all makes sense. Garrett's secret is that he was married to Lucy at one time." I pondered for a second before deciding I needed to hold up my end of the bargain. "The one thing I found in Lucy's room was Garrett's business card with a note on the back stating the two of them needed to talk and asking her to give him a call."

"What could they possibly have to talk about after all these years?" Danae tugged on her hair as she thought. "I did some deeper digging and found out the two of them went to high school together in upstate New York. They must have been high school sweethearts, because they got married shortly after graduation. They stayed in their hometown, both worked blue-collar jobs; Garrett as a gas station attendant and Lucy waiting tables at a Speedway truck stop out by the interstate. Lucy took classes at the local community college, and then they divorced a few years later. I didn't find any juicy gossip about either one of them."

"No kids?"

Danae shook her head. "Nope."

I chewed my lip, not so sure about that, but not ready to disclose Sunny and Lucy's relationship to Danae. It wasn't my story to tell.

"How unlikely do you suppose it is that, all these years later, Lucy comes to the town where Garrett has made a new life for himself, and winds up dead?" Danae took three chocolates from the box, popping one in her mouth and chewing slowly.

"It sure seems like a weird coincidence, doesn't it? There's got to be a connection. Garrett made it sound like they hadn't been in touch in years, so maybe it was just serendipity. But why would the world-renowned landscape photographer accept an invitation to judge a contest in tiny Bobwhite Hollow? The whole thing seems strange to me."

"Unless she knew her ex-husband lived here and was hoping to reconnect?" Danae popped another chocolate into her mouth. "I have a feeling Garrett Rogers is up to his eyeballs in this. We just have to find a way to prove it."

I trained my gaze on Danae to judge her reaction before asking my next question. "To make things even more complicated, now Alex Bell has been murdered as well. In your research, did you find any threads tying Alex to Lucy, Garrett, or anyone else involved in this investigation?"

Danae blanched. Her hands shook as she closed the screen on her laptop. "Not a thing, but I'm sure there's a connection I just haven't found yet." She stood abruptly. "Sorry to cut this short, but I think my blood sugar just spiked. I'm shaky and need to eat something that isn't chocolate. I'll let Sunny know you stopped by."

Before I knew it, I was kicked out onto the doorstop like the cat on the old Flintstones cartoon opening clip.

Chapter Thirty-One

"You'll never guess what I just found out," I told Tristan as soon as I came into the farmhouse and peeled off my coat.

He was lounging in the library with Uncle Will and Aunt Ellen. All three of them had books open on their lap, but I only felt bad for two point four seconds for interrupting their reading time. Uncle Will placed a bookmark in the latest William Kent Krueger he was reading, and Aunt Ellen set aside her Louise Penny title.

Tristan held his finger on a sentence in his copy of *Upgrade* by Blake Crouch and slowly looked up. "What?"

"You'll never guess what I found out," I repeated.

He grunted. "I heard you the first time. Exactly what did you find out?"

All eyes were on me now, so I filled them in on Danae's revelation about Lucy and Garrett's former marriage and subsequent divorce.

"Even so," Uncle Will chimed in once I finished, "I stand by my declaration that Garrett Rogers is no killer."

"I couldn't agree more. For what it's worth, if I was poking my nose into other people's business, I'd be more concerned about finding out why our two guests were screaming at each other this afternoon." Aunt Ellen arched her eyebrows, her cornflower blue eyes steady as she delivered the news.

"Screaming at each other? Sunny and Danae?"

Tristan looked at me like I was a dim lightbulb. "Nobody else staying at the farm is a guest."

I chose to ignore the sarcasm and addressed Aunt Ellen. "When was this? How did you hear them arguing?"

"Oh, probably close to two hours ago now. I went out to collect the eggs and give the chickens the kitchen scraps. The two of them were inside the cottage, but yelling so loud it was hard to miss. The only thing I made out was one of them calling the other a selfish so and so before Sunny stormed out and slammed the front door so hard I was afraid the window would shatter. She ran off in a huff."

"Danae said Sunny had texted her to let her know she was going for a walk, but I'm going to guess the only text was the slamming door."

Tristan shrugged. "Everybody lies to cover their own bad behavior."

I'd have to mull that over later, because from the corner window, I caught the reflection of Sunny returning to the guest cottage from her walk. "Back to Garrett. Maybe he's not a killer, but what if he *is* Sunny's father? I'm sure she doesn't know it. When I mentioned his name, she said she'd never heard of him. I think Sunny and I need to talk to Garrett in person. Do you want to go with us, Tristan?"

"Not this time. I'm going to sit with Grandpa so Grandma can go to church."

Aunt Ellen rose from her chair. "We're getting ready for our Harvest Craft Fair, and I promised I'd help the ladies prepare this afternoon."

"That reminds me, Grandma. Does Jen Earley go to the same church you attend?" Tristan asked.

"She does. Jen works as the church secretary and is active with all of our women's activities. Why do you ask?"

"No reason. Callie and I were visiting with her earlier today, and she mentioned needing to prepare for the craft fair, too. I was just curious," Tristan replied.

"Good deal. Glad you're able to get out for a while, Aunt Ellen." I shoved my arms back into my coat and raced out the door to catch up with Sunny. "Hey! Wait up," I called out.

She whirled around and met me halfway. "What's up?"

Might as well cut to the chase. "Do you remember the business card from Garrett Rogers we found in Lucy's room?"

Sunny cocked her head, her long dark hair falling forward over her shoulder. "Sure. The forest ranger, right? He left a note saying they needed to talk. Did you find something else out about him? Do you think he killed Lucy?"

"Danae hasn't told you what she found?"

Sunny glanced back toward the guest cottage, then frowned my way. "No. She's always so wrapped up in her work, she barely talks to me. What did she find?"

"A divorce filed between Lucy and Garrett."

Sunny's eyes flared like a spooked horse. "From when? What year?"

"Twenty-five years ago, give or take a month or two."

She sucked in a sharp breath. "The timing adds up. Garrett could be my biological father. Maybe that's why he needed to talk to her. Maybe they were going to try to find me."

"My thoughts exactly, though they didn't know their baby grew up to be you." I made a sweeping gesture at Sunny with my hand. "Are you up for having a chat with Garrett?"

"One hundred percent." Sunny spun on her heel and beat me to Old Rusty.

I ran back into the house to get directions from Uncle Will to the Rogers house.

When Tristan reached for his coat, I told him to leave this one to the girls. "What's Skip doing this afternoon? Maybe you should give him a call," I added slyly.

Tristan slid his coat back onto the hook and wiggled his eyebrows. "I like the way you're thinking."

Hehehe. My evil plan to entice Tristan to move to town is coming together. I rubbed my hands together with glee.

Aunt Ellen pulled out of the driveway on her way to the church right behind Sunny and me. She followed me to town, where I waved out the window as she pulled into the church parking lot to the left, and I made a right-hand turn onto Egret Way. The houses in the neighborhood were a mixture of classic, charming bungalows and mid-century ranch-style homes with neat and tidy yards.

Sunny gazed out the passenger window. "Right here, right here." She rapped on the window when she saw the correct house number, virtually thrumming with what I could only guess was a combination of excitement and anxiety.

I pulled Old Rusty to the curb in front of a well-tended bungalow with a dormered window on the roof above the candy apple red front door. Pumpkins, gourds, and baskets of colorful fall mums lined both sides of the four concrete steps leading to the front porch. A long wooden welcome sign painted on barnwood leaned invitingly against the siding near the door.

Sunny pointed to the sign. "I hope he's still welcoming when he finds out what we've come to say."

I reached for her hand and gave it a quick squeeze before ringing the doorbell. A dog's bellowing bark accompanied the chime of the bell. Sunny and I both took a giant step back from the doormat that was printed with a black Gothic fence and invitation to "Enter if you dare."

The door wrenched open, and Garrett, wearing a long-sleeved green Henley shirt, jeans, and stockinged feet, greeted us. "Hello there. Can I help you two with something?" He glanced between Sunny and me, then shot out a leg to keep the big chocolate lab from escaping. "Buddy, sit," he commanded the dog. Buddy obeyed, though his quivering muscles indicated he was jonesing to have a meet and greet with the two of us.

"We're hoping so. I'm Callie Haybeck, and this is Sunny Hammond," I started in, but it was clear Garrett wasn't listening to a word I said. His entire focus was on Sunny, a look of pure confusion on his face.

"Are you my father?" Sunny got right to the heart of the matter.

Garrett nearly choked on his own tongue. "Your father?" he finally managed to spit out.

"Lucy Thorne was my biological mother. We just found out the two of you used to be married."

Garrett shook his head, his mouth still gaping open. "But Lucy and I...we didn't...we never had any kids." His eyes were still glued to Sunny's face.

Avery, Garrett's high school-aged daughter, came up behind Garrett from inside the house. "Who is it, Dad?"

Sunny and Avery's eyes locked on each other, Garrett's head swiveled between the two, and I wanted to smack myself on the forehead. No wonder Avery looked so familiar at the soccer game. The resemblance between her and Sunny was uncanny.

"How old did you say you were?" Garrett asked.

"I didn't," Sunny replied, "but I'm twenty-four."

You could see Garrett doing the quick calculations in his head. He glanced between Avery and Sunny once more, then turned back to Sunny. "I think there's been some secrets kept from all of us. You better come inside." He held the door wide open and ushered us both into the house while Buddy ran circles around our legs, sniffing at our shoes.

Sunny and I settled into two small armchairs while Garrett hustled Buddy into the backyard before sitting next to Avery on a creamy sectional couch opposite us. Father and daughter had the same striking jade green eyes. Sunny's eyes.

Garrett leaned forward, focused on Sunny. "Tell me everything. When exactly is your birthday?"

When Sunny told him, he blanched. "That's eight months after Lucy left. How could she not have told me about you?"

"Maybe she didn't know yet before she left," I inserted. "A month is pretty early in a pregnancy. I had a friend who didn't realize she was pregnant until she was nearly five months along."

"Quite possibly, but there's no excuse for not telling me once she found out." Garrett sighed. He stood and paced the room, running a hand through his hair. "You asked if I was your father. Did your mom never tell you about me?"

"No." Sunny shook her head. "Lucy didn't even know she was my mom."

He reared back. "What? If she gave birth to you, of course she knew. That makes zero sense. Are you trying to pull something over on me?"

"Not at all. I truly think you are my biological father. I was born in Alaska and given up for adoption as a newborn. From what I understand, my birth mother most likely never even held me. She just signed her rights away." Sunny's voice remained under control and calm as she told her story. "You're telling me the truth when you say you didn't know anything about her pregnancy? About me?"

"Lucy left New York for Alaska. It was the one thing she told me when she left. That she was going to Alaska for a job opportunity in Anchorage that was too good to pass up. She was adamant that we'd outgrown each other and didn't want me to go with her. I wanted kids and a house with a white picket fence. She wanted a career. End of story." He stopped pacing, sat back down beside Avery, and looked at his young daughter. "I think you have a big sister, Ave," Garrett said breathlessly.

"You think?" the girl repeated sarcastically. "We look exactly alike. There's no thinking about it." Avery jumped up and wrapped Sunny in a bone-shattering hug, then squeezed into the chair beside her newly found sister. "I've always wanted a big sister. But just wait until you meet your super annoying little brother."

Sunny wiped tears from her eyes. "I have a little brother? What's his name?"

"Mason the terrible," Avery joked.

"Now, not so fast." Garrett made a stop motion with his hands. "We don't know for sure. I mean, how do you know Lucy was your mother? You said she didn't know, so how do you?"

Avery snorted. "Come on, Dad, really? Look at us." She tipped her head to lean her face against Sunny's and grinned.

Looking slightly embarrassed but pleased, Sunny pried herself out of Avery's grip. "I took a DNA test. It matched me with a woman named Lisa Thorne as my maternal aunt."

Garrett nodded. "Lisa is Lucy's older sister. There were just the two girls in their family."

Sunny matched his nod. "Which makes Lucy my mother."

"Seems that way. You were at Lucy's workshop the morning she died, but you didn't introduce yourself to her?"

Sunny glanced at me.

"Go ahead. Tell them everything," I encouraged.

She launched into her backstory, from losing her parents in the plane wreck, finding out she was adopted, the foster placements, and finally turning eighteen. Then taking the DNA test, tracking down Lucy, and securing the job as her assistant. "But I hadn't worked up the courage yet to tell her I was her daughter. I was afraid she wouldn't want anything to do with me."

"Yet you knocked on my door the minute you found out Lucy and I used to be married."

Tears sprang to Sunny's eyes. "I waited too long with Lucy, and now I'll never get to know her. I didn't want to make the same mistake twice."

Garrett crossed the room and enveloped both his daughters in a healing hug.

I studied my hands as if I'd never seen them before and tried not to make any noise in order to give them the space they needed. After a couple of minutes, I was getting uncomfortable. Glancing at the door, I contemplated pulling off an Irish exit, but then how would Sunny get back to the farm? Better to wait it out. Another full minute passed before the front door swung open. Garrett's wife and a dark-haired boy about ten years old stood in the doorway.

"What's going on here?" Heather asked as she slung her purse onto a hook by the door and approached the four of us.

"Hey, Avery, you're never going to guess…" The boy came to a skidding halt as both Sunny and Avery glanced over at him. The boy threw his hands up and spread his fingers wide. "Whoa! Who cloned Avery? We didn't need two of her. Aaargh!" He screamed and ran up the stairs. Seconds later, a door slammed.

Heather's eyes were wide. "I mean…Mason's not wrong. Can somebody please fill me in here?"

Garrett made the introductions. Between him and Sunny, they explained the circumstances to Heather, who seemed to take it all in stride.

Lots of questions and answers later, Heather smacked her hands together and addressed Sunny. "Well, I think we will want to have both you and Garrett take another DNA test, just to confirm. But I'm pretty confident what the results will show." She smiled. "Welcome to your new family, Sunny. You'll stay for dinner, won't you?"

Tears poured down Sunny's cheeks as she nodded yes.

"Would you like to stay, too, Callie?" Heather asked.

"Thank you, but no. I better get back to the farm and get the chores done. The animals are going to be yelling for their dinner." I stood and zipped up my coat, then glanced at Sunny. "Just call when you're ready for a ride."

"I'll run Sunny out to your place later," Garrett said. "No need for you to have to come back to town."

"Thanks, I appreciate it." The business card I'd found in Lucy's room popped into my mind. "Oh, there's one more thing I meant to ask you, if you don't mind."

"Sure, shoot."

"We found the business card you left for Lucy that said you needed to talk. If you didn't know the two of you had a child, what in the world did you need to talk about after all these years?" I glanced at Heather apologetically, afraid the answer wasn't something she'd want to hear.

"Lucy and I haven't kept in touch since our divorce. I was a wreck after she left, but a couple of years later I met Heather, and everything changed for the better. Lucy wasn't a part of my life anymore, and I didn't keep up with her career. It felt like the Twilight Zone when I found out she was in town to teach her workshop and judge the photography contest at Soul Dust."

"I bet that was weird," I agreed.

"Completely surreal," Garrett confirmed. "Anyway, my mom passed away a year ago, and since Lucy was in Bobwhite Hollow, I wanted to let her know. Back in the day, they used to be really close. My mom talked to Lucy for several years longer than I did. I just thought she'd want to know Mom was gone. That was all."

"So nothing nefarious? You didn't kill Lucy up on Weaver Mountain that morning?" The feelings I got from Garrett and his family were completely cozy and warm. If I thought there was much of a chance he was truly the killer, I wouldn't have been so glib with my remarks.

Garrett placed one hand over his heart and one arm around his wife's shoulders. "No, I solemnly swear, I did not kill Lucy Thorne, or Alex Bell, for that matter."

Garrett followed me outside and pulled the door closed behind himself. "Callie, I can't thank you enough for bringing Sunny home. When I think about all the years we lost…" Tears welled in his eyes. He shook his head. "There's no sense dwelling on what could have been, but seriously, thank you."

"You're more than welcome. Sunny really needs a family, and you all were so kind and welcoming." I hesitated, but had one more question for him. "You just mentioned Alex Bell."

"Yeah, what about him?"

"I don't want to upset you, but I heard a rumor today connecting your name to Alex's murder."

Garrett jerked his head back. "In what way?"

"The person said you may have killed him out of jealousy, because rumor has it Alex had been making a play for Heather."

"Heather? My Heather?" Garrett pointed to his own chest.

The front door of the bungalow flew open, and the woman in question strolled out holding her phone. She held it up and pointed to the screen. "Ring camera. Thought you might like my take on the wild rumor you heard."

"Are you spying on us?" Garrett asked playfully.

Heather grinned. "Not so much spying as wondering what was taking you so long." She turned to me. "The only dealings I've ever had with Alex just so happened to be on the day he died. Avery had her senior pictures photo shoot with him that afternoon. After the shoot, Alex was flirty, trying to get me to purchase a bigger package, but that's all there was to it. No flirting back on my part, I promise you."

I frowned. "Was anyone else in the studio?"

"No." Heather shook her head. "Well, wait a minute. There at the end, Jen Earley came in to change her daughter's appointment time."

Garrett made a sweeping ta-da motion with his hands. "There you have it. If Jen's privy to anything, it's going to be amplified a thousand-fold and spread around town like wildfire."

"Gotcha," I said. "Sorry to even bring it up."

"No worries. We'll make sure to nip that nasty little rumor in the bud before it finds traction."

Garrett and Heather waved as I turned and walked back to the truck with my mind racing a mile a minute. After our conversation, I realized I could place all of my potential murder subjects at Alex's studio sometime during the day of his murder. All except for Sunny. Tristan and I had seen Danae leaving as we arrived, Jen had come in during our session, Chris blew in in a rage as we were leaving, and now I knew Heather, which was nearly the same as Garrett being in the studio, had been there. The waters were as muddy as ever.

Chapter Thirty-Two

Leaving the Rogers sweet bungalow, I jumped in Old Rusty and headed for home. The afternoon light was already turning dusky even though it was only a quarter to five. I was halfway across the covered bridge when my cell phone rang. As soon as I was over the bridge, I pulled off the road to take the call.

"Hello. This is Callie from the Zen Goat," I answered, not recognizing the number that came up.

"Callie, hi. It's Claire Kennison. Sorry it's taken me so long to call you back. I ended up spending the night at my sister's in Stonehaven last night and only just got home. One too many spiked apple ciders, don't you know!" She giggled. "Anyway, Pete said you have a question or two for me?"

"Sounds like you had a fun time with your sister." I smiled, picturing the grandmotherly Claire tipping back the cocktails and getting silly.

"Oh, boy, did I ever, and you can bet I'm paying for it with a wonky head today, but never mind. It was all worth it!"

I chuckled. "So, Pete mentioned you used to be a member of the Bobwhite Hollow Photography Club, and I was wondering if you could tell me a little bit about why the club imploded."

Claire made a disgusted sound deep in her throat. "It's such a shame. We'd been together for a handful of years without any problems until Jen and Alex joined and were elected to the board. If we could've figured out a way to get rid of those two, we'd still be going strong."

Was it too soon to mention that with Alex no longer among the living, it seemed like half their problems were solved? Probably a little morbid to bring that point up right now.

"What kind of things were going on?" I asked instead.

"Like I said, they'd both finagled their way into officers' positions, since the rest of us were tired of doing it. Alex was elected president, and Jen vice president. We thought having new people in those positions would freshen things up. That they'd bring new ideas and challenges to the club. Boy, did they bring the challenges all right. Be careful what you ask for."

"They were like oil and water?"

"Hot oil, cold water, and a lit match thrown into the mix, more like. The bickering was hard enough to handle, but after the trip to Acadia National Park, the backstabbing and accusations were too much for all of us. We disbanded the club after that fiasco. It shocked me when I heard Lucy Thorne had agreed to judge Soul Dust's photography contest. And teach a workshop on top of it? I'm surprised she wanted to be in the same state as our club members."

"Why? What connection did Lucy have with your club?"

A few cars rattled over the bridge behind me. I watched their taillights disappear down the road as I sat talking with Claire.

"Well, the workshop we attended at Acadia was with Lucy, don't you know. I have a picture of all of the club members with her around here someplace. I could dig it up for you if you'd like. A nice tourist took the photo for us before the whole thing went south."

I racked my brain. Hadn't Jen told me she'd never met Lucy before this weekend? I'd swear that's what she'd said. "What happened on your trip to make things so bad?"

"Besides Jen accusing Lucy of stealing her photos, you mean?" Claire scoffed. "As if. Can you imagine a world-renowned landscape photographer stooping so low as to steal a small-town hobbyist's photographs? Please. Give me a break."

"Whoa! Hold up a minute. Jen really accused Lucy of stealing from her?"

"Indeed she did. Are you familiar with Lucy's iconic photograph from a couple of years ago, taken at Acadia? The sky is lit up with a golden sunset, and the ocean waves are crashing against boulders in the foreground?"

"I know the one. My mom has a canvas print of it hanging on her dining room wall. And I've seen the same photo on calendars, notecards, everywhere, really. In fact, Brittany sold a few at Soul Dust today in the short time I was in the gallery. Don't tell me that's the photo Jen claims is hers?"

"The very one," Claire answered. "The club was divided in half. Some of us thought Jen was completely off her rocker, but other members were adamant there was something to her claims. I'll be the first to admit Jen Early is not my cup of tea, so who's to say? Maybe I'm biased against her."

"Do you know if she tried to do anything about it?"

"While we were in Acadia, Jen screamed and yelled. Threatened to sue Lucy, but it never went anywhere. We hadn't been home from the trip a month, though, when Jen and her husband bought that fancy new house on the hill and left their home down in The Bottoms sitting empty."

"The Bottoms? The neighborhood that floods if the river crests its banks?" The one Jen scoffed at during yoga the other morning and acted like the people who lived there were beneath her?

"Yes. They were worried about flooding yesterday, in fact. Good thing we didn't get quite as much rain as they predicted." Claire paused for dramatic effect. "Between you and me, I've never been sure how the Earleys could afford that brand spanking new house on a mechanic's and church secretary's salary."

Remembering the comment Jen made about her winning photograph finally getting her the recognition she deserved, I sucked in a breath. "Do you think Lucy paid her off?"

"That's what the club members who took Jen's side believe," Claire answered. "Anyway, dear, I better go supervise Pete. He's got chicken on the stovetop, so I need to make sure he's not burning it beyond all recognition if I want to eat dinner tonight. It was nice talking to you. Don't be a stranger."

Before I had a chance to say goodbye, Claire disconnected the call. I sat in stunned silence, going over everything I'd learned about Jen up to this point. Things started to click into place. Her lie about using the outhouse when Lucy was killed. Her refusal to show the other workshop participants her photos taken during the morning. Her willingness to point an accusatory finger at everyone in a ten-mile radius. Her Jekyll and Hyde personality Tristan and I experienced at the soccer game. Her volatile history with both the Bobwhite Hollow Photography Club and with Lucy herself that Claire had just divulged. And hadn't Heather mentioned Jen had stopped back into Golden Bell Photography the afternoon Alex was killed? She must've realized he was on to her and decided she had to take care of him, too.

I dialed Chief Barnhart's number. His voicemail clicked on. Fudge nuggets!

"Jen Earley is the killer. Please call me back as soon as you can."

Chapter Thirty-Three

With only two miles to go, I flipped on my brights and broke the sound barrier as I sped home. Sliding sideways into the driveway, I killed the engine and jumped out of the truck. From the barn, Bugsy yelled his displeasure at not having been fed his dinner yet. It was a whole ten minutes past his usual feeding time and completely unacceptable.

"I'll be there in a minute," I yelled back.

My plan was to swap my sneakers for my barn boots, change my coat, and head out to feed, but Aunt Ellen called to me from the kitchen.

"In here, ladybug," she said.

I hustled down the hallway. "Yum. What smells so good?"

Uncle Will and Aunt Ellen sat at the table while Tristan pulled dinner plates out of the upper cabinets.

"We're having a one-pan meal tonight. Roasted pork tenderloin, sweet potatoes, and brussels sprouts with a side of pear sauce," Aunt Ellen answered. "Half an hour to dinner."

"Perfect. That gives me time to get all the critters fed and watered. Be back in a flash."

As I turned to go, my gaze landed on a disposable cup sitting on the hutch.

"Where did that come from?" I pointed at the cup. A gruffness in my voice must have startled my family, because they all turned to stare at me.

Aunt Ellen stood. "Oh, I meant to throw that thing away."

When she reached for the tan paper cup with the rippled sleeve, I slapped her hand away. "Don't touch it. Where did you get it?"

"From the church. We always have a big urn of coffee available when we're working on a project. Why are you acting so strange?"

I swiveled my head and glared at Tristan. "Did you not notice this?"

He nearly dropped the plates as he shook his head. "I-I didn't."

"Enough of this nonsense." Uncle Will raised his voice. "Enlighten us, please. What seems to be the problem?"

I continued pointing an accusatory finger at the cup. "That's the exact type of cup the poisoned coffee was in that killed Alex. Chief Barnhart asked Tristan and me to keep an eye out for the place who serves coffee in them."

Her hand flew to cover her mouth as Aunt Ellen gasped. "Oh, my soul. Jen and MJ are the only two photographers who are members of our church. The killer must be one of them."

I nodded. "It's Jen. I figured it out on my way home, but this solidifies I'm on the right track. I've already left a message for Chief Barnhart." I gave them a quick rundown on my conversation with Claire and why I'd come to the conclusion Jen was the killer. "There are still a few loose ends, but hopefully Chief Barnhart will call back soon. Now, I'm going to go feed the animals before Bugsy comes knocking on the door. In the meantime, nobody touches that cup until I get back."

Chapter Thirty-Four

Bugsy must have been listening for any little noise, because as soon as I cracked the front door open, he started screaming bloody murder. I laughed and jogged to the barn, hitting the light switch as soon as I made it inside.

"Sorry to keep you waiting, your highness." I scooped a pitchfork full of a fragrant mixture of orchard grass and alfalfa hay into his manger.

The silly goat immediately grabbed a mouthful and chewed contentedly. I gave him a quick scratch behind the ears. "I'm going to go feed everyone else, then I'll be back to say goodnight. Enjoy your dinner."

Out of the corner of my eye, I caught a dark shadow moving on the far side of the barn.

"Tristan? Are you there?"

Maybe my cousin had followed me out to help with the feeding. I listened for a second, but didn't get an answer. Probably just one of the barn cats. The lights in the barn were dim at best, so the corners and crevices always remained in the shadows. I'd gotten used to it and didn't startle and look over my shoulder when I was in the barn after dark nearly as much as I used to the first few months I'd been living at the farm.

I tossed hay into the covered enclosure where the other goats were used to being fed. They had access to the stall Bugsy had claimed as his own, but he was territorial, butting any of the goats out of the way who were brave enough to attempt to eat out of "his" manger. It hadn't taken long for them to learn their lesson and wait to be fed in the shelter on the backside of the barn. They were all food-driven, but none of them were quite as impatient as Bugsy.

Next, I grabbed a flashlight and headed out to the sheep shed. Daisy barked as I approached her herd. "Good girl, Daisy. It's okay. It's just me," I reassured the big dog.

She pranced around me, excited for praise, a pat on the head, and dinner. I filled her bowl from the kibble we kept in a container at the sheep shed, then tossed hay to the sheep. I checked their water tank, glad to note the self-waterer was working like it should.

Next, I jogged through the dark to the chicken coop, wishing I'd had the foresight to grab a flashlight. The minute it barely started to get dark, the flock went to bed. When I entered the coop, they were perched on their roosts, hunkered down for the night. They let me know they were content with soft chicken murmurs and trills, almost like a goodnight song. I hurriedly gathered the eggs, and locked the birds in for the night, effectively locking Mr. Fox out in the process. He wouldn't be indulging in a chicken dinner on my watch.

From the barn, Bugsy let out another ear-splitting bleat.

"Hush up, buddy," I yelled back.

He'd been fed but apparently demanded a bit of attention now. Or had decided his full belly also required an apple. Even goats craved dessert after a good meal. I set the basket of eggs on a wooden stool just inside the barn and grabbed an apple out of a bucket while Bugsy continued to attempt to raise the dead with his commotion. With a pocketknife, I sliced the apple into wedges as I walked toward his stall.

"Settle down, mister. Here you go." I held out a slice of the apple, but Bugsy looked past me and let out another ear-splitting scream, his ears standing at attention. Something was up. Bugsy never passed up an opportunity to wrap his lips around an apple. "What's the matter with you?"

I swiveled around to see what he was looking at. This time, there was no doubt a shadow figure scurried into the corner on the far side of the barn. Bugsy let out an ear-splitting scream again.

"Tristan, stop messing with me. I mean it."

I stomped across the barn floor and peered into the wedge of space between the ten-foot-tall stack of hay and the barn wall where the shadow seemed to have gone. Something moved. I grabbed a flashlight from the workbench and clicked it on.

Jen Earley flung a gloved hand up as the bright light illuminated her face. She stood sideways in the small space, her back against the barn wall and her chest pressed to the stack of hay bales. I flicked the light down her body. She held a red gas can with a yellow spout by the handle and shook it at me. "Don't you dare come any closer, Callie. I'll burn this place to the ground with you in it." Her nostrils flared as she pulled a lighter out of her pocket and brandished it in the air.

I widened my stance, not taking my eyes off of her. Behind me, the barn door stood wide open while Bugsy kept up his frantic racket. If I yelled loud enough, would someone hear me in the house? Doubtful, since all the windows and doors were sealed tight to keep the chilly night air out. No, I was going to have to figure this one out on my own.

I tilted my head and studied Jen. "Since you're the one backed into a corner here, I'm not sure you've thought that scenario out thoroughly. If you light the haystack on fire, you'll be the one going up in flames with it while I scooch out the door to safety." I crooked my thumb at the open air behind me, hoping my nonchalant tone would talk some sense into her.

Jen's wide eyes resembled a frightened goat as her head swiveled around to take in her predicament. She chuckled uncomfortably and tucked the lighter back into her pocket. "Obviously, I was only kidding. Why in the world would I do anything to hurt you or your family? No, it was just a joke, Callie. Simmer down."

"Just a joke? Then do you mind explaining what you're doing in our barn with a container of gasoline and a lighter?"

She looked down at the gas can as if surprised it was there. "Oh, gosh, it's a simple explanation. My van ran out of gas down the road a piece and came by to see if Will or one of you could help me out. When I saw the lights on in the barn, I naturally assumed someone was in here. I called out, but you must not have heard me. The gas can was sitting by the door, so I decided to grab it and be on my way. I'll fill it up and bring it back to you tomorrow.

Will that work?" She nodded as if I'd agree.

I crossed my arms and glared at her, surprised at how calm I felt. If I held my position as long as possible and kept her talking, my hope was to get her to confess to the murders. It wasn't ideal for me to confront Jen alone, but there didn't seem to be another choice. Better roll with it. "And what's the reason you wedged yourself into this tight spot here? Is it a simple explanation, too?"

Bugsy continued to scream his displeasure while Jen attempted to blink innocently and pointed at the deep, dark corner at the back of the haystack. "I thought this was the way out. You mean there's not a back door this way?"

"Nice try. Tell you what, why don't I make a quick phone call and get us both out of this sticky situation? Deal?" With any luck, Chief Barnhart would answer my call this time. I patted my coat pockets, searching for my phone. Fudgesicles! I'd changed into my barn coat before coming out to do the chores. My phone was still in the pocket of my other coat, hanging uselessly inside the house.

Jen took advantage of my moment of panic. She dropped the gas can on the floor and lunged forward, trying to get around me. I reached up and grabbed hold of a bale of hay, pulling it with all my might and shoving it toward her. The seventy-five-pound bale of hay knocked Jen sideways. She fell onto her left side.

"You broke my ankle," Jen screamed, clutching at her leg.

"It's the least I could do for the woman trying to burn down my uncle's barn," I replied sweetly. "You're welcome."

While she scrambled to stand, I took the opportunity to swiftly lean into the crevice, retrieve the gas can, and move it out of the way, kicking the can behind me. I grabbed for another bale of hay, pulling it down onto the top of the first, then going back for a third. The last one, I maneuvered until it stood on its end, locking Jen into the tight spot she'd managed to create for herself.

"Callie Haybeck! You let me out of here right this instant," Jen yelled. "I need a doctor."

"What is wrong with that ridiculous goat? We can hear him screaming inside the house. And Grandma said she's not going to hold dinner for you much longer, so you'd better hurry it up." Tristan strode into the barn but stopped short when Jen yelled again. He pointed at the wayward bales of hay. "Do you have a wounded animal trapped back there?"

"Tristan? Is that you?" Jen's voice floated over the stack of hay. "It's me, Jen Earley. Can you help me out here? I think my ankle is broken, and I know for sure Callie's lost her ever-loving mind. I promise not to press charges if you'll just help me get out of here."

Tristan made a shocked face and glanced at me. "How did you manage to get her cornered in our barn? Has she confessed to the murders yet?"

"Confessed to the murders? What are you talking about? I've never been so offended in my entire life. Why would I kill anyone? I didn't even know Lucy, for heaven's sakes, and Alex? Alex was my friend." She scoffed. "You're way off base here."

Tristan and I climbed up onto the haystack and peered down at Jen in her mouse hole as I lit her up with my flashlight beam. Bugsy must've realized help had come, and he'd stopped screaming. In the quiet, the sound of gravel crunching under tires as a vehicle came down the driveway reached us.

"Oh, really? You didn't know Lucy, huh? Then how do you explain the photograph Claire Kennison showed me today? The entire Bobwhite Hollow Photography Club, including yourself, on your trip to Acadia National Park two years ago? You must know the one. Lucy was standing smack in the middle with you right beside her." Claire hadn't shown me the picture, but it was easy to guess Jen would have weaseled her way to stand beside Lucy for the photo.

Jen's pale face peered back at us as she stuttered to find the right words to defend herself. "Well, uh…um…I said I didn't know Lucy personally. I didn't say we'd never met. There's a distinct difference, you know."

"Or how about your accusation that Lucy's award-winning Acadia photograph was actually yours?" I continued.

Jen's gaze shifted away, and she clamped her lips tight, for once.

"By the way, I have it on good authority that some of the members of your old photography club believed your allegations against Lucy. Did you know that?"

Jen gasped and placed a hand on her heart. "No they don't. Are you sure? If I knew people believed me, it could have changed everything."

Tristan poked me, placing a finger over his lips. He pointed to the barn doorway. I turned my head slightly to watch as Chief Barnhart silently edged his way up to the stack of hay blocking Jen's exit. Thank goodness. He must have finally listened to my half-panicked voicemail. The chief made a motion for me to continue questioning Jen.

"But the photo did change everything, didn't it? Lucy paid you handsomely. That's how your family could afford your new house, isn't it?"

Jen's face crumpled. "You can't blame me. Our house in The Bottoms was killing us. We had black mold in the walls from the flooding, and my girls were getting sick. They've both been so much healthier since the move. It was all worth it. I'd do anything for my daughters."

"So why kill Lucy now?" Tristan asked. "It sounds like her payoff to you was a blessing? Unless you got greedy and wanted more." He snapped his fingers. "I'm right, aren't I? You hit her up for more money, and she wasn't about to give it to you."

"That obstinate woman laughed in my face. What was I supposed to do?" Jen's own face turned red with rage. "I tried to talk to her from one professional to another the evening she arrived in town. I wanted to explain why she owed me more money, but she was just so condescending. I hate to admit it, but I lost my temper and punched her. Anyone would have. But instead of trying to work our issues out, she slammed the door in my face and wouldn't listen to anything else I had to say."

"Wait a minute. You're the one who gave Lucy the black eye?" The mop of doll hair I'd seen in the tote bag in Jen's van flashed through my mind. It hadn't been a doll's head at all. "You wore a wig when you went to Lucy's room at the inn to confront her. And then again later, to gain access to her room. You told Greer you were Lucy's assistant."

Jen waved her hand. "Oh, that Greer is an idiot. The girl has known me her entire life but the second I put on a wig and a hat, she no longer recognized me. It was perfect."

"I'm surprised you attended Lucy's workshop the next morning," I said. It took a lot of gall.

Jen chuckled. "Lucy was surprised, too, but to her credit, she hid it well. I figured she'd had time to sleep on my proposal and would see the benefit for both of us. I waited until everyone else was off shooting their little pictures, then went in search of Lucy. It didn't take me long to find her."

"And that's when she laughed in your face," Tristan guessed.

"Exactly. What can I say? I lost my temper there for a second. Next thing I knew, Lucy was on the ground with those spikey tripod feet buried in her heart. Guess I blacked out for a minute, there. Whoopsie."

"And what about Alex?" I asked. "You claimed he was your friend."

"That little punk," Jen grunted. "Don't be ridiculous. That loser was no friend of mine. Plus, he was even nosier than you, if you can believe it. Getting all mouthy and looking at me sideways like he knew something. Taking him a coffee on a busy day was a nice gesture, don't you think? I told him I wanted to mend bridges, and that moron believed me. He had no idea I'd spiked his drink with a lethal dose of liquid nicotine." She chuckled again. "Listen to me rambling on and telling you two all of my dirty little secrets. Too bad it's all hearsay. I'll deny my little confession to my last breath, but you guys will be looking over your shoulder for the rest of your lives. Which I predict won't be long ones." She cocked her head and flashed a demonic smile at us. "If you'd just left well enough alone, Callie, I wouldn't have had to come out here to frighten you off, and this little scenario wouldn't have had to happen."

"But unfortunately, it did, and now you're the one who seems to be in a pickle. Your family is going to be so proud." I clicked my tongue. "By the way, there's somebody else here who wants to say hello."

Tristan and I scooted apart and made room for the big man climbing the haystack.

Chief Barnhart wedged in between the two of us, poked his head over the edge of the bales, and waved a handheld voice recorder at Jen. "Hey there, Mrs. Earley. Fine evening, isn't it?"

Jen shook her fists and let out a wail rivaling the decibels of Bugsy's loudest bleat.

"I thought they say it's always the quiet ones," Tristan joked.

"Not this time it sure isn't." Chief Barnhart shook his head.

Chapter Thirty-Five

"Sit, ladybug. Let me get you some dinner." The spoon tapped against the porcelain plate as Aunt Ellen added a serving of pear sauce next to my pork and vegetables. She placed the food in front of me and gave my shoulder an affectionate squeeze. "You really need to stop confronting killers. Your grandfather is probably turning over in his grave right now."

"My brother would be mighty proud of you, Callie-Cat." Uncle Will pointed his fork at me. "The only reason he'd be turning over in his grave would be because he wanted to get out here and help you."

I cocked my head. "Did Grandpa Orville want to solve crimes?"

"Orville was all about helping people out, and I think finding out who murdered their loved ones is the ultimate way to help somebody. You and your grandfather are two peas in a pod."

As I ate my dinner and contemplated Uncle Will's words, my heart warmed at his comparison. I'd never known my grandfather while he was alive, but I was proud to carry on his tradition of helping people down on their luck, even in my own small way.

After dinner, Tristan drove me into town, where I spent an hour giving my statement, then cooling my heels in the reception area while Tristan gave his.

By the time we were finished, Chief Barnhart came out of the interrogation room looking exhausted. He ran a hand over the five o'clock stubble on his chin, sighed, and looked at us through saggy basset hound eyes. "Come into my office for a minute. I'll give you two a quick rundown."

Officer Bishop brought the three of us mugs of the blackest coffee I'd ever seen.

I thanked him before blowing on the coffee and tentatively taking a sip. "Whewie! That stuff could strip paint off the wall." My eyes watered as I set my mug on the desk and pushed it as far away from me as it would go.

Chief Barnhart frowned and took a gulp of his own. "What's wrong with it? Don't tell me you like those sugary sissy coffees."

"Guilty," I said around a parched throat. "Not to mention this stuff has been boiled down to a sludge."

Tristan pursed his lips while quietly setting his own untouched mug on the corner of the chief's desk. "I'm tempted, but I'll never sleep tonight if I have caffeine this late in the day."

Bull honkey. I'd seen Tristan down a giant mug of coffee at ten at night and still be sleeping like a baby an hour later.

Chief Barnhart cleared his throat. "Anyway, I thought you'd be interested to know Jen not only officially confessed to the murders of both Lucy Thorne and Alex Bell, she also admitted to planting Lucy's stolen camera in Alex's desk drawer. We have her dead to rights, thanks to your efforts. Good work."

"Will anything be done about her claim Lucy stole her photographs?" I asked.

The chief shrugged. "If Jen decides to pursue a case, she'll have to do it from behind bars in her prison cell. Besides, as her motive for murder, the stolen property claim won't have a bearing on her murder trial. Anyway, I wanted to thank you for all of your help in finding Lucy and Alex's killer."

I glanced at Tristan. "I'm glad we could lend a hand."

"Hey, I didn't help do anything but talk through a few scenarios," Tristan told the chief. "Honestly, I was convinced the only reason Callie wouldn't let the Jen thing go was because she didn't like her. My money was on the ex-husband."

Chief Barnhart chuckled and shook his head. "Like I said early on, Garrett is a solid guy. He was never a suspect in my book." He stood and pulled his car keys out of his vest pocket. "How about we call it a night?"

Chapter Thirty-Six

"This family tree builder will give you a good place to start." I gestured to the small tree I'd helped Sunny begin by plugging in first her information, followed by Lucy's, and then Garrett's. "Once you get a library card, you'll be able to access the various genealogy sites the library subscribes to."

Sunny's jade green eyes sparkled. "I can't thank you enough. I'm so excited to gather all those hints and learn about my family history."

I clapped my hands together three times in slow motion to underscore my next words of advice. "A word of caution, and I can't stress this enough. Be careful. Be diligent with your own research, and cite your sources. It's easy to get excited and follow those hints down a rabbit hole. The problem with public trees on genealogy sites is that if you don't verify the information is correct, you're simply inheriting other people's mistakes. You'll end up chasing entire lines of people who turn out to not be your ancestors because someone connected the wrong person to their tree."

Her jaw dropped open, and she nodded. "I guess I can see how that could happen. How do I make sure I'm researching the right people?"

"Go slow and check the documents."

"Like my birth certificate? It should be here by the end of the week." Sunny had found that Alaska allowed adoptees to request their original birth certificates. She immediately ordered hers, paying extra for the rush service they offered.

"Yes, exactly. You want to start the tree with yourself, so getting your birth certificate is the perfect first step. There's a ton of information online available to access, so as you start climbing your tree, you'll even be able to look at digital versions of many of the documents, like census records, marriage and birth records, for example. Go over them with a fine-tooth comb to make sure the names match up to your people, the dates make sense, and the place it was filed matches up to where your ancestors lived. Not only will you be looking at your great-great grandparents, but you'll need to look at their siblings, their aunts and uncles, and cousins. It all works together to form the picture of their lives. A rule of thumb is to verify you have the right person with at least three valid sources before moving on."

Sunny gritted her teeth. "Yikes. It sounds daunting."

"It can be, but also super addicting. You've been warned." I laughed and stood up. "Come on. Let's go say our goodbyes to Danae."

Sunny and I stepped out into the October sunshine as Danae was loading her suitcase into the trunk of her car.

"I'd say I hoped you had a good stay, but I know better. You'll need to come back one of these days to experience some Zen at the Zen Goat as opposed to pure chaos."

Danae held up her hands. "Hey, this trip wasn't what I expected, but it turned out to be a productive time for me." She turned and took Sunny's hands in her own. "I'm so, so sorry for your loss. I wish I'd known sooner about your relationship with Lucy and could have provided you with way more than I did. You're a strong woman, Sunny Hammond. You're going to be okay. Better than okay. And I'm sorry I ate your mac and cheese." Danae pulled Sunny into a tight hug.

"And my Oreos." Sunny laughed as she squeezed Danae back. "I'm sorry I screamed at you and called you a selfish bit—"

"Shh," Danae interrupted her. "We're not talking about that little incident. It never happened."

Well, that cleared up the question about what the two of them had been screaming at each other about the other day. I couldn't blame Sunny. Imagine searching for your biological mom, finding her, but not telling her who you were before she is tragically killed. And then someone has the audacity to not only scarf down your mac and cheese but steal your dang comfort cookies on top of the whole debacle. I probably would have lopped off her fingers.

"I wish you could stay for the bonfire tonight," Sunny said as she released Danae from the hug.

"I wish I could, too. It sounds like a blast, but my producer is adamant I show my face at the morning meeting tomorrow. Duty calls." Danae got into her car, put it in reverse, and executed a perfect three-point turn before heading down the driveway. Before she turned left onto Old Canal Road, Danae shot her arm out of the window and yelled, "See you in the news!"

Chapter Thirty-Seven

"Nothing beats good friends around a crackling fire." Uncle Will raised his mug in a toast. "Even if you've been reduced to toasting with peppermint tea as opposed to a hot toddy," he chortled.

"Hear, hear," Chief Barnhart agreed, raising his own mug, which I suspected held something a tad stronger than peppermint tea. "And to a few less murders in our village in the future."

We all raised our mugs to that.

"We might have to send our little murder magnet back to the Pacific Northwest to let things settle down here for a while," Sweet Pete quipped with a wink in my direction.

Rude.

The yard between the farmhouse and the guest cottage brimmed with all the folks from Bobwhite Hollow I'd grown to love in my short time here, along with a few others I was only getting to know. The twinkle lights had been turned on, but couldn't compete with the stars shining in the midnight blue sky overhead. The bonfire crackled and sparked while kids squealed in the darkness as they zoomed back and forth, playing hide-n-seek in the shadows.

Earlier in the afternoon, Uncle Will and Tristan had ventured into the woods in search of the perfect hot dog roasting sticks they'd whittled down the ends on to create a fine point, while Aunt Ellen and I had spent the afternoon in the kitchen brewing up ginormous pots of chili and a cauldron of hearty chicken stew.

It had been my idea to pull a last-minute party together to celebrate

Autumn and take advantage of the dry evening. Other than tonight, the forecast predicted rain and sleet for the next ten days, so it had been now or never. Fortunately, most everyone had jumped at the invitation to spend the evening at the farm.

Sunny, sitting in a lawn chair surrounded by her brand-new family, grinned at me. "Well, I'll be moving out of your guest cottage tomorrow and into the spare room at Garrett and Heather's." She stretched her back like a cat, her expression saying she could barely believe her good fortune.

"I sent in my DNA test yesterday," Garrett said, "but it's really just a formality. There's no doubt she's my kid."

I was glad Sunny had decided to stick around in order to get to know the Rogerses better.

"Oh! And did I tell you Garrett and Heather are buying me a pickup so I'll have something to drive?" Sunny asked.

"No, you hadn't mentioned it. That's awesome," I said.

"Chris Shields gave me a great deal," Garrett added. "It'll be perfect for Sunny."

"Now I just need to find a job," Sunny said.

Brittany and Chris slipped up beside me. "Did you say you're looking for a job?" Brittany asked Sunny. "Because if you are, I would love to have you and your knowledge at Soul Dust. The gallery is growing, and I'm having a hard time keeping up. I've been thinking about bringing on another full-time employee for a while now. What do you say?"

Sunny's eyes sparkled as she nodded vigorously. "Yes, please. It's more than I could hope for. When do you want me to start?"

"Would tomorrow be too soon?" Brittany asked.

The two women wandered off to stand closer to the fire and hash over the details of Sunny's new position.

I turned to Chris. "It's none of my business, but I'm curious. Is the pickup Garrett's buying for Sunny the same one you were selling to Alex?"

Chris nodded. "Not to speak ill of the dead, but Alex defaulted on his agreement with me."

In case Brittany hadn't mentioned to him that she'd told me all about it, I simply grunted.

"With Alex's death, I planned on just writing it off as a lesson learned, but the other day, his wife brought the truck over and handed me the keys. I parked it on the street with a For Sale sign taped to the window. Not half an hour later, Garrett called. He'd just started looking for something for Sunny when he saw the pickup, so the timing was perfect."

"Sweet. I'm guessing you didn't carry the financing this time?"

Chris shook his head and chuckled. "They only got the keys once the hard, cold cash was in my grubby little hands."

"Good plan," I laughed.

Levi strolled over with two roasting sticks in hand. "It's come to my attention that you've been too busy gabbing to eat."

I raised my eyebrows. "Have you been watching my every move?" I teased.

"You can't fault a guy for being concerned about your nutrition. I've seen you when you're hangry, and it's not a pleasant experience." He held out a stick. "How about we remedy that situation before it happens?"

I sent him a mock scowl and grabbed the stick. "Lead the way, kind sir."

Ten minutes later, I pulled my perfectly roasted hot dog off the stick and into a bun, topping the whole thing with a scoop of chili, shredded cheddar cheese, and diced red onions. Levi completely copy-catted my plate, grabbed us forks and napkins and suggested we sit at the picnic table so I didn't end up with chili dog in my lap.

"I have seen you eat, you know," he added with a smirk.

I scowled for real this time. And took four more napkins.

To my surprise, Levi leaned over and planted a quick kiss on my lips.

This morning, I'd completed my second shift at Stonefield Veterinary Clinic. I'd been nervous things would be tense and weird between Levi and me after the awkward goodbye hug the other night, but he'd acted perfectly normal. It hadn't stopped me from dwelling on the strange hug, however.

Digging a fork into my chili dog now, I decided to address the topic. "So, the other night after dinner…" I started, glancing at Levi.

His light complexion flushed pink. "Yeah, that was painful, wasn't it? I hoped you'd forget all about my blunder."

CHAPTER THIRTY-SEVEN

"I thought maybe you didn't want to see me anymore, now that I work for you."

Levi dropped his fork and gaped at me. "No. That wasn't it at all. Never think that."

I shrugged. "Then what was it? You couldn't get away from me fast enough."

"You're not going to let this go, are you?"

"Most likely not."

"Fine." He hung his head and let out a giant sigh. "The steak I had for dinner didn't sit well with me. I needed to get home quickly."

Heat rushed into my face to match Levi's. "Oh."

"Do you mind if I sit?"

I glanced up at my friend Nancy, our local cat lady, grateful for the change of topic. "No, of course not. There's plenty of room." I didn't even need to scoot over.

She smiled and glanced down as if embarrassed. "Maybe you two want some privacy. I don't want to intrude."

"Believe me, you're not intruding. Tonight is all about spending time with all my favorite people, and that includes you," I assured her.

Levi leaned over and whispered in my ear, "You just said I'm one of your favorite people."

I glanced over my shoulder at him. "Settle down." He didn't need to know I was talking to the butterflies in my belly.

At the far end of the table, Nancy giggled and took a big bite of her tofu dog. I wouldn't dream of ratting her out, but earlier I'd seen her slip one of the one-hundred percent beef dogs into a plastic bag and put it in her purse when she thought no one had been looking.

"I've been meaning to ask about your plans for yoga this winter," Nancy said.

I shook my head. "I think we're pretty much wrapped up for the season. It's already too cold most days for outdoor yoga."

"Are you open to suggestions?"

"Sure." Most goat yoga studios closed down for the winter, but might as well hear her out. "What are you thinking?"

"I'm a member of Moose Creek Grange Hall. We have a nice open space once the benches are pushed back. We hold dances there a couple of times a year, and I got to thinking that it would be the perfect spot for yoga during the winter. Now, I know there wouldn't be any goats involved, but it might be a good alternative for you for the winter. And I know I would love to continue to practice yoga. Without it, by spring I'm worried I'll lose all the flexibility I've gained."

"Do you think there would be enough interest?" I questioned her between bites of chili dog. In Seattle, I'd taught traditional yoga, but my gimmick in Bobwhite Hollow had always been the goats. What if nobody was interested in my classes if the goats weren't a part?

"Oh, absolutely. You can't imagine how many people are lamenting the loss of your classes for the next handful of months," Nancy gushed.

My excitement level rose. "Okay. I'm totally interested. Do I need to prepare something for the members of the grange to approve me teaching there? Or go to a meeting and plead my case?"

Nancy grinned and shook her head. "Nope. I added it to our agenda for our last meeting, and we already voted you in. The last step was asking you if you'd be interested. Oh, and you need to know that we would charge a twenty-five-dollar fee for using the building." She squinched up her face. "Would that be acceptable?"

"Seems perfectly reasonable to me." I grinned and held out my hand to shake. "You've got yourself a deal."

"Now, slow your roll a minute here," Levi interrupted my deal-making. "You already have a winter job. You're going to be working at the veterinary clinic with me, remember?"

As if I could forget. I held up a finger. "Hey. That's a part-time job. I'm perfectly capable of doing both and still taking care of the farm."

He threw his hands out in surrender. "I have no doubt. Just wanted to make sure you don't fill your plate too full."

"Too full for what?" My dander was rising. How dare he suggest I couldn't hold up my end of my obligations.

Levi tipped his head and lowered his voice so I was the only one who could hear him. "Too full to be able to spend time with me."

My heart melted as I touched his hand. "We'll work it out. I promise."

A smile teased at the corners of his lips.

Nancy wore an expression of concern when I turned back her way. "All good?" she asked.

"It's perfect. When do I start?"

Before we got another word in, a ringing sound filled the air. I stood and turned toward the bonfire. Tristan stood in the middle of everyone with a sheep bell swaying from his hand.

He rang it one more time. "Listen up, I have an announcement." Once we all quieted down, he raised his voice again, "One month from today, there will be a new hair salon opening in downtown Bobwhite Hollow."

I gasped and glanced at Uncle Will and Aunt Ellen, who gawked at Tristan in confusion. "Are you serious? Did you rent the space?" I jumped up and down, too excited to listen to his response.

"What space? What are you on about?" Aunt Ellen demanded.

"Grandma, I'm moving to Bobwhite Hollow," Tristan took her shaky hands. "By the beginning of December, you will have a standing appointment at Timeless Tresses."

"Don't you be messing with us, Grandson." Uncle Will pointed a weathered finger in Tristan's direction as tears sprang to his eyes.

"I promise you I'm not. It was all Callie's idea. I signed the paperwork this afternoon." Tristan flashed a giant smile. "And guess what? There's an apartment over my salon. It's absolutely perfect."

My gaze flew to the handsome nurse standing off to the side. Skip's smile radiated as much joy as my heart felt.

"Until I get the apartment and the salon ready, I'll be staying here," Tristan added.

"Good," I bumped him with my shoulder. "You can pay for your bread and butter by helping me with all the chores."

"Somebody has to, since I've been relegated to the couch. You'd be better off to put me out to pasture, for all the good I'm doing around here," Uncle

Will lamented.

Aunt Ellen's eyes sparkled. "Which is why I think it's finally time for Will and me to pack our bags and take one of those vacations we've been talking about for so long." She smiled at her family and friends gathered around the warm fire.

"Vacation? I just want to go fishing," Uncle Will grumbled.

"You can fish later. I want to do some traveling before it's too late," Aunt Ellen insisted.

Tristan jumped in between his grandparents and put an arm around both. "Have you considered starting with Florida? There are all kinds of exploring for you to do, Grandma, and Pop-Pop can go fishing to his heart's content."

"I had planned on seeing Italy, but I guess it might be wise to start closer to home. And I've always wanted to see the six-toed cats at the Hemingway House in Key West," Aunt Ellen said with a thoughtful nod.

"You might be on to something here, grandson," Uncle Will added. He leaned around Tristan to look at his wife. "What do you say, sweetheart? Should we go enjoy the sun and sand in Florida for a few weeks and let the young'uns mind the farm?"

"Listen to you, making it sound like it was all your idea." She smacked him lightly in the chest. "I say yes. Have we left yet?"

Uncle Will had an extra pep in his voice that had been missing lately as he and Aunt Ellen began excitedly discussing their plans to book motel reservations in Key West, Florida, first thing in the morning. The Barnharts and Kennisons chimed in with suggestions for places to eat and all the must-sees while visiting the Florida Keys.

"You've got to go snorkeling off of Key Largo."

"Stop at the bird sanctuary."

"Don't forget to get a big slice of key lime pie."

I was starting to feel a little jealous of their Florida excitement when my phone rang.

"Hey Dad, what's up?" I braced myself, half expecting for him to have changed his mind again and start haranguing me about moving back to Seattle. It had been his m.o. ever since I'd moved to New Hampshire, so I was more than a little gun-shy whenever he called.

"Hi, sweetie. Just wanted to touch base with you. Your mom and I have been talking…"

Ugh. Here we go.

"…and we'd really like to experience a Bobwhite Hollow Christmas."

"Dad, I'm not moving home." Wait. What had he said?

On the other end of the line, my dad laughed. "We either have a bad connection or you didn't listen to what I said. I'm not asking you to come home, I'm telling you that Mom and I want to spend Christmas with you in New Hampshire."

Tears sprang to my eyes. It was everything I'd hoped for. "Yes," I screamed into the phone. "You said you'd never come visit. What made you change your mind all of a sudden?"

"I can be a little stubborn when I've set my mind to something, can't I? It seems like I inherited that trait from my mother."

"I may have gotten a smidgeon of a stubborn streak as well," I joked, trying to appear nonchalant about his announcement, even though my heart was about to explode with happiness.

"Believe me, you inherited more than a smidgeon. Anyway, the research you and your sister have done has convinced me that maybe my father wasn't the bad guy my mother made him out to be. It's hard to argue when the documents are sitting in front of me in black and white. Why your grandmother found the need to lie to me my entire life and make me feel like my father didn't want anything to do with me is something I'll never know or understand. To be honest, Uncle Will's health scare scared me, too. With both my mother and father gone, Will and Ellen are the only ones left who can fill in those blanks for me. I've decided I want to meet him before it's too late. I've nursed my hurt and anger long enough," Dad said around a voice choked with emotion.

My own voice shook as I replied, "We will roll out the red carpet for you. I can't wait to hug your neck and am beyond excited to show you and Mom around Bobwhite Hollow."

About the Author

When Janna Rollins isn't writing, she likes to sit on the front porch and thumb through New England-based magazines while drooling over the pictures. She has a love of red barns, goats, and genealogy. She is the author of the Zen Goat Mysteries, as well as the Hometown Hardware Mysteries written as Paula Charles. Janna is a member of Sisters in Crime, the national chapter, and the Columbia River chapter. She lives, with her extremely patient husband, in a 125-year-old house on the Washington coast where the sound of crashing waves and seagulls calling can be heard from every window.

AUTHOR WEBSITE:
  www.paulacharles.com

SOCIAL MEDIA HANDLES:
  Facebook: Rainy Day Mysteries
  Instagram: rainy_day_mysteries

Also by Janna Rollins

The Zen Goat Mysteries
An Escape Goat
Goats Just Wanna Have Fun

The Hometown Hardware Mysteries (written as Paula Charles)
Hammers and Homicide
Axe Me No Questions
A Zappy Little Christmas

www.ingramcontent.com/pod-product-compliance
Lightning Source LLC
Chambersburg PA
CBHW060531160726
47991CB00001B/272